ACCIDENTS IN THE HOME

Tessa Hadley was born in Bristol and studied English
Literature at Cambridge. She has an MA in Creative
Writing from Bath Spa University College, where she
now teaches English and Creative Studies. She lives
in Cardiff with her husband and three sons. *Accidents
in the Home* is her first novel: she has also written a
book on imagination and pleasure in Henry James.

D1322469

ACCIDENTS IN THE HOME

TESSA HADLEY

Jonathan Cape
London

Published by Jonathan Cape in 2002

2 4 6 8 10 9 7 5 3 1

First published in Great Britain in 2002 by
Jonathan Cape
Random House, 20 Vauxhall Bridge Road,
London SW1V 2SA

Random House Australia (Pty) Limited
20 Alfred Street, Milsons Point, Sydney,
New South Wales 2061, Australia

Random House New Zealand Limited
18 Poland Road, Glenfield,
Auckland 10, New Zealand

Random House (Pty) Limited
Endulini, 5a Jubilee Road, Parktown 2193, South Africa

The Random House Group Limited Reg. No. 954009

A CIP catalogue record for this book is available from the
British Library

ISBN 0-224-06230-1

Papers used by The Random House Group are natural, recyclable
products made from wood grown in sustainable forests. The
manufacturing processes conform to the environmental regulations of
the country of origin

Typeset by Palimpsest Book Production Limited,
Polmont, Stirlingshire
Printed and bound in Great Britain by
Biddles Ltd, Guildford and King's Lynn

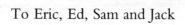
To Eric, Ed, Sam and Jack

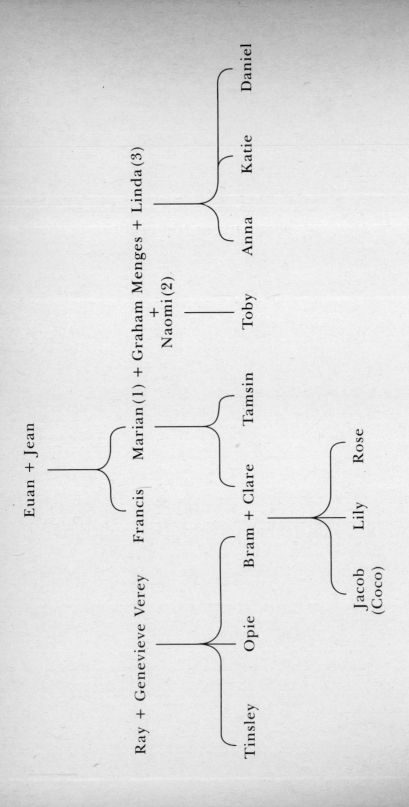

accidents in the home

Lost and Found

The weekend that Helly brought her new boyfriend down to meet Clare, Clare's younger brother Toby was also staying with them, following them round with his video camera, making a documentary about the family for his college course.

Clare gave the camera one quick exasperated glance when the doorbell rang and the guests arrived. The food should have been ready but she was still chopping hurriedly amidst a debris of vegetable leavings; her fingers were stuck with parsley bits.

—Oh Toby, *stop* it!

Her deep glance at the camera – she looks at the lens and not at Toby, as if it was his eyes – is caught forever on the tape. She is wishing she had had time to change into the nicer clothes she had planned. Her hair is in a short, thick black plait on her shoulder, fastened with a rubber band. She looks tired. When she is tired (she believes) all those things which, at her best, make her look like an intellectual just make her look like a librarian: small eyes, neat straight brows, thin lips, a square high forehead. She has good skin but it is pink and hot because she is flustered. Her glance is naked and hostile – her last moment of free expression before she has to put on a smiling face.

She might be hostile to Toby; she is sometimes bossy and arbitrary with him.

Or perhaps to Helly, who comes and finds her out in her humiliation, dragged down by the children, without make-up, with wet red hands.

When Helly introduced her new boyfriend to Clare she said:

—You two should know each other. David comes from round here too. We must have all been at teenage parties together. He knows people we knew.

But the man was a stranger, an alien in Clare's house, with sunglasses hiding his eyes and an exaggerated presence she flinched from, curvy big cheekbones and chin with blue-black stubble, a thick beautiful leather coat, loudly and confidently friendly in a way that suggested immediately to Clare that he didn't want to be here in the provinces visiting his girlfriend's friend who was nobody. When they all kissed, the Londoners smelled expensively of bathrooms full of bottles of scents and lotions, and Clare was aware of her limp T-shirt which had soaked up the smells of the onion soup she was making for their lunch. The onion soup, with Parmesan toasts baked in the oven, would be delicious. (It was.) And Helly couldn't cook. But Clare feared that everything brilliant and savoury about her might appear to have drained into that onion soup, leaving her wan and dull and domesticated.

Helly was her best friend.

Recently, Helly had been paid thirty thousand pounds (twice as much as Bram, Clare's partner, earned in a year) to make a series of television advertisements for ice cream; as well as on television, they were used in the cinema and on hoardings. Everywhere Clare went she was surprised out of her reverie by Helly's golden face or the misty curves of Helly's body, intently and extravagantly inviting her into a larger-than-life golden vanilla space concealed inside the prose of everyday. These images got in the way for a while whenever she was with the real Helly: the real Helly would even seem for the first few minutes slightly contracted, smaller and more precise than she should be, and muffled in surprising clothes.

Helly was embarrassed about the advert. She was a serious actress. She did get work, in fringe and in soaps, but not enough. She was still waiting for her break. And no one, no one, could have turned down thirty thousand pounds. The advertisements paid for the serious work: that was the theory. But her friends couldn't help feeling that something momentous had happened, that she had stepped into a golden current of money and frivolity and glamour that would carry her off. Anyway, she wasn't strikingly talented as an actress. Although none of them quite acknowledged it, this was more exciting, really, than if Helly had got a good part in a play. They watched to see what would happen next.

Clare could remember that when she and Helly were fifteen, one of their shared night-time fantasies had been to imagine their nakedness projected lingeringly onto a cinema screen in front of an audience. So she couldn't be sure just how genuine Helly's contemptuous indifference was to those golden simulacra plastered everywhere. Or how genuine her own contemptuous indifference was, either.

The two visitors filled up the little terraced house with noise and cigarette smoke and with their things. They had brought in from the car a camera and bags of presents and bottles of wine and flowers and a portable mini-disk player and a heap of leather luggage, even though they were only staying the one night; also a laptop on which David had already tried to access his e-mail. (He worked as a lighting technician, designing systems for stage shows and clubs: this seemed to necessitate frequent contacts with his associates and long sessions on the mobile.) They talked more loudly and constantly and laughed more than Clare was used to.

Clare was taken aback at how profoundly she coveted Helly's beautiful clothes. She liked to think she was fairly indifferent to material possessions. Under Bram's influence she had given away lots of her CDs, deciding she had outgrown them. They had a house full of books but no television, and Clare made her own bread and ground her own spices and salted lemons to put in salads and chicken dishes. She bought most of what she wore in charity shops: not grudgingly but pointedly, because it was more original to put together your own bits and pieces. But when she saw Helly's long lilac-coloured dress and her green velvet jacket sewn with mirrors and her toenails painted green, she was reminded that there was something else you could do with your clothes, something better than just original, something that amounted to power and joy. You needed money, to make the look of you so mysteriously arouse longing and satisfaction at once: although you had to have a gift, too, to choose the right things so inventively and surely.

Helly was grievously good to look at: tall and spare, all flat planes, wide shoulders, big hands and feet, with big cheekbones and a long mobile mouth. Her eyes were pale green and her skin was really quite pale, not golden like in the adverts. Her spiky hair was blonde out of a bottle, with the roots left deliberately dark. The children came and watched

Helly and David as if they were a show. Lily reached out a finger and stroked the velvet of Helly's sleeve; Rose put on her Superman cape especially for David, who didn't notice. He never knew what he was supposed to say to people's children, he confessed. Helly was the one who made all the efforts. She'd brought them things, and she talked to them in a chaffing ironic voice that Clare knew (she knew Helly very well) meant she was slightly afraid of them, not sure what they were thinking or how to please them. Coco, the oldest and the boy, was deeply suspicious of both visitors. He winced at Helly's silver lip-ring and ignored her as if it was kinder not to draw attention to how she shamed herself by wearing it; but he was drawn, almost against his better judgement, to the laptop. Even Toby – infuriatingly because he was twenty-three and should have been backing Clare up as a fellow adult – sat dumbly smiling and blushing in spite of all Helly's efforts to bring him out (she would be much more confident of how to please him, not because she had known him since he was a boy, but because he was a man now, and couldn't take his eyes off the lip-ring).

Ten years, eleven years ago, they worked out, David and Clare and Helly had all lived in this city, but had not known one another. David had even been in the sixth form with a boy Clare went out with for six months. They'd had so many teenage haunts in common, a pub, a club, even the city reference library where they revised for A levels: so many mutual acquaintances, it seemed impossible they hadn't met.

—I'm just beginning to remember, said David. —When I see you two together. It's starting to come back to me.

—Don't believe him, laughed Helly. —He's just flirting.

He was flirting, although Clare presumed he was only using his flirtation with her in some game with Helly. She was as aware of the unaccustomed aura of flirtation in her house as she was of the unaccustomed cigarette smoke: both things made her anxious and excited at once, and she was bracing herself already for when Bram came in. He would sniff them both out immediately, and disapprove of them, although he would be as always – infallibly – courteous and friendly. This was why Clare didn't see Helly very often any more. It stretched her too painfully, having to defend Helly from Bram's disapproval while mobilising inside herself all her best arguments against how Helly's life tempted her and invited her and made her envious.

—Did you know someone called Tim Dashwood? David asked.

—Tim Dashwood? No, said Clare.

—Yes we did, said Helly. —Remember? We went to parties at his flat. Very naughty parties. *Pas devant les enfants.* Where we got up to all sorts of things.

—What did you do at the naughty parties? asked Lily.

—Lots of rubbish I expect, said Coco.

—That's exactly right, said Helly. —You're so right. Lots and lots of rubbish. And d'you know what we used to wear? I'll bet you can't imagine your mummy dressed entirely in black clothes, with a black bustier, and black eye make-up and fingernails and lipstick and earrings. We were briefly gothic. It didn't last. But that was the Tim Dashwood period. We didn't know him well. He wasn't particularly gothic. Bit of a bloodsucker perhaps. He and his friends must have been older than us.

—Black lipstick! Yuk! said Lily. —What's a bustier?

—Something silly that ladies wear, like underwear on top of their clothes.

—I suddenly had a feeling that that was where I was remembering you from, said David. —I'm sure I can remember Clare at one of Tim's parties.

—No you can't, said Clare quickly. —Not if I can't remember it. I don't even remember such a person.

—Can you remember me there? Helly asked him.

—Perhaps. Did you use to have long plaits?

—Long gothic ones, naturally.

—Then maybe, maybe.

—If I ever look in my old diaries from those days, said Clare, —which mostly I don't, it's too hideous – I feel as if I'm reading about someone else. Not just people I knew that I can't remember, and places I went and things I did: but feelings I felt, things I wanted. It doesn't connect to me as I am now.

—You keep a diary, do you?

—Oh: not any more. I wouldn't keep one now.

—She's got volumes of it. She used to write pages every night.

—It's so embarrassing. The entries begin with things like: 'calories so far today, 5: one centimetre of toothpaste'. Or: 'I know that now I will never, ever, be happy again in my whole life', about some boy whose name I can't even remember from his initials.

—So what do you remember from Tim Dashwood's party, David? asked Helly.

He was simply the wrong scale for the little room crowded with books and pictures and delicate ceramics (Clare's father was a potter). He was sitting in his leather coat, jammed with one leg crossed over the other knee into the most comfortable chair in the house (which was not all that comfortable). He vibrated his leg restlessly, showing a stretch of big brown hairy calf above his scarlet sock, drumming his fingers on the arms of the chair. At least he had taken off his sunglasses. His eyes exposed without them were comical, doleful, as if they were pulled down into his cheeks; he had a large head with decisive features and thick dark hair standing straight up from his forehead. He smiled consideringly. Rose put a small fat hand onto his knee, which he ignored.

—I don't remember much. You know what his parties were like. That used to be the general point, didn't it? To get so out of it you couldn't remember much.

—Out of what? asked Lily.

Clare and Helly had met at Amery-James High School for Girls: from twelve to twenty they had lived in an intimacy they would never attain again with anybody else. In the very process of their formation they were intertwined, like two trees growing up in the same space. They learned to smoke together, practising at home (Clare's home, with more liberal parents) under one another's critical scrutiny until it looked right. Now Clare, who had given up, saw that Helly still tilted up her chin and blew her smoke off to one side in the way they had decided was most flattering.

At school they made a secret pact of resistance (the school motto was 'so hateth she derknesse': they determined to love it); the pact was sealed by an exchange of drops of menstrual blood on tissues folded and wrapped around with hairs pulled from one another's heads. They went shoplifting together (for clothes, mostly, and make-up) setting it for themselves as a significant test, an initiation into the kind of adulthood they aspired to: transgressive, toughened, disrespectful (the opposite to the one Amery-James aspired to on their behalf). Helly carried the shoplifting off with flair, Clare was cowardly and full of dread. Clare was the theorist and Helly was the one who acted. Clare was the feminist – when they were fifteen they read her stepmother's old copy of *The Female Eunuch* together, squeezed side by side on their stomachs on Helly's bed – but it was Helly who later rode a motorbike and went out on her own to pubs and clubs and mostly dismissed, contemptuously, the boys who asked her out. Clare always suspected and concealed a secret abjection in herself, some treachery of neediness towards the other sex which seemed to fulfil itself when they were in their early twenties, and the serious business of life became men. The girls turned their backs on one another then, ruthlessly cutting away old lives and connections because they thought they had found, at last, the life they really wanted.

Clare was putting the Parmesan toasts in the oven when Bram came in through the back door. He was working on a two-year project recording the ecology of an area of mudflats and coastal grassland which would be covered by water when the new barrage for the city's marina was completed. At weekends volunteer groups came down to help and he had to be there to supervise: but he'd promised to be home for lunch. She was relieved that he came in the back way because it meant Helly and David would not see him in his unflattering cycling helmet. He was so without vanity (genuinely, she was sure: she had probed for it deeply enough) that she sometimes thought he looked for ways to make himself ugly, to undo the effect of gentleness he couldn't help; he was blond and delicate with a forward-thrust lower jaw that made him soften his consonants when he spoke.

—So what's this one like? he asked, taking off the helmet, running his head under the cold tap, scouring himself with the towel.

—He's perfectly friendly. I think he's nice. After the last one, anyway. (After Helly brought the last one to visit them Clare had found scorched silver foil in the bathroom, and feared the worst.) —He's a bit too *much*, though.

—Too much of what?

—They sort of fill the place up.

—She always brings several changes of clothes, doesn't she? Just in case.

—You can hardly get past their luggage in the hall.

—And I suppose you've been hearing all about the cultural delights of the capital?

—Oh, they've been everywhere and done everything. And know everyone, of course.

This rehearsal of mutual ironic judgement felt comradely and consoling: but as soon as Bram went to talk to the visitors and Clare was left setting the table she was filled with unreasonable resentment at his tone. They hadn't really talked much about London; mostly she and Helly had talked about the old days. It was Clare's own fault if she had taken away any impression that things in London were more brilliant and thrilling than down here.

The lunch went off alright. At least the soup was good, and there seemed to be plenty of talk, although perhaps most of it was Helly's and David's: Helly told them funny stories about the shoot for the ice cream advert (she imitated the voice-over for them: 'Forgive yourself: it's irresistible'), and David seemed to hold forth on every topic; he knew someone or he'd read something or he'd once worked somewhere. He even managed to find some kind of software program to talk about to Bram: mostly Bram didn't try to compete whenever the conversation was noisy. Clare was used to presuming, wincingly-defensively, that Helly must think Bram was dull and stolid. She always made a point of trying to coax him out of what she probably imagined was his shell. Clare winced

12

defensively for Helly too: she had no idea how Bram recoiled from her coaxing.

Toby got it all on his video. Both the visitors tried encouraging him out from behind his viewfinder, David had friends in a video production company he should get in touch with, Helly lit his cigarette for him (Clare hated Toby smoking) and tried to draw him on the subject of himself. But he couldn't resist how the shots framed themselves around David and Helly, how their clothes and scent and cigarette smoke and loud lunch-party laughter crowded all the space, and how dingy they managed to make ordinary family life seem. Rose tipped over her orange juice. Lily and Rose wouldn't eat the onion soup. Coco had broken his glasses, which had to be mended with sticking plaster until they could get to the optician's on Monday. For some reason Clare was exasperated at this, and at how patiently Bram mopped up Rose's orange juice with a cloth, although she knew this was unfair, and knew how much more exasperated she would have been if he hadn't mopped it.

She had taken a few minutes before lunch to change into a dress and brush out her hair and spray on perfume. She wasn't sure whether she was really flirting with David, at that point: she was making up to him, flattering him, because that would make everything go smoothly, Helly would be satisfied, and he would be at least kept sweet for the afternoon. She could see herself, when she watched the video later, backing away in front of them down the path of their weekend, his and Helly's, sweeping and sweetening it ahead of them with her interest and her attention, helping to damp down David's impatience to be gone.

They went out in the afternoon to look at Bram's project. Bram had been amused that Helly had to change her clothes first; although actually she reappeared in sensible scruffy trousers and shirt, in which she still managed to look spectacular. It was Clare in her dress who got her legs bitten and scratched in the long grass. They walked round the bay which would eventually become the marina: now it was low tide and the ruined jetties of the old harbour marched out up to their knees in sleek grey glinting mud. Oystercatchers and curlews (Bram identified them) picked their fastidious way between them. Across the ring of the bay the piled up buildings of the city loomed, glinting and flashing from plate-glass office-block windows whenever the sun flew out from between ragged slate-coloured clouds. It was May; there was a wind which flattened the pale mauve-green grass like a pelt and sent it racing in liquid waves; from time to time the sky shook out cold drops of rain. David was taking photographs. Bram left them to go and find his group of volunteers who were counting lug-worms further on round into the estuary. They climbed down some concrete steps with a rusted handrail onto a scrap of beach heaped up with stones and sticks and plastic rubbish and cans which the sea had bleached to the same opaque pale pastels.

As soon as she saw water, Rose began to take her clothes off. She was an ironic, wilful, huge-eyed baby with rolls of translucent pale flesh at her wrists and chin and waist, and she despised clothes. She stripped at every opportunity, winter and summer, streaking triumphantly just out of reach of pursuing adults, flashing in triumph the long tender crease of her vagina and the pink cheeks of her bottom. Clare worried that Rose's taste for nakedness was outgrowing her innocence – she would be four in a few months – and she thought she needed to be taught to protect herself.

Rose protested that this was the seaside.

—No it's not, it's dirty water, and you're not to go in it.

Rose seemed to concede defeat.

But a few minutes later, she was suddenly nowhere to be seen, and there was a little pile of her clothes dropped down beside an oil can with the bottom rusted out. It seemed impossible that she could have gone anywhere out of their sight in so short a time. Everyone stared around them, calling her name, looking for her along the beach and back up the steps. The crescendo of dismay, from the first exasperated flutter of worry ('What a pain she is!') to hollowing uninhibited panic only took a few minutes: Clare screamed at the other two children to stay where they were and kicking off her shoes ran barefoot across the shingle and the potentially lethal debris of glass and tin, to stand soaking her skirt in the scummy edge of the water, shrieking along the waterline to right and left, fumbling in the water with her arms to try and feel for anything pulled under and washing in that dirty tide of sluggish brown waves that hardly broke, hardly made spume. She couldn't see through the water, she couldn't imagine what she ought to do next, or whether she ought to somehow submerge herself in it and try to open her eyes: wasn't this always how it was, with accidents, that the parents tinkered grotesquely, futilely, in the wrong place, failing confusedly as you fail in dreams?

David shouted for Helly to go one way and he ran the other, back up the steps. Clare felt a passionate revulsion from her guests. It was in her preoccupation with them that she had taken her attention off Rose: she had been talking to David, pretending she was interested in cameras. If Bram had been here this would never have happened. Frantically, puritanically, Clare linked up her dereliction with other falsities, with her efforts to impress upon Helly and David the charms of family life, with the perfume she'd sprayed on, with their money, with

Helly's advertising contract, even with the scorched tinfoil in the bathroom.

It occurred to her that there was a literary tradition of guilty women whose children pay for their mother's momentary lapses of attention, their casual betrayals (in the mornings when Rose was at nursery she was writing a PhD thesis on George Sand). Wasn't there a scene in Flaubert – or Balzac? – where an adulteress watches over the cot of a sick child, pledging the whole of her selfish future happiness against the few degrees his temperature must come down for him to live? At that moment she imagined such a scene, if it existed, quite without irony, the cheap irony that smirks at literary machinery. It seemed a revelation of a naked truth before which irony could only grovel.

Also, she suddenly dimly remembered someone called Tim Dashwood, and odd details of a party she had gone to at his flat when she was a teenager: a plastic armchair pocked with cigarette burns, the suspect slickness of a greasy carpet under bare dancing feet, men with ponytails and slow-burning smiles who brought her and Helly drinks in plastic cups and didn't even bother to learn their names. Like good little girls they swallowed and smoked everything that was put in front of them. The slow black ink mushroom-clouding in her mind came back to her, a fearful sensation of cold deep water slipping past, tugging the ground out from under her. All sorts of things could have happened to them – did happen to them – at those parties. She splashed out of the water and ran along the shoreline, staggering with the pain in her feet, shouting for Rose.

A high sheer stone wall came down into the water, too high for Rose to have climbed. Clare ran back up the beach alongside it, her breath coming jaggedly in sobs, stopping to peer into a hollow runaway that pierced the wall, wide enough for a child to crawl into: it was dark and foul and stank inside, with nameless black shapes half-submerged in an oily black puddle, but no Rose. Clare became convinced again that she was being dangerously distracted from the real disaster, which was happening somewhere else: and she ran back down to the sea.

David found Rose. She was quite unhurt and only thirty yards from where they had been standing and shouting, hidden from them by a grassy bluff. Clare made him show her the place afterwards, at the back of the beach where a wet trickle that might have been a stream and might have been sewage emerged from a big concrete pipe set into an earth bank: Rose had been dabbling her feet where the water spilled over the lip of the pipe. She might possibly have been contemplating crawling up into the pipe; and possibly if it had rained (as it proceeded to do shortly after she was found) there might have been a rush of water off the land. But these dangers were too remote to count, or even to produce any retrospective jolt of imagination at a horror narrowly skirted: the only one hurt was Clare, who had cut her foot on something in the water.

David looked funny – improbable – holding a pink naked toddler, balancing her as he picked his way down the beach, wary and concentrated: Rose clung on with her arms round his neck. Clare had known all the time they were looking for Rose that if anything bad – anything sickeningly terrible – had happened, she would have never seen either of them again, David or Helly. There would have been a few hours of unspeakable practicalities with doctors and police and then they would have got out of it as soon as they decently could, and driven back to London in their special Citroen that rose up on its wheels when you started it, and she would never ever in the remainder of her ruined life have been able to forgive them their association with that day. But now they were all reprieved: now she could like these friends again, and smile at them. David was pleased with himself for finding Rose, and tickled her awkwardly on the cheek, like a man who has not had practice at such things; she clung on to him as he handed her over, and Clare, up close, felt gratefully the friendly heat of him. Now she would be able to tell Bram that they had lost Rose and it would only mean an ordinary manageable hitch in the day, he would not be able to see through it to any deep dereliction, any dangerous absence of mind.

Helly put her cardigan round Clare's shoulders as the rain came pattering in dark spots on the stones, and tried to help her get Rose dressed, pulling tight socks on the wet feet, T-shirt on the twisting little body.

—You're a naughty, naughty girl, said Clare. —You mustn't take your clothes off, and you mustn't wander away. Mummy was seriously frightened.

Helly looked abashed at what the moment had unleashed in Clare, the excess of reaction. It was excessive, Clare supposed: all that shrieking and thrashing about in the water, and the cut foot, which was now bleeding into her shoe. But she felt rather recklessly as if she'd shown Helly something, something she couldn't know about, being childless.

Clare sat with her knees drawn up under her chin on her big unmade brass bed, opposite Helly, cross-legged at the pillow end. She had bathed her cut with antiseptic and checked that her tetanus injection was still in date (Bram kept meticulous records of these things). Her foot was aching. David had taken Coco and Lily out for a drive in his car, 'to leave the girls to talk', as he put it; Rose was asleep in her cot.

—So what's he like? Clare asked.

—He's nice, said Helly. —Nicer probably than you'd think. He can seem a bit full of himself.

—I like him better than the last one.

A little involuntary spasm of pain and regret twisted Helly's expression. —Everyone but me could see it. But David's much more steady: don't you think?

Clare thought of him finding Rose. —Oh yes, she said. —He seems kind. And sensible.

—I know he shows off a bit.

—Not in the least, Clare protested stoutly. —He's just exuberant. He knows how to enjoy himself.

—Oh yes. He certainly knows that.

Helly thoughtfully closed her teeth on the cuff of her shirt sleeve and pulled at it, not meeting Clare's eyes, sharing some joke with herself. Bram probably thought it was just a sensible shirt; Clare had recognised something expensive and perfect of its kind, all the better for being casual and crumpled.

Clare stiffened. —Meaning?

—Oh, you know . . . Do you remember Moments of Beauty?

This was a private jargon from a game they had played when they were teenagers: winding pop videos and films backwards and forwards to isolate the 'moment of beauty' for their favourite male stars, the summation of what melted and undid them, some grin, some sleepy inadvertent glance, some lazy look of sexual appraisal. They had even tried for a while to isolate their own (female) moments of beauty in the mirror, so as to work on them: they gave up when their faces were beginning to freeze into perpetual self-consciousness.

19

—Well?

—David's very good, sexually. You couldn't really know him – I mean, what's so appealing about him – without sort of knowing that. It's his Moment.

Clare braced herself against the end of the bed. She felt caught out in the very scene of her decent connubial satis-factions: the duvet cover they sat on was faded and flowery and its poppers were missing so that the innards of grey duvet spilled out of one end. One of Rose's teddies lay between their pillows with an air of baleful occupation: and for some reason she was visited by a memory of Bram calling out to her in the bathroom not to run the tap while she was cleaning her teeth because it wasted water.

—I see, she said.

—We do all kinds of things I never thought I'd do.

—Oh? Such as?

—Well: mirrors.

—You mean mirrors on the ceiling and all that kind of thing?

—And cameras.

—Oh God, Helly, that's awful.

—No, really it's not. Helly laughed.

—But it's so cold! I just don't think that would give me any pleasure, thinking about it and setting about it in that deliberate kind of way.

—You'd be surprised.

—Isn't it supposed to just happen spontaneously? Isn't there something wrong if you have to plan for it? It seems unnatural.

—He naturally likes women, Helly said. —You think you can take that for granted – I mean, under the circumstances – but believe me, I'm beginning to realise, lots of men don't like women, whatever they say . . . Really, he likes them; it's special, he has this look . . .

To her dismay Clare found herself imagining it.

—I can always tell when he likes someone. And we've done three in a bed.

Clare genuinely shrank in disapproval from all this: even talking about it seemed to her a betrayal of what she believed was her grown-up self, watching over the kind of sacred bedroom secrets decent grown-up couples share. At the same time she was seized with curiosity urgent as a cramp: and she noted that Helly presumed that David didn't like her, or she surely would have mentioned it.

—With another woman?

—Yes.

—God, Helly. What was that like?

—Oh well, you know: strange and familiar.

—Strange and familiar? So what was strange?

—You ought to try it.

—No, thank you. I'm quite happy as I am.

—Do you know what I found the other day? Helly said suddenly, with a blithe quick laugh. —I found a little box of earrings.

—Earrings?

—Among David's things. Just single earrings. At first I thought maybe he had had his ear pierced at some point. But I asked him if he ever had. Anyway, some of these just weren't that sort of earring, not what a man would wear.

—So what on earth do you think?

—I think he's collected them. In the past. From other women.

—You're joking. Like trophies?

—Not exactly like trophies. That would be too ridiculous. More like souvenirs.

—Oh no, said Clare. —Surely not. That can't be.

—I didn't tell him that I found them. The box was dusty, down at the bottom of a drawer full of old things, and the earrings were sort of dingy, the shine had gone off them. There wasn't anything very good. So I don't think he collects them any more. And anyway, maybe I made it all up in the first place: he could have them for any odd reason. Perhaps he had an old girlfriend with only one ear pierced and she left them.

—How many were there?

—I didn't want to count. I don't know. Quite a lot: they were all in a tangle together. I put them back and I haven't looked at them again.

—It doesn't matter, anyway, said Clare. —As you say, it was probably all years and years ago.

There is a minute or two on the video where Toby catches David sitting alone in the front room in the not-so-comfortable chair. David looks up at him and then away again, absorbed in thinking about something. He's photogenic; all those things about him which seem exaggerated and over-eager in the flesh – the hard curved cheekbones, the standing-up thick hair, the big mouth full of talk – are toned down by the camera. Clare rewinds the video (this is weeks later, when Toby sends her a copy of his final version). She likes his smile, the lazy look he gives Toby, lids half closed, eyebrows raised, long cheeks in shadow. She rewinds it because she can't work out what he's doing in there. He isn't – he might have been – taking a few relieved minutes off from a dull afternoon to commune with his precious laptop or check his e-mail. This is after he brings the children back from their trip in his special car which rises up on its wheels. (Lily's face at the door was portentous with tales to tell of how he drove along, entertaining them by making it dance, taking his foot on and off the brake in time to the music on his stereo. Coco was disgusted at his showing off. Only Rose liked him, she chose him, there on the beach, Rose the child Clare thinks of as most like herself.) Helly is in the kitchen helping Clare get supper ready (only not helping much). Bram is taking a shower. The children are playing something noisy on the stairs which involves tipping out all the contents of the toy basket (it's one of those moments where she wishes they had a telly).

David is looking at her books. He isn't looking at them as a reader might, getting close to see the titles, pulling them out and opening them up. He isn't a reader, he's hardly read anything, she's already worked that out. He's just sitting with his head thrown back and one leg propped across the other, surveying her books with a kind of thoughtful smile as if he's putting together some idea of the sort of person who might want to read all these, someone whose life was hidden under these covers.

Clare feels slightly uneasy, and amused, watching him looking. He may of course have completely the wrong idea of what is in her books. People who don't read often imagine that a life lived with books is serenely truthful, perhaps rather idealistic, elevated to a higher sphere above the trickeries and treacheries of real life. Combined with the children, and the little house without television, and the making of her own bread and the salting of lemons, the books may make him think she is wholesome and sane. He may think that he is much more devious than she is.

Three days after the visit an envelope came in the post

addressed to Clare. Bram had left for work, she was on her way to take the kids to school, pinning Rose down in her pushchair to fasten her straps. She didn't recognise the handwriting: she tore it open, shouting at Coco to get his lunch box. Inside, wrapped in a slip of tissue paper, was a single earring. Of course.

As soon as she got home from delivering the children she dug out an old jewellery box she kept in a drawer in her bedroom (the box had once played music and been her grandmother's); inside was a jumble of souvenirs and junk, museum tickets, suitcase keys, bills from cafés she and Bram had been to in Venice and Stockholm, picture hooks, the tassel from an old embroidered belt. She scrabbled in the mess of tarnished, damaged jewellery and drawing pins at the bottom of the box, and found the matching earring to the one she had been sent. It was black, of course, gothic black and silver: to go with the lipstick and the nails.

She would never have recognised him: it was only when Helly told her about his collection of souvenirs that she remembered what had happened at that party of Tim Dashwood's. David had never given her any sign, all weekend, that he remembered. If he had said anything, or even looked significantly at her, then the whole thing would only have been funny or embarrassing. As it was, the broken token that had been restored (that's how Clare thought of it: she kept the two earrings buried far apart from one another in different hiding places) seemed to have an occult power to frighten and excite her, so that for a while she simply didn't know what would happen to her next, or what she might do.

The Axe

Once, Toby found an axe.

It was when he was about twelve; he was playing one evening with a gang of other boys in a grassed over area with benches and young trees near his home. They were not allowed to play football there but they did, until late, until it was too dim to see the heaps of their coats used as goalposts, and their shouts bounced eerily against the sky slipping higher and higher away from them behind the dark.

Toby went to fetch the ball from behind some bushes and found a small cairn of pale stones, each about hand sized, neatly built in a concealed place between the bushes and a wall. The pile was as high as his knees; he almost fell over it, looking for the ball. He crouched down beside it and began taking off the stones one by one to find out what was underneath. He could hear the other boys calling for him and then one of them broke through the bushes and breathed strenuously down at him.

—Where's the ball, Tobe?

—I want to find what's underneath.

—Underneath wha'?

The boy bent down to watch Toby's painstaking dismantling. The others pushed in and soon they were all, five of them, pressed into the awkward space between the bushes and the wall, watching. You could see the stones because they were pale in the murky light, like Toby's hands moving them.

—Who made it? one of them asked.

—Fuck knows.

—Where'd they get those fucking stones from anyway?

—I can't *see*, Toby complained sharply back across his shoulder at one point, and they moved obediently out of what light was left. He thought incredulously sometimes of this moment of command and obedience; afterwards, when through his long illness and absence he had lost his place in the hierarchy of boys, and did not know any longer how to speak to them in a way that would effect any response or claim attention.

Under the last stones of the cairn lay something wrapped up in thick polythene. The boys squatted round it, portentous with the mystery. One of them skewed suddenly to look behind them through the gap in the bushes. —What if someone comes?

—It's a gun, one said.

But it wasn't.

Toby unfolded the polythene cautiously and the last light found out a pale gleam in the shining head of a new axe. He picked it up by its handle and felt the sheathed smoothness of thick-varnished wood.

—There's blood on it! one of them said hoarsely, playacting their fears and frightening himself. Toby dropped the axe back hastily onto the polythene. They all recoiled: a clotted shadow stuck to it might not be merely shadow.

—Fuck off, he said, and picked it up again, turning its head this way and that. It was quite clean. He weighed it on his palm: heavy, and cold, and with a film of grease.

★   ★   ★

The boys in the gang, although each had a family life which was quite distinctive and unrepeatable, belonged together in a social class apart from the one Toby's family belonged to, and Toby was anxiously aware of this separation and of himself dissimulating it. Kingsmile was a mixed area of the city; the big cheap houses appealed to a few 'arty' families, as Toby's mother called them (the word would never have passed Toby's lips), but most of them were turned into flats and bedsits and student lets. Since Toby had been playing out in the street, facts which had once been merely the warm enfolding substance of his life – his father the ceramicist, his mother with wings of long hair who sat cross-legged on the floor and rolled her own cigarettes – had to be steered around, the others had to be distracted from them. 'He makes mugs and stuff,' Toby threw out when pressed, with calculated roughness, as if it was as incomprehensible to him as it was to them. He wished he lived in a home where the television was always on, he wished his mother would buy big plastic bottles of blue pop.

None the less the crowd of boys spent a lot of time in Toby's room, because no one in that house ever questioned their coming or going, no one bothered to catch them out smoking cigarettes. The house was already full anyway with a constant stream of visitors, the doorbell and the phone were constantly ringing, mostly for Toby's two older half-sisters from his father's first marriage. The other boys never said a word against Toby's parents, but still his shoulders went into a hunch of embarrassment when he led the sheepish file past his father's workshop or past his parents drinking wine at the oversized kitchen table.

It was to Toby's dad they took the axe.

First they carefully rebuilt the cairn. They were all agreed they should not put the axe back.

—If it was just for cutting wood why would they hide it here? Al sensibly said. So Toby rewrapped it in its polythene and stuffed it under his shirt, the others crowding around him for camouflage. No one mentioned what they all imagined, that whoever owned the axe and had hidden it might be watching them, and might be enraged at this disruption to his plan, whatever it was. Solemnly they collected up their coats and gear and accompanied Toby home. Leaving the grassed area they had to walk along beside the high wall of a disused small engineering works before they turned into the street before Toby's street: involuntarily, they kept glancing upwards, half expecting to see Him outlined maniacally against the sky, crouched on the top of the wall where broken glass was set into concrete, poised to throw himself upon them and reclaim his property.

Toby's mother had been crying.

The bottle of wine between his parents on the table was empty, they hadn't cleared up the meal around them, the salad was wilting into its dressing. Toby wasn't embarrassed by the mess, but wished it had been something more normal than salad and vegetable crumble. His mother blotted her cheeks with the backs of her hands, then with a tea towel. The black lines she always drew inside her lower eyelids were smudged and there were flecks of black in the tears in her eyes; her lips and teeth were stained blue by the wine.

—Do you want anything to eat, darling? There's plenty left. Anybody hungry?

The others refused politely; bringing the axe wrapped in its polythene out from under his shirt, Toby didn't deign to reply. He addressed his father.

28

—We found this. We reckon we should take it to the police. It wasn't just lost, it was hidden on purpose.

His father looked as if he had to draw his mind from far away to attend to their polythene package, but also as if he was pleased to have it drawn. He stood up in his slow and powerful way (at least there was that: he was six foot two and thirteen stone and used to box for his college), combing his fingers hard up into his chin through his beard. Toby's half-sisters said he did that when he felt the world was against him and he was wilfully misunderstood: they had the whole repertoire of his gestures decoded.

—Now, he said, in his rumbling big voice. —Found what? Where?

They unwrapped their trophy from its layers of soft thick opaque polythene, they explained the strangeness of their finding it. The axe looked brash against the old pine table.

—But I expect it's just a tool someone's bought and wrapped up to keep it dry, Dad said. —We need to take it back to them.

—If he was going to chop wood with it, why hide it under a pile of stones? Foggles repeated what Al had said earlier. Usually they didn't talk much to parents, but in the importance of the moment the boys were forthcoming and serious.

—And he specially brought the stones. There's no stones round where he hid it. He must have brought them on purpose.

—It's like he didn't want to keep it at home, in case anyone saw.

—You shouldn't have touched it, Tobe, Haggis said. —Police might want to fingerprint.

Dad smiled knowingly into his beard but he didn't pick

the axe up. —I don't know if the police'll really be very interested. There haven't actually been many axe murders round here recently.

—It's interesting, Toby's mother said, —that we all presume it belongs to a man, planning violence against a woman.

His dad didn't look at her. —*Do* we all presume that, Naomi? I don't think I'm presuming anything.

—Well, that's what I'm picking up. That's what we're all imagining. Some man planning some horrible secret thing, some way of hurting and destroying someone close to him. Somehow that's what it makes me think of, the horrible ugly thing. It's like a sign, a sign of cruelty and abuse. I don't even want it in the house. Seizing the tea towel again she turned her back on them all and started opening another bottle of wine.

There were a few moments of polite apologetic silence, while the boys let the woman's words pass. Toby's dad rested his ten fingers on the edge of the table, his head slightly bowed. (The girls said this meant he was reflecting sorrowfully on the bottomlessness of his extraordinary patience.)

—So what d'you reckon we ought to do with it, Dad?

—I still think it's a tool somebody bought and wrapped up to stop it from rusting. Maybe whoever prunes the trees at the park.

Naomi snorted over her corkscrew. —With an axe!

—Well, we'll take it to the police tomorrow. See what they say. What shall I do with it for now? Naomi?

She shook her head in abandonment without turning round.

—In the outhouse? OK? Everybody happy?

He rewrapped the package with that scrupulously responsible concentration he always brought to minor domestic tasks, managing to communicate at once (the girls said) extreme willingness to do his bit with the helplessness of the creative artist who couldn't be expected to do it very often.

He and Toby took the axe to the police station the next day. The police were as mystified as they were, wrote the details down on a form, and kept the axe. Haggis, who was often off school and who lived alone with his mother in a flat overlooking the place where they played football, said he saw a policeman poking about once behind the shrubs where Toby had found the cairn. Three months later when everyone had forgotten about it, a card from the police arrived at Toby's house saying that the axe had not been claimed and that therefore if they wanted it they could collect it.

They didn't want it, of course. Particularly, they didn't want it, because in the meantime Toby's dad, Graham, had left Naomi and Toby and Clare and Tamsin and had gone to live with the woman who would become his third wife, and with whom he would go on to have three more children even though he was already in his fifties.

Also they didn't want it because Toby had started, shortly after the night they found the axe, to be ill. He began by suffering from headaches and a general feeling of weakness and malaise. For several months their general practitioner insisted he was malingering. Probably he thought it was something Naomi was making up, or that she was producing in her son as a hysterical response to her husband's leaving her. Naomi at that time would not have inspired confidence in her powers of diagnosis or in her authority as a responsible mother. Every night she drank a bottle of wine. She once went round to where Graham was living with his new girlfriend and stood yelling her opinion of them in the street and threw the bottle and broke a window (in the wrong flat, as it turned out). Another night she took an overdose of pills and although she almost immediately threw them up again Clare and Tamsin called an ambulance just in case. She gave up the job she had had in a shop specialising in Native American crafts, and the household had to manage on social security and whatever Graham gave them, which wasn't much and was naturally another source of grievance.

It was suddenly a very female and a very aggrieved household. Naomi and her two stepdaughters talked and talked about Graham and his vanity and his weakness and his lust and his selfishness and his fear of ageing until the conversation ached and winced and they couldn't bear to touch it any more, for a few hours at least. Clare and Tamsin wouldn't have anything to do with their father for almost two years. (It was the *babies* that coaxed them round to a reconciliation in the end.) Even Marian, the first wife and Clare's and Tamsin's mother (they lived with her at weekends), came round and joined in the 'Graham conversation', as the girls called it, on one or two occasions.

But Naomi knew there was really something wrong with Toby. In the mornings when she struggled out of her poisoned drunken sleep to get him up for school, she was at least sensible enough to tell the difference between an ordinary unhappy boy and this listless deadweight huddled under his Star Wars duvet. He even smelled sick.

—Darling, she said, her tongue thick with shaming fur, the broken pieces of her life taking up their swollen lurid waking places in her mind. —Just describe to me exactly how it hurts, and where.

But he only moved his head once in frowning denial, not opening his eyes, his mouth clamped shut, keeping her out.

In the doctor's surgery, her puffy pale face without make-up and her velvet skirt stained and crumpled, she insisted on knowing which tests could be done to find out what was the matter. The doctor even joked that she should try some herbal remedies, or 'Red Indian charms'. In the end the tests showed that Toby had a form of viral encephalitis, an inflammation of the brain; and he was off school for two years, with almost constant pain in his head and all over his body. He spent months in hospital, because the encephalitis weakened his immune system and made him prone to other illnesses: he had pneumonia twice. Naomi lost interest in the Graham conversation. She cut down her drinking; whenever Toby was in hospital she slept every night there too; she was silent, fixated, dull company except when she was talking to other mothers with ill children. The girls moved back to live full time with Marian.

At one point when Toby was very ill his name was mentioned in Assembly at school, and his class collected money for flowers. Two or three years later when he was better, he once bumped into Haggis (Haggis's real name was James, and that was how Toby hailed him from across the street). Toby and Naomi meanwhile had moved to a flat in a different part of the city, and Toby had started back at a different school. Haggis looked surprised to see him, and told him they had all presumed that he had died.

When Toby was twenty he went away to University, where he studied for a Visual Arts degree specialising in film and video. When he came home at the end of his final year he planned to spend some of the summer with his mother, and some with Clare and her husband and children, before he went off travelling with his camera. Naomi had moved again since he'd last seen her, and had got out of an abusive relationship with a man with a mental health problem (before that there had been a married businessman who imported shoes). She was now living with another woman, Angie. Tamsin couldn't deal with it and wouldn't visit them, but Clare said it was a good thing. She said that Naomi had fallen into a pattern of being treated badly by the men she got involved with, and that this relationship with Angie was a sign of her wanting to break that pattern. She said that women were kinder to women than men ever were, more appreciative and gentle and sensitive; and that Naomi's choice of Angie was a sign that at least she wasn't willing her own destruction any more.

Naomi picked him up from the bus station in her old VW Beetle. The car was as scruffy as ever and she had to move paper tissues, crisp packets, Tampax box, secateurs and rolling tobacco before he could get into the front seat; but she looked pretty. She was wearing an embroidered silky top and jeans; she had had her hair cut shoulder length and as Clare said, it made her look younger because she didn't look as if she was trying to. The lines at the corners of her eyes and mouth were still there, but crinkled with smiling. She was buoyant and childish and seemed rather overexcited, unlike his usual idea of her: small, dark, concentrated with suffering. Her silver earrings had some sort of symbol on which might be a lesbian thing: Toby didn't mind, as long as she didn't try to corner him with it and make him say something.

—We're nearly there. Look, Toby!

They were driving round a mini-roundabout at the end of a suburban street; an improvised banner was tied between two young trees. In red paint on a white torn sheet was written: 'Welcome home, Toby Menges, BA!'

There were tears in her eyes. —Did you see, sweetheart?

Realise how proud of you we are? Let's go round again, what the hell!

This time she sounded the horn, blaring out one of the rhythms he used to clap at football matches with his friends. A car following them onto the roundabout sounded its horn too, probably in protest rather than sympathy.

Toby's face was hot; he stared ahead, blinkered with embarrassment.

—The banner was Angie's idea. She hung it up last night, after it was dark. We were just praying it wouldn't rain. She was so determined it would be the first thing you'd see.

Angie and Naomi had found the house together; it was a maisonette, with a front door up concrete steps round the side of a white-painted nineteen thirties semi. It didn't look like Naomi's usual sort of place – not 'arty' – but the gardens were full of flowers and there were trees everywhere, as if the suburb had been tucked inside a little wood. Angie was waiting for them at the top of the steps before the car had even stopped. She was small and slight like Naomi, but younger and more definite; when they were together Naomi seemed dreamier and vaguer than she really was. Angie had short-cut hair and very bright eyes with a distinctive extra fold of firm flesh beneath them which made them pixie-like; her glances like all her gestures were quick and pointed and compact.

—Hello Toby, she said, reaching out a small cool brown hand laden with silver rings. She had a butterfly tattooed on her upper arm and another one appliquéd onto her sleeveless white vest. —Meet Angie: I'm the new light in your mother's life. We're both very proud of you.

Toby felt large as an elephant – or perhaps a giraffe – between them in their little home. Their tables and chairs only seemed to reach somewhere around his knees, and he kept walking into doorframes as though they were built to a different scale. They had baked him a cake with three candles for the three years of his degree and decorated it with the University logo, which he didn't recognise until they pointed it out. The sitting room was hung with paper chains and balloons and more 'Welcome Home' banners: it was very tidy and bright and full of plants and pictures; there was even a colour scheme, with a blue sofa (which would turn into a bed for him later), blue curtains and yellow walls. They got out a bottle of champagne from the fridge. Toby didn't know how to open it so Angie did, and they drank a toast to him.

—I only got a 2.2, he protested, blushing. —It's honestly not worth all this.

—Nonsense, said Naomi, putting her arm around his waist and her head against his chest. —We've had such hard times and such a lot of bad luck. Now everything's turning out to be for the best. Here's to you, my brilliant boy. Here's to us. Isn't this a bit better than where you last saw me?

—I'd say so, said Angie. —Better than that tip.

Naomi and Angie had planned out the whole evening. They showed Toby round the garden, which belonged to the owners who lived downstairs but which they were allowed to use. It was a big garden, rather neglected, overtaken by clumps of pampas grass and wandering up among trees at its far end.

—I'd love to get to work out here, said Naomi, who was good at plants. —Perhaps they'll let us put a few things in and do a bit of tidying up.

—Perhaps, said Angie tolerantly. —If we get the time.

Then there were cocktails and hot home-made nibbles, followed by vegetarian lasagne and expensive ice cream. And for after dinner they had rented a video, *Shine*, which they thought would be suitable.

—I know you're not into blockbusters, said Angie.

He politely didn't tell them he'd seen it already, or that he hadn't liked it.

Over balloon glasses of brandy last thing, when they had pulled out the sofa and made up his bed, Angie explained to Toby that her name wasn't short for Angela. She had been rushed into hospital when she was only a few hours old, and the nurses had called her Angel because they didn't think she'd live. A man walking his dog in a park had found her abandoned under a bush, wrapped up in someone's bloody nightdress. They never found out whose nightdress it was.

—I'm the original babe in the woods, she said. —Now, wouldn't that make a great film? Haven't I given you a fantastic subject? Complete with a happy ending too.

Naomi poured herself a second brandy. She watched Angie with a private smiling concentration, nursing her glass in her warm palms and breathing the fumes, slightly drunk and exalted. Then she turned to Toby expectantly as if he was their audience and might applaud what she loved and had had displayed for him.

When he settled down to sleep Toby pulled the duvet tightly up over his ears. Their bedroom opened directly off the sitting room where he lay. He dreaded overhearing Angie making love with his mother (although no more than he had dreaded it with the men).

Angie was a playworker on a council scheme. Naomi had been doing office work for the RAC for a couple of years now: it was dull but it was safe, it brought the money in, she didn't hate it. So they were both out all day; they stepped around

Toby in his bed in the mornings while they were getting ready, and made their arrangements in hurried undertones. When they pulled the door shut behind them at half past eight he sank back down into a sleep that ballooned with relief and lightness into the empty space.

They left him notes in the kitchen: 'Supper at six thirty if you'd like some (aubergine bake)'; there were two boxes to tick for yes or no. He worried while he ate his cereals over what to put, and how often he could say no without offending them; it was always possible that they felt as grateful as he did on the nights he ate at Clare's or bought himself chips. When he said yes, he had to spend all day trying to remember to get back in time. There was only one bus from town that came anywhere near the house and it only ran once an hour; if he got out of bed around midday that didn't leave him much time for getting things done. If he was late for supper Angie would be silent and smiling and Naomi over-emphatic in her reassurances that it didn't matter and hurrying to warm things up.

He did have things to do. Each day he set himself one task to accomplish: the travel agents to visit, or the doctor's to organise his inoculations, or some item of clothing to buy, or insurance to arrange. He didn't always accomplish it. Toby's 'task for the day' became a sort of jokey catchphrase with Angie: and it was true that he wasn't very good at focusing single-mindedly on his purpose. However much he determined not to be distracted or to allow himself to be waylaid, there must have been something in his face that gave away an openness to suggestion like a weakness. Anyone eccentric or garrulous always sat next to him on the bus. People selling political newspapers or giving out religious tracts or tickets for a club homed in on him from across a crowd, or refugees with an album of photographs of torture injuries and a petition to sign which turned out to involve contributing money. He never managed not to catch the eye of the *Big Issue* sellers, so that he always had to stop and explain to them that he didn't have anything to spare. Then he'd find himself in a long conversation while the crowd flowed past as if he'd never been a part of it, on his way somewhere.

The day he went to see his father he happened to have a book in his pocket which he had just bought from a man selling *Socialist Worker*; when he had tried to explain that he didn't want to buy their paper because it seemed to him that their approach to politics was superficial and sloganising, the man had produced from somewhere inside his coat a book of essays in tiny print on shiny paper, assuring Toby that he would find inside the deep-level analysis that he was looking for. Toby accepted it rather than make a fuss, and then the man asked him for two pounds. Graham got very excited about the book.

—God, I can't *believe* that anyone still reads this stuff. Wonderful old Trotskyite *nonsense* . . . Listen to this: 'Sooner or later, and despite all the immense obstacles on the way, the working class and its allies in other classes will bring into being an authentically democratic social order . . .' Ah, those were the days. And you paid two pounds? For this? Of course I was in the CP when I was at college. We'd have thought this was dangerous revisionism.

He had to lend Toby two pounds to replace what he'd spent (Toby needed it for the bus fare) and he went on reading out sentences about workers and mass movements in delighted irony until the toddler he was minding fell over his baby-walker and had to be picked up and consoled. Graham's third wife Linda worked in a psychiatric unit for teenagers and was the family breadwinner; Graham looked after the children who were aged nine and five and two.

—I hear your mother's having a lesbian fling, Graham said, expertly hoisting his little son's legs in the air to change his nappy, wiping him with a sequence of torn-off chunks of cotton wool soaked in baby oil which he had laid out ready in a row alongside the plastic changing mat. He was looking austerely patriarchal; his hair and beard had turned a soft clean white. Clare had told Toby that he had played Santa Claus for Daniel's playgroup, and also that he wasn't selling much work. 'Whether it's because he's not producing much, or because nobody wants it, we're not sure . . .'

—Yes, kind of, said Toby.

—Poor old Naomi! Why can nothing ever be straight-forward with her? Still holding up the baby's feet, he spread a clean nappy deftly underneath its bottom with his big right hand. —And is it all going to end in tears as usual?

—They've got a nice flat, Toby said.

—In Leigh Mills, of all places! Frightfully respectable.

—It's got a nice garden.

—I'm sure it's all very nice. But rather her than me.

Graham and Linda still lived in Kingsmile, near where Graham and Naomi had once lived together; but it had changed, and most of the big houses that had been bedsits and student lets had been renovated and repainted, their floors were sanded and the old fireplaces put back in. On the way to catch his bus (Graham had wanted to drive him back, but had to pick up his nine-year-old daughter from ballet) Toby walked past the scrap of park where he used to play football with his friends before he got ill. A few boys now were scuffling or riding their bikes desultorily in and out of the trees. The trees were fatter and heavier and the boys had expensive bikes and names like Dominic and Jake and Noah.

Toby got himself so entangled with a couple of young evangelists that he ended up spending an evening at a house where one of them lived, not an ordinary family house but something like a youth hostel for religious young people. Different residents, lots of them African and South-East Asian students, came and went during the evening, heating themselves solitary suppers in the microwave. They didn't seem to know one another very well. Notices on pieces of paper were sellotaped onto cupboard doors in the kitchen: instructions, complaints about stolen food or washing up, and a fluorescent poster for a concert, 'Christ Takes the Rap'. The kitchen had a sickly smell like margarine.

Toby had been invited, without quite realising it, to a sort of prayer-meeting. When the two young men had stopped him in town, asking him how he felt about consumerism and materialism, he had given them his telephone number without thinking, trying to get rid of them without seeming rude. Then when they rang him at Angie's and Naomi's flat he had thought he had better agree to meet them somewhere so that he could explain that it would be awkward if they kept telephoning him because it was his mother's number. He found himself sitting drinking instant coffee with seven or eight others round a bare formica table under a central light. Only one of them lived in the house, and they were not all young. There was a man with a grey goatee and a paisley cravat whose wife had died of cancer (rather a long time ago, it turned out), and a middle-aged woman who was a buyer for Marks and Spencers and said, reproachfully, she wished she'd thought to bring some 'nibbles'.

Toby listened to them talk. He didn't recognise their experience; he couldn't imagine what it would be like to feel as they felt that God was involved intimately in every tiny twist and turn of their experience, as interested in their lives as they were, partaking of their hopes and anxieties and indignations. Outnumbered by them, he wondered how they could possibly all be wrong. The buyer described how her faith had helped her to her latest promotion at work. The young man who lived in the hostel explained how God had given him a sign that he was to leave his college course in business studies and find work helping in the community (he hadn't really found it yet, apart from stopping people in town and asking them how they felt about materialism). A girl from a family of refugees from Laos told how her secret prayers (her mother disapproved of her conversion) had ended in her father's release after fifteen years in a re-education camp. The man with the goatee said that his wife's spirit often visited him, touching him and reassuring him as he went around doing the housework that she used to do.

There was something attractive and disquieting about how casually they used words like faith and spirit and love, and how they mixed together fantastic assumptions of God's reality and agency with ordinary everyday knowhow. Toby contemplated the possibility that perhaps the world was really this shimmering yielding fabric of opportunity and love and he was simply closed to it. With a banality that irritated him he kept coming back in his mind to the question of the shower rail he had broken in Angie's and Naomi's bathroom the other day, grabbing it and ripping it out from the wall when he slipped under the shower because he'd forgotten to put the rubber bath mat down. There was no possibility – even if he prayed, even if God was real, even if there was a transcendent redeeming meaning to life and death – that that shower rail could be back in the wall and never have come out, that the big dirty holes in the plaster, full of a mess of screws and Rawlplugs, could be unmade, or that his mother could have not rushed in and looked at the disaster with such a frightened face (Angie was out). —We could pretend I did it, she had said.

This was a trivial point, he knew. He knew such trivial things could be interpreted as mere distractions from a larger theme. But he felt it none the less as a blockage, a stopping point that prevented him seeing God's transformations. It was the real small accidental things that happened in time, he felt, that could not be altered or loosened. And he felt those real small things as implacably strong, stronger than all the rest.

There was only one thing he could think of from his own experience to proffer modestly alongside all the signs and instructions and intimations these other lives had bristled with. Occasionally when he was facing a flat surface, a door or a wall – and especially when he was tired – he saw a brilliant flickering on it like the reflection of a conflagration behind him; when he looked quickly, instinctively, over his shoulder there was never anything there. He wondered for a while whether to mention it. Then he decided not to. Told baldly, it would seem pretty insignificant. And he had always known it might only be a trick of the brain left over from his illness.

One Saturday, after he had been staying there for about a fortnight, he came back to the maisonette at supper time and found the door open at the top of the concrete steps. Outside the door were some gardening things: trays of bedding plants, a trowel with earth stuck to it, muddy gardening gloves. From inside he could hear Angie's voice. He thought she might be telling one of her funny stories, because his mother didn't reply and Angie's voice was pitched rather exuberantly rhetorical. When he got to the top of the steps he stopped, embarrassed, not quite able to make out what was going on inside. The room was shadowy at first in contrast to the bright summer's afternoon. The white of Angie's sleeveless sweatshirt came and went in the shadows.

At first he thought it was sex. His mother was lying on her back on the floor, Angie was crouched astride her, athletic in tight leggings, rocking backwards and forwards hard and rhythmically, slowly; taking the weight on her arms when she hung over Naomi, lifting her bottom; then pushing off her hands, pulling her back straight and banging down hard onto her, crotch to crotch. They were both fully clothed. Naomi was lying with her head away from the door, Toby couldn't see her face, nor Angie's, Angie was busy with her back to him. When Angie brought her weight down hard on Naomi, Naomi's feet leaped weakly in the old stained canvas espadrilles she kept for gardening.

He realised it wasn't sex, it was violence.

—He doesn't make his bed, Angie was saying, in a tone of mock surprised delight, banging down on Naomi once for each separate complaint. —He puts the sofa back but he just bundles up the sheet and duvet on top of it. The wastepaper basket's full of his nasty tissues. He leaves a scum of shaving foam around the sink. He leaves the tap running. When he washes up he puts all the pans to soak and then doesn't do them in the morning. His trainers stink the place out. He puts his dirty washing in the basket and expects you to take care of it, even though he's here all day with fuck all to do. And he's been smoking in here. Apart from the stench, I found the butts. Didn't you hear me ask him not to smoke? Didn't you?

Toby thought his mother might be dead.

Then while Angie hung over her, weight balanced on her arms, Naomi turned herself over in one movement, face down onto the floor, wrapping her arms round her head, crying abandonedly.

—You see? said Angie, thumping down on her again, crotch to arse, making Naomi bounce and give out a sobbing grunt. —Didn't I?

Then Toby saw, very clearly, a package lying on the carpet beside the two women, wrapped in soft thick opaque polythene, real with the banality of real solid things. He looked at it without recognition for a few seconds, but curiously, wondering what it had to do with the scene. As soon as he remembered what it was, and was properly astonished at seeing it there, it disappeared.

Angie was rocking more gently now on top of Naomi, back and forwards and from side to side. The crying grew duller and quieter. Angie bent forwards and spoke in a different, coaxing, tone into the hair on the back of Naomi's neck. —So what are you going to do? she said, huskily, as if it was a tease Naomi would enjoy too. —What are you going to do with him? Come on.

Toby retreated down the steps. He tried not to crunch the gravel on the path round to the front of the house. The leaves of the trees dappling the bright sunshine as he made his way through the suburban street reminded him of what he'd just been watching as if he was seeing it on film.

—That *neanderthal*, Angie had also said. —The *graduate*. You've got to be joking.

It occurred to him that from inside the shadowy room the

doorway must have been a brilliant oblong of light; and that when he stood blocking it he must have cast a deep *film noir* shadow, changing everything inside. His mother might have had her eyes closed all that time. She might have. But Angie must have known that he was standing there.

Weeds

A corridor ran the length of the big house, from the top of
the stairs at one end to a tall arched window at the other
end, looking out over a sloping field down to the lake.
Five bedrooms opened off each side of the corridor, and
the last room before the arched window was a bathroom, the
only bathroom. The bath had feet and thundering taps and
peat-brown not quite hot water; the toilet had an overhead
cistern and a chain to pull. The children had never had a chain
to pull before, and they all wanted to use it. Only Coco was tall
enough to reach by himself; Clare had to lift up Lily and help
her give the sharp tug that emptied down more peat-brown
water (they thought it was dirty). Then Rose, who was three,
balanced anxiously gripping with her hands on the edge of the
big wooden seat, and dribbled her tiny wee into the bowl.
They waited for the cistern to finish its slow self-absorbed
water-music and be full again for her turn.

This was County Clare, Ireland.

There were enough bedrooms for everyone staying there
that summer to have slept alone if they had wanted; but out
of lack of experience in such solitude-bestowing living space,
they all clustered together into the four bedrooms nearest the
bathroom. Even Bram's two sisters, aged twenty-seven and

thirty-one, slept in a twin bedroom together to 'catch up on their chat'. Clare's and Bram's bedroom had damp-blotched nineteen-sixties orange and pink flowered wallpaper and a green satin bedspread and orange-striped curtains in a felty synthetic material which floated rather than hung and kept out no light at all.

You could see the lake from their window too. When Clare woke early, earlier than she ever ever did at home – by nature she was sluggish in the mornings and clung to the warm odorous den of sheets and blankets – she got up and stood in her nightdress in the window recess behind the floaty curtains. She saw dawn, she heard the dawn chorus, she saw mists lying like a layer of white milk on the fields and water, she heard the day start up outside with the multitudinous lives of animals and birds and plants, hours before the humans stirred inside the house. The cold climbed up inside her nightdress from her feet on the bare boards. She stood in a kind of ecstasy until her feet got so cold she was uncomfortable: then she put socks on, and retreated back to bed to warm herself up against Bram.

This ecstasy of hers was probably absurd, in relation to the man she was obsessing about (she couldn't call him her lover, he wasn't that yet). As far as she knew, he – David – wasn't in the least interested in natural things, he liked London and cars and sound technology. It was Bram, her partner, and not David, who was the early riser, the bird-watcher and morning-lover and fresh-air enthusiast. David's taste as far as she knew (she hadn't been to his flat yet) was austerely urban and contemporary. Austerely: she felt a quiver of pleasurable chastisement at the thought of how he would cut through the half-considered shell of her homemaking with its cosy clutter.

David's preferences excited her as if they were messages to

her. At home she had taken to watching all the television programmes he had said he liked; she had brought on holiday with her tapes of music he had recommended, obscure jungle and drum 'n' bass, types of music Clare had hardly known about a couple of months ago. Whenever she got a chance to drive the car down to the shop on her own she played them, imagining him watching her to the soundtrack of the music, imagining him taking pleasure in the competence of her driving and the chic of her sunglasses. There was a moment's dislocation when she turned off the ignition and the music stopped; a flicker, like shame, of self-consciousness left high and dry.

It would be a fine day. They were incredibly lucky with the weather on this holiday. The mini-market was cave-like, dark, humming with freezers, thin on temptations, odorous with cauliflower. They only seemed to sell one flavour of crisps; when she wanted a pound bag of flour, they opened a three-pound bag in spite of her protests and weighed out a third for her; they sent presents of sweets up for the children every time. Usually Clare was exaggeratedly deferential on her holidays, scrupulously aware of her outsider's ineptness. She knew enough about Irish history to have felt apologetic for her English yawing vowels and her problems understanding what was said to her, and to have felt wincingly what reverberations might be touched off by an English family renting a Big House, even a small Big House, for their holiday. But that summer she felt licensed in her privilege, lordly in her assumption of the pleasures of the place. (Because of it she was probably friendlier and better liked.) She imagined she was responsible for the fine weather, too.

Genevieve Verey had been so disgusted by the burden of

romance in the name her mother gave her that when it came to names for her own children she simply looked up surnames in the *Times* deaths column and chose something. So her son was Bramford and her two daughters (one older; one younger than Bram) were Tinsley and Opie. Clare could imagine Genny getting over the whole business of the births with the same pragmatism, the same slightly theatrical gestures of contempt for other people's fuss. She had seen photographs of the young Genny, recognisable – in spite of the white hair and the thickened flesh that had come since – because of that bright scornful readiness in her expression. The old-fashioned kind of childbirth would have suited her, enema and pubes shaved, jollying injunctions to be a good girl and not make a row, new baby taken off to a nursery so Mother could get a decent night's sleep. It was impossible to imagine her in the midst of all the palaver of Clare's generation, beanbags and water births, bonding and demand feeding; impossible to imagine hers as one of those middle-class households thrown into a kind of slack excruciated martyrdom for years on end by sleep problems and the crisis of belief in adult authority.

While they were all on holiday together Clare tried to keep out of sight that potential in her own family life for spilling over into martyrdom and hysteria. Coco worked droopingly through a whole sequence of symptoms from a sore throat to a sprained ankle; Lily made nightly scenes about spiders; Rose's moaning and struggling ruined every trip they tried to take her on so that in the end Clare and Bram took it in turns to stay behind with her in the house. Clare was sure that when Tinsley and Bram and Opie were children they wouldn't have wasted time quarrelling about TV channels (the house had Sky), but would have escaped outdoors every possible minute to the lake and the woods and the ruined mill. Of course she couldn't have let her children do this even if they had wanted to, she would have thought it much too dangerous. That was a perception that had changed with the generations too.

Whenever Bram and his sisters did tell stories from their childhood, which wasn't often because they had been brought up to be shy and sceptical of talking about themselves, the stories were never about fights but about projects carried out as a little team of siblings, loyal, intimate, peculiar, with passions distributed conveniently between them: Bram with his birds, Tinsley with her rocks, Opie with her snakes. One summer they built a tree house in their back garden in Oxford and slept in it every fine night. One holiday in Northumberland they repaired an old boat they found by the river and caulked it and painted it and gave it a name and took it on leaky trips out on the water. (They named it *Shimmershy*: Clare wondered which one of the girls – it must have been one of the girls – had given way to romance for an inspired moment.) Such stories, as far as Clare was concerned, belonged inside books and were unimaginable as real childhoods; it seemed wholly characteristic that while Bram and his sisters had been busy living these adventures she had only been busy reading about them.

Genny took Coco and Lily and the others on an expedition looking for bones in the Burren; she was chief technician for the University Bone Collection at Oxford, trained as an animal behaviourist and now working for the Archaeology Department. Lily, under her grandmother's tutelage, was getting quite bold and had even poked at a very dead cat at the side of the road with a stick, having the structure and articulation pointed out to her. (Unfortunately it didn't make any difference to her feelings about spiders.) Bram had managed to persuade his mother not to bring the cat home and boil it up for its skeleton – they had already done several voles and a pigeon, filling the house with a stink Clare had to wash out of her hair. She had learned long ago never to look under the lids of Genny's saucepans. Coco had helped to bleach the bones and lay them out like exquisite puzzles on old seed trays in the plant-less ruined conservatory. He had a pigeon wing too, and had showed Clare condescendingly how it folded like a fan.

When they went to the Burren Clare stayed at home with Rose and played David's tapes on Coco's Walkman. She sat on the grey crumbling steps of the portico at the front of the house to smoke one of the cigarettes she had bought on her last visit to the mini-market: the cigarettes too were a fetish item from her obsession, as if by accumulating around her objects and habits associated with David she could somehow translate herself inside his real presence. No other building except some unused outhouses and one wall of the ruined mill was visible from where she sat; she could see the lake, the islands, a field where the hay was gathered into old-fashioned beehive-shaped stooks you never saw in England any more. It was a ten-minute drive down to the village; at night, partly because of the trees planted closely round the house, you couldn't see another light.

Rose had taken all her clothes off and, having achieved her point in getting out of the trip to the Burren, was rewarding Clare with her deep absorption in some rite involving small stones picked from the drive and carried off to a sorting place behind the rhododendrons. Clare made a pot of real coffee and brought it out into the sunshine for herself and Ray, Bram's father, who was painting at the bottom of the rough sloping lawn with his back to her. In this household of practical people (Tinsley was a geologist in plate tectonics, Bram worked on a conservation project, Opie was a physiotherapist) Clare and Ray tended to get lumped together, as if they might help one another out and understand one another's mysteries. Today it was possibly true that they shared a sense of respite in the absence of his wife and his children. He was really startled, coming up from concentration, when she brought him his coffee; he had the same forward-set lower jaw as Bram, so that his mouth closed with an expression of gentle trustingness like a ruminant, a vulnerable deer.

She sat on the stone steps with her novel turned face down beside her because she couldn't concentrate on it. This was one of those moments given on earth like a promise of what's possible: the palely veiled creamy blue sky, the water glinting, the sunwarmed stone against her skin, the heat on her shoulders, the loved child happy playing in the earth, all the loved family spread safely and at their proper distances like a constellation, so that she in her place, part of it, was both holding and held. In literature though, Clare thought, there is a notorious problem with heavenly peace. It is well known that it can only be appreciated through the glass of loss. It is only after Raskolnikov has struck the blow that cleaves him forever from ordinary happiness that he can perceive its possibility. It is only because Emma Bovary's provincial Normandy is in the irrecoverably lost past that what seemed to her banal and smothering seems to us charming, mysterious, desirable. It is only from Paris that Joyce can love Dublin. She listened to the heartbeat-stimulating rhythms on her headphones that were like a message from another place.

Rose began to weave her into her game, including her in the circuit between the drive and the bushes, offering her little stones squeezed in earth-grubby fingers; every time she came close enough Clare captured her and kissed her, drinking in the smell of hot baby skin and hair and earth and vegetation, repentant already that this was not enough, that there was always more that one greedily wanted, more than whatever precious thing it was that one held real and live and finite in one's hands. She was thinking about telephoning David. She hadn't ever intended to telephone him from her holiday; her idea had been that if she simply held off from contacting him or from making any arrangements to see him, then her decision about what she was going to do with him would make itself. But his telephone numbers were written in her diary, and the thought of them had begun to eat like caustic into her idea.

She had written down the numbers, the mobile and the home number, a month ago, on the day she went up to meet David in London, telling Bram she was going to work at the British Library on her thesis. She had fully expected that David would take her into his bed (the bed with the mirrors that she knew about from Helly, her friend, David's girlfriend); she had not known if she would even use her return ticket. The numbers were in case David wasn't there to meet her at the station; but he was, with his jacket slung on one finger over his shoulder, his thick brush of black hair that grew upwards like an exclamation mark, his loud voice that overfilled wherever he was, his oblivious gifted swagger in the great city. Bram wouldn't have understood how she wasn't disappointed by David's showing off, wouldn't have understood how she drank that down as the very element of her pleasure.

But confusingly David hadn't taken her into his bed or even to his flat, but had taken her out for a Thai meal and then to an exhibition of disconcertingly sexual Helmut Newton photographs at the ICA. With everything she knew about him – from Helly – she had presumed that he would be the one who would know how to bridge the unbridgeable transition between the animated conversation of friends and the first fumbles of acknowledgement, the first frank reachings out. She had surely done enough by simply turning up. Didn't he know to read that as her absolute surrender to whatever he wanted? But the more they talked the more the talk had seemed to pile up between them, solid and sensible as stone, separating them. All the time she was smiling and talking, putting on to the utmost an appearance of happy charm, her calculations were racing. Had she misunderstood him from the beginning; when he telephoned and said they should get together, had he meant just this, lunch and galleries? And she thought too, humiliatedly, that unlike her he wasn't desperate, he could afford to wait and see, he could afford to treat with respectful seriousness all the good reasons lunch and galleries was quite enough. She smothered a panicking sense that she would be betrayed into making a scene, that she simply couldn't bear to go home without the initiation she had come for.

Then as they stood in the idle wide space in front of the departures board at the station, he had kissed her, and in such a way that she was quite certain after all that there had been no mistake. One of those motorised yellow litter sweepers bore down on them noisily. The sight of them kissing must have enraged the bored driver, he nudged towards them several times before they retreated out of his path, then he came round at them again for good measure.

—Can you stay? David asked, into her ear, into her hair. —Stay, please, stay. Phone home.

She shook her head. Really, she couldn't stay. No, now they were on the far side of the unbridgeable gap, she was full of doubt suddenly. She had forgotten that she would be there with a stranger.

★　　★　　★

She telephoned David that evening while the others were swimming. Every day Genny and Tinsley and Opie and Bram and even Ray went swimming in the lake, taking it in turns to stay with the children in the shallow water by the little stony beach while the others struck off, racing one another for the islands. They all swam a strong crawl; when Bram and Tinsley and Opie were children they had competed in galas and worked for life-saving badges.

Clare couldn't. She could, just, swim; a stately slow breaststroke with her head held out of the water, which was one of the few things Bram ever laughed at her for. But only in a swimming pool, in clear chlorinated water where she could see to the bottom and the worst (bad enough) one might bob up against was a stray used sticking plaster. She was too much of a coward ever to bring herself to swim in the agitated murky sea where jellyfish or crabs or bits of decomposing fish might be washed against her or in the lake which was calm but thick with brown weed growing up almost to the surface, sheltering a whole dark suspect world of underwater life and death. Slippery weed was sometimes wrapped in dark strips like stains around the swimmers' legs when they waded out, blowing and streaming water and shouting breathless exhilarated comments on the shared ordeal to one another.

So while they swam she put out supper onto the plates in the kitchen, washed limp lettuce that was all you could get at the shop and boiled eggs and cut tomatoes and mashed tuna with mayonnaise. She sliced two loaves of floury soda bread. She stood wiping her hands on her apron, hearing the raised voices of the children from the beach. The house had been used as a hotel at some period, so although they only had a dingy miscellany of utensils and a tiny electric stove to cook on (including boiling Genny's voles), the kitchen was full of the relics of past grandeur: a disused Aga and two deep enamel sinks and huge wooden plate racks on the walls like something from a giant's kitchen in a fairy tale. Opie had pulled up a corner of the Vinolay flooring and found stone flags underneath.

Then Clare fished in her handbag for her diary and for coins for the payphone and shut herself into the small cloakroom off the passage behind the kitchen where the phone was mounted on the wall. It smelled of polish and disinfectant because the cleaning things were kept in there. With shaking hands she dialled David's number. She pressed herself back among the coats and waterproofs, distinguishing textures with exactitude against her face with her eyes closed: a button, a pocket fastened with Velcro, a corduroy trim, Rose's ladybird mac.

Helly answered the phone.

Clare had told herself that if Helly answered she had the perfect alibi; why shouldn't she be phoning her best friend from Ireland? She would be phoning to complain, comically, about the Vereys; to let off steam over the well-worked theme of their imperturbable impossible decency and straightness. Helly would recognise the phone call as belonging in a long line of such calls. In the split seconds after Helly's voice was real and close in her ear Clare actually imagined she could hear herself with utter naturalness beginning:

—Hel, can I just be truly ghastly with you for a few minutes? I need a break. They're all *swimming*. You know, not just splashing about at the edge like ordinary people do, but powering up and down across the lake. His sisters are the sorts that actually knew how to inflate their pyjamas for lifesaving at school. D'you remember that? How mine had a rip in and wouldn't blow up? Look, I'm having such an incredibly wholesome time here – it's really nice – that I just need to say a few desperately dirty words to somebody.

It would feel so natural that she would believe as soon as she began that this was what she had called for, the other thing would be so completely instantly submerged that she wouldn't even be lying.

But instead she pressed down with quick silent decision the little metal rests that cut her off. Then she sat listening to the tone in the phone as though she might hear in there the aftershock of what had happened, traces of how Helly had taken it at the other end. Two things occurred to her, each sending through her a pulse of dismay like a too-rich heartbeat. If she had spoken to Helly she would have had to explain how she came to have the telephone number for David's flat; she always spoke to Helly at her own place, Helly had never given her David's number. She couldn't believe she hadn't thought of this, that she had come so near to jeopardising herself. And then as if she could see her doing it she knew that Helly would dial the 1471 recall as soon as the phone went dead, to find out who had been calling. But surely 1471 didn't work for Ireland, surely the mechanical voice would simply say that the number had been witheld, and Helly would have no reason to imagine it was her? Would the message specify that it had been an international call? An international call would be enough, Clare thought, to give her away.

She went back to cutting up spring onions in the kitchen, focusing intently on chopping off the ends and then slitting them shallowly down one side to slip off the coarser outer layer. She put them white end down in a glass on the table so that everything was pretty, and then rapped the shells of the boiled eggs under the tap in the sink and peeled them and distributed the cut halves with blobs of mayonnaise from a jar around the plates beside the tomatoes. When the others came in with wet hair and loud relishing complaints about the coldness of the water, it seemed soothing and consoling that what was happening to her was quite invisible to them. She was even grateful to them for their safe insensibility, and glad she hadn't betrayed them by making fun of them to Helly. She listened with real absorption to Genny explaining to Coco and Lily about how you could tell from the spinal bones of a horse whether or not it had been ridden, and about how she was working with an archaeologist to establish the period in which horses were first domesticated.

Rose started spattering her tomato with the back of a spoon and Tinsley smartly took away her plate. Possibly this meant Tinsley was finding the children annoying – or finding Rose annoying, anyway – and that she disapproved of how Clare and Bram indulged them. But Clare felt wrapped away from her usual sensitivity to such criticism in the thick wadding of her private thoughts.

Tinsley – the dry humorist of the family – was tall, with wolfish lean sexiness and blonde-streaked hair she pushed out of her way behind her ears or stuffed in a rubber band; she dressed in yellow waterproofs and yellow and blue and red clothes that always looked, even the dresses, as if they were bought in a shop selling mountaineering equipment. No one knew much about Tinsley's love life; she was spending months at a time cooped up in a research station in the Arctic where they were drilling long cores of ice from deep below the surface for the geological record, and she was sometimes the only woman alone with ten or fifteen men. Occasionally she turned up at home with some snow-tanned expert man in tow – once a bearded fat boozing American mineralologist whom Clare suspected just because he was so improbable – but she never offered any elucidation of their relationship and Genny never asked.

Opie was smaller and darker and plumper than Tinsley and Bram, with her dark hair cropped short; she was neat and watchful and devoted to her boyfriend. She was a secret smoker; it was not so much, she told Clare, that she didn't dare tell her family, as that she wouldn't in a million years have been able to enjoy smoking in front of them anyway. So several times a day she absented herself discreetly and hid herself to smoke in a little den she had found, tucked behind a ruined wall above where the river flowed out of the lake and towards the mill. She even started keeping her tin of rolling tobacco and papers and lighter behind a loose stone in the wall. It was just what Swallows and Amazons would have done if they'd taken up smoking, Clare thought.

That evening, when the children were finally asleep, Clare came out and sat in the den with her. It was late; the sun was setting behind the plantation of trees in a sky like a sea, all brilliant with orange and mauve, one dark navy cloud sailing in it like a boat. The lake was dim. The den on its little mound was in a last pocket of light and warmth above the shadows.

—Good look-out point, said Opie. She trickled tobacco along a paper, refusing Clare's bought cigarettes.

—I telephoned a friend this afternoon, said Clare, —but she wasn't in. I wonder if 1471 works from Ireland?

—Golly, I don't know. I shouldn't think so.

—Just wondering whether she'll know I've called. It doesn't matter.

—No, but I know what you mean. I hate that. Sometimes you have an impulse to talk to somebody and they're not in and then the impulse passes and you really hope they don't do 1471 and get your number, because the point of you calling them is completely finished. Once I rowed with Jamie, before we lived together, and I phoned him to make up and he wasn't in, and about half an hour later I was so furious because I'd completely changed my mind about forgiving him, but I knew he'd know I'd called.

—I can't imagine you rowing with Jamie.

—Oh can't you! Laughing, she blew out smoke and contemplated an inner happy place. —We're both so stubborn. And then we're always both utterly miserable until we're friends again.

—But not real rows. Not like me and Bram.

Clare didn't know why she'd said this; she and Bram very rarely argued, and she certainly had no desire to try to tell anyone in his family what was happening between them that summer, unspoken, quite unacknowledged.

—Oh dear, said Opie, surprised. —Is there something the matter between you two? Not *you* two.

—Not in the least. Not really. But you know what Bram's like. I mean, he's wonderful. He does so much with the children, he's so patient. He's so fair about my studying, he makes time for me to get on with it in the evenings, even when he's been at work all day, he puts the children to bed for me, washes the dishes . . .

—But?

—But nothing, really. He really is good. He makes me feel like a lower form of life sometimes.

Opie was dabbling in the leafmould, making a shallow hole.

—I remember once, she said, —when we were teenagers, I had deliberately broken something, a china bird Mum had brought me back from one of her trips. I broke it because she wouldn't let me go out to a club for a friend's birthday. Then I felt terrible. I had the broken pieces wrapped up in a T-shirt at the back of my drawer, I was hoping she wouldn't notice.

One day when I came home from school Bram was glueing it on the kitchen table. And Mum was all nice about it, thinking it had been an accident. And I was so angry with them both, how did they dare look in my private drawers, how dare they touch my things, they were never ever to go in my room again without permission, and so on. It was just the way he was sat there *fixing it* for me.

She put the nub end of her cigarette in the hole and palmed leafmould across it, burying it.

—So I do see what you mean.

Something had happened between Bram and Clare that summer. Or rather – that sounded too much as if it had happened to both of them, impartially – there was something she had done, to him, although neither of them could have named it. She had an image; it was as if with fiendish cunning she had contrived to lower around him out of the clear blue sky, without him once being able to be sure she was doing it, an invisible all-smothering deadly force-field of antagonism. It was like a dome of glass, cutting him off from her completely: but quite transparent. She knew there wasn't a word he could say to complain of her. She was punctiliously generous and cheerful. She not only entered into but initiated holiday enthusiasms. She overflowed with just the right measure of affectionate names and touches, not overdoing it. Only a flaw in the quality of their eye contact could possibly give her away – she felt it on her side almost like a momentary ugly squint, that when she looked at him her glance didn't reach his eyes straight, but slipped off him, off the falsity of the bright reflective surface between them. Then, for a moment, anyone might see revealed the rictus of her hostility. So she didn't look directly at him very often.

The only place that what was happening was even half acknowledged was in bed. Under the green satin bedspread, inside the bleak box of that stained orange wallpaper, they were cast out of the cocoon of their familiar things; they confronted one another alertly across a raw terrain. Clare simply dispensed with the whole years-long accumulation of their intimate habits and signs and codewords.

—Let's pretend, she whispered to him, when the light was still on and he was reading. —That I'm English and you're Irish. I own the house; you're my tenant. You're a republican and I'm a unionist.

They had never spoken before of their fantasies. Bram, the first time, smiled in bewilderment at her. It was as if his face was shallow – not like hers, hers was deep, opaque – and she saw running across it like shadows across water his efforts to follow her meaning. She was seized with a brief spasm of sympathetic understanding for him. But the words she had used could not be taken back; they drew her on, she was escaping up through them into an open, new, heady space.

—You hate me. You would like to burn my house down; probably, one day, you will. You've been taught to hold my luxury in contempt. But at the same time you can't resist my things. The sheets I lie in. My expensive silk underwear. My perfume. My soft skin. I hire you to carry furniture around the house. But in the bedroom I stand before the open door carelessly so that you have to squeeze past me, sweating, struggling with something heavy. I have on a thin summer's dress, with nothing underneath. You feel my heat.

—Don't, said Bram, smiling. —What are you doing?

—Play, she said. —Play with me.

—I don't want to. I don't hate you.

—When you first kiss me – you smell of peat smoke and

63

animals – you think of your mother who already looks like an old woman because of her life of hard labour. You want to refuse me, you pull your mouth away. But I touch you – like this . . .

Bram never spoke a single word that she could seize as token that he had lent himself to her games. But he couldn't close his ears; she cheated her way – that was how she thought of it – inside his desires, contaminating them. And if he was sullen and reluctant and half-disgusted then he only played the part she had devised for him.

It wasn't only unionist and republican. She did Miss Julie and her servant; the society beauty tempting the hermit in his hut; the young trade union leader and the spoiled factory owner's wife. She did Bertha Mason and Mr Rochester. 'He used to visit her, you know, in the attic. Even when Jane was sleeping under the same roof.' They were all costume dramas and period pieces. She detailed the furniture of the rooms; and the clothes, which came off, or half off, the complicated olden-times knots and hooks and buttons which had to be fumbled with hasty, sweating hands.

She was disgusted with herself, she winced with shame next day, remembering. There had been months at a time in her life when if she caught sight of the suckings of mouths or the slithering of oiled bodies on someone's television she only felt ennui and numbness. Now her obsession was a burden to her, heavy and distorting. Just before they came away on holiday she had been to the optician's for a routine test, checking the prescription for her reading glasses. The examination was carried out by a young man she had not seen before, rather shy, with a mop of dark fluffy hair and Wallace and Gromit socks. It was all perfectly straightforward. And yet when he turned the lights off her heart had pounded with excitement.

—Which looks brighter, red or green?

—Is it clearer with this one? Or this one? Clearer now?

His woolly hair brushed her cheek, he was breathing close to her face, he held up for her to follow his little torch with a lit bulb the size of a seed pearl. She thought: now, now, he'll touch me. But all the time she actually had on her face those grotesque test frames full of lenses, or he'd been instructing her to look left, look up, look down, peering into the red of her peeled up lids or pulled down rims. How could she have thought of sex? What was this sickness that made the whole world reach her through its prism, suffused in its slippery drugged rainbow excitements?

This rainbow-revelation that then like a light went out?

Eventually Bram refused her.

She whispered, —Pretend I'm a senior figure in the KGB. You're a dissident, a young physics lecturer who's also written a book on Dostoevsky. You're brought to my room, for interrogation . . .

—Oh for Christ's sake, he said. —Don't you think that's a bit off?

—A bit off? Her laugh was meant to convey insouciance, amusement at his priggishness. But she also felt a wince of exposure, the same as when she turned off the ignition in the car and the throb of supporting music died. —What d'you mean by a 'bit off'?

For some long minutes he didn't answer. Her perky smile hung in the dark like the Cheshire cat's.

—If you don't know, he said, —then I can't tell you.

She sat up in bed. It was cold in the room, the nights were cold because the days were so clear. She felt the chill strike her bare shoulders, she took it like a punishment. It was hours before dawn.

—OK, she said into the dark, perkily, bleakly.

Bram and Tinsley showed the children how to build a dam. (A 'barrage', the children called it, because they all knew about the one that was being built at home; Bram was employed on a two-year project to assess its ecological impact.) Tinsley, in cut-off jeans, stood with the water riding against her knees in the deepest part of the river and assumed command. The children, who had been prised unwillingly from in front of the Discovery Channel and turned out into the sunshine blinking and wincing, were soon organised into an eager workforce.

Clare watched from her vantage point in Opie's den, where she had taken her book.

—We need big ones! shouted Tinsley. —Big ones to make a strong base.

Bram helped Coco with an over-ambitious huge rock that came away from its bed like a tooth from a socket; he solemnly accepted the handfuls of wet grit Rose brought.

—Too small! said Tinsley.

—No, this is fine for filling in, said Bram equably. —Good girl, Rose.

—How deep is it going to get? Coco asked Tinsley; he pushed his glasses up on his nose and stood with his hands on his hips surveying the work. Clare feared he was more like her than like his father whose every gesture he slavishly copied (except the one with the glasses, which Bram didn't need).

—How deep d'you want it?

Coco shrugged his skinny shoulders. —Deep enough to sail the inflatable dinghy?

—Put your back into it then.

Clare had thought the children would lose interest after fifteen minutes, but an hour later Coco and Lily were still doggedly, silently working, lost in the task, all their awareness focused on supplying the steady line of stones advancing across the burbling evasive water. Rose was filtering dirt through her fingers at the river's edge, imagining she was part of the project because she was in its orbit. Conversation had narrowed to a soothing transactional minimum.

—We need a good one to go in here.

—Alert! Alert! We have a collapse.

—Pass me that one, quick.

—Help me with this, Daddy!

Clare thought, they will remember this, when they think about why they love their father.

It was what she had loved him for too: his quiet competence, a remote unassailable presumption of the one way to do things, a right way. She watched his hands, placing stones, helping Lily pick her way in the current, pushing back his tangled hair from his hot forehead. He had that kind of fine fair hair that separates naturally into curling strands, like a renaissance painting. He let it grow too long because he didn't care about it. She wished he would have it clipped fashionably close. His hands were like his father's, brown and small and firm. In the evenings these hands moved chess pieces patiently, teaching Coco or losing to Tinsley (she played in the station in the Arctic); or they chose cards in family games of solo whist where the Vereys could not completely disguise their relief that Clare didn't want to make an awkward fifth player (Opie didn't play either). Of course Bram was talking to the children all the time as well, he probably talked to them more than she did, explaining how things worked, explaining why it was better to do things in a certain way, explaining to them what was dangerous. He sometimes told Clare off, for driving with her tyre pressures crazily low, or using a vacuum with a broken plug whose live wires were exposed.

She couldn't think how to complain of him. She ought to have a complaint, oughtn't she, for an alibi? He was uncommunicative sometimes. And he didn't like many people, much: he was always friendly and polite, but in private he was unforgiving if he found out anyone's vanity or pretension. He knew things but he didn't invent things. She couldn't think what to accuse him of. Those didn't sound like accusations; they sounded like goodness.

When the barrage was built there was a little lip of captured water behind it and they did just manage to skull the play-dinghy across it amid shrieks of triumph; the children splashed and scooped the water with large exaggerated gestures, as if the pool they had made was deeper and more miraculous than it actually was. After tea there was consternation because Lily found three little dark fishes swimming up and down in it. She was dismayed at the idea of the bewilderment of the little fish and she haunted the bank, coaxing them with chirruping calls to a place where they could swim over; eventually Bram (who might even in his calm way have also been concerned for the fish) broke down the barrage and made a channel for them to escape through. Coco and Tinsley disapproved and the evening ended on a sour note. The fish, anyway, stayed swimming around in the pool, although they were gone by the morning.

The sister of the woman who ran the mini-market was married to the man who owned the garage, and it was from her that they had collected the key to the house at the beginning of the holiday. The owner lived in London and rarely visited; his wife had asthma and couldn't manage the house's dampness. Mrs

Tierney was also supposed to come on their last day, a Friday, to read the electricity meter; they were leaving very early on Saturday morning to catch their ferry. For some reason she turned up with a car full of friends in the middle of Thursday night. Into the deep seclusion of their sleep there burst the roar of an engine with a squealing fan belt, the slushy bite of tyres in the gravel, the ill-suppressed sounds of partying from the car. A car door banged, there was incomprehensible calling, a scream of laughter abruptly broken off. Then someone pounded on the great front door knocker.

—Go round the back! someone else shouted.

All the adults within the house were at once bolt upright, startled out of themselves, expecting for split seconds whatever dreadful thing it is that one expects to break in roughly and unceremoniously in the small hours upon one's sleep. Bram jumped out of bed and grabbed his bathrobe, but Ray, in pyjamas, was downstairs ahead of him, pulling open the big front door they had learned from the locals not to bother to bolt.

—What in heaven's name . . .

Bram and Tinsley and Opie and Clare loomed supportively behind Ray in the hall.

Mrs Tierney, with black dyed hair and a worn face and lipstick applied approximately to her mouth, was very much the worse for whatever was in the bottle they were handing round in the car. She swayed and came to rest against the door lintel. She was wearing some kind of pale trouser suit which, as they stood confronted, looked farcically like a match with Ray's pyjamas; perhaps that was why when he swung the door open there was another outbreak of laughter from the car, abruptly choked off. Inside the house the English family in their nightwear were sober and frowning. A crumple-faced man

69

they didn't recognise pushed his way in front of Mrs Tierney on the steps, waving his cigarette that left its trail of odour on the night, sounding as if he was placating them and offering a long explanation which they could only partly follow.

—She's come to read the meter, Tinsley snorted in disbelief.

—That's right, missus, said the man. —We've come to read the meter.

—But it's the middle of the night, objected Ray.

—Sure it is, said the man. —Only tomorrow she has a nephew coming up from Cork (he pronounced it Cork-e). —The t'ing was, she would have come over here earlier . . . He circumscribed a significant shape with his cigarette on the night.

—Only she's pissed out of her mind and doesn't know what time of night or day it is, said Tinsley.

—I thought it best, said Mrs Tierney, swaying in hostile dignity, —to wait til you'd have finished using the electric.

—Oh for God's sake, let them come in and get on with it.

The Vereys in their pyjamas traipsed through the downstairs rooms of the house after Mrs Tierney and her friend. Mrs Tierney couldn't remember where the meter was; they all offered more or less helpful suggestions, opening cupboards, poking round in the cloakroom and under the stairs. Others from the car drifted after them into the house, a teenage girl in a short dress and an overweight young man with a bald patch like a tonsure and a worn shiny brown suit. Clare could not be quite sure how much the party's air of suppressed hilarity was directed at the English holidaymakers; in the dining room the girl heaved up one of the sash windows and shouted something out to whoever was left behind in the car. There was another explosion of laughter from outside, and a thick waft of black cold humming night air into the room, dispersing the smell of their sausage and cabbage supper.

Strangely, when they looked into the room they called the library, Genny was sitting up in all her clothes in front of the embers of the peat fire. She must have heard the noise of their arrival and crazy progress round the house: there was something prepared, theatrical, in the way she lowered her book and frowned over the top of it.

—What on earth is going on? she exclaimed.

—Stay where y'are, missus, soothed the crumple-faced man. —We've no need to disturb you.

—Jesus, Michael, where the hell is it? Mrs Tierney focused for a moment in perplexity.

—Cast your mind back now, Michael coaxed her.

—Could you possibly meditate elsewhere? said Genny. —Only I'm trying to read.

When Bram eventually found the meter in an outhouse built behind the kitchen, they then had to find a pen and paper for Mrs Tierney. Michael called out the numbers and she wrote them down with breathy concentration, then shoved the paper carelessly into her handbag. The party raggedly departed, calling farewells that might or might not have been mocking, their extravagance a blare that hung on the night behind them after the sound of the car engine had nosed its way far down towards the village.

—Why is Mum up? asked Opie.

—Couldn't sleep, said Ray.

—But she's in her clothes.

—She's not been sleeping well.

Clare felt a thickening of meaning around this exchange, a familial alert that excluded her. In the library Genny sat holding her book on her knee, keeping her finger in her place.

—Weren't we just wonderfully po-faced! exclaimed Tinsley.
—They must have been delighted!

—Insufferably rude. Whatever did they think they were
playing at, at this time of night? Have they woken the
children?

—You were up. Why didn't you answer the door?

—Didn't hear it. Until they came bursting in here.

—Are you going to bed now?

—Mum! said Opie. —You've hurt yourself.

In surprise Genny turned the back of her hand towards
herself, where three parallel weals trickled drips of blood.
—Blast, she said. I didn't realise I'd made such a mess. I did
it on the metal tape around the peat brickettes, just now. I
should get some tissue or something.

But she didn't move. In fact she sat in her chair with a strange
heaviness as if she couldn't move, her head collapsed back and
her mouth slightly open; there was an effortful delay each time
before she spoke, although when she did she sounded sensible
and normal.

Silently Tinsley handed her a tissue from her sleeve.

Ray offered to make tea. His pyjamas flapped emptily over
the hollows of his skinny chest and legs; he didn't make eye
contact with his wife but looked hopefully at his children.

—I suppose now we're up, said Bram, —we might as
well.

—I don't want tea, hissed Genny, with an intensity that was
a moment's glimpse of something hidden, lethal, gleaming.
—Why don't you all go back to bed? Leave me alone. I
don't know why you let those people in in the first place.
In the baggy skin of her weathered face the pouches under
her eyes were purple thumbprints from lack of sleep.

—You're probably right, said Ray. —It is too late for

tea. But we could hardly have left them hammering away at the door.

Clare thought that one of them would ask Genny what was the matter. That was what would have happened in her own messy family with its rich history of betrayals and divorces: and then there would have been recriminations, counter-accusations, raised voices, tears. But instead the Vereys did quietly what Genny asked and filed off to bed and left her alone, and Clare, for the moment, went along with that.

—Goodnight, Mum, Opie said. —Don't stay down too long.

Perhaps this was the way that families managed to stay together. There weren't any guarantees, anyway, that what came out in tears and recriminations was any more truthful than this evasion. She didn't even ask Bram, when they were alone in the bedroom, what it had all been about; even though she had seen for herself that the tape around the brickettes wasn't broken and that Genny hadn't put any new peat on the fire. He said something about 'one of my mother's moods'. If she accused his family of evasion then he might ask her to look straight at him.

Clare woke on Friday morning very early. The sunlight and the sounds of the birds from outside were thrilling presences in the room, irresistible once you wholly opened yourself to them. Rose had joined them at some time during the night and was asleep face down between them, hot little limbs flung abandonedly as if the bed was all hers, small hard feet kicking and pushing into free space, leaving the adults only a straitened margin which in their sleep they had submissively adapted to. Clare eased herself from under Rose's embrace and slipped out of bed, then, without forming any articulate plan, picked up her sandals and a jumper and went downstairs and out of the back door into the morning. It seized her – still warm from her bed – like a gulp of ice-water, waking her immediately and completely. She took the shortcut across the meadow down to the lake shore; there was a heavy dew on the long grass and soon her feet were slipping wetly in her sandals and the hem of her stretch nightshirt was soaked and clinging to her ankles. Arbitrary looking puffs of milky mist were still lying about here and there on the fields and the water, not blotted up yet by the clear hot day.

There was a wooden dinghy drawn up on the shingle beach which was theirs to use. Clare had been out in it twice with the others and knew more or less how to row. She fetched the oars which were hidden across the joists of an old outhouse and pushed the dinghy out into the water, holding her nightshirt up above her knees. For a split second she queried what she was doing, incredulously returning into her normal self and doubting – what if the boat leaks, what if I'm pulled by the current out of the lake down the river towards the mill, what if I get tangled in the weeds, what if there's something essential the others know that I just don't know about – but danger seemed unreal, the unpopulated golden morning felt like a promise of safety, a charm that meant she could do nothing wrong. The dinghy rocked and tipped wildly when she slithered across the side onto her knees in its wet bottom, but it didn't spill her out; she manoeuvred herself up onto the seat and remembered which way to face and pushed away from the shingly shallows with an oar.

She could do this. Buoyant, sweating, panting, a hundred yards from the shore, she shipped her oars (Tinsley had taught the children all the nautical terms) and took off her jumper. She closed her eyes and held her face to the sun; on her lids were crimson trees growing upwards, twisting into flames. When she opened them she saw that the water round the dinghy was thick with brown weed; because of a trick of the early slanting light she could see deeply in. The water was glassy and luminous between the brown stirring wafting fronds, she was looking into an illuminated drowned forest. In an impulse that was more physical than like a thought, she stripped off her nightshirt too. If anyone was watching from the edge of the lake she was too far off for them to see much – she even imagined there was someone, she supplied for her voyeurs the teenage girl and the brown-suited man left over from some Arcadian pastoral coupling the night before. She convinced herself, but quite without any alarm, even with a sense of fitness and mutual appreciation, that she could make out his brown suit and her pale legs against the camouflaging russets of a stretch of bank.

Holding the dinghy with both hands she stepped over the side and into the water. It slipped over her naked body like a glove of cold, clenching her tight in its shock. The weeds touched her – not clingingly or spongily as she'd imagined, but intimately, lightly, like prompts and hints. She swam because there wasn't anything else to do but move to keep alive; if she had stopped still her lungs might have seized up with cold and forgotten how to draw in air. So she cleaved the glassy water with her slow breaststroke, the sound of her own gasping breathing loud and strange in her ears, and the weed ends brushing along her naked breasts and stomach. Birds on the water took flight; she heard the crack and beating of their wings. She'd never swum before without a costume, her body felt unbound and loose, and as if it was actually mingling and exchanging substance with the lake. At the same time she was so distinct from the lake, she cleaved it and it parted

75

ahead of her in obedience to the strong shapely movements of her limbs.

One part of her mind was already thinking that it would be difficult to get back in the boat, but another was still able to marvel at herself, at the reality of her doing this, this epic and improbable thing, not just imagining it, but doing it, in the flesh, in the astonished and jubilant flesh.

It was difficult, getting back in the boat. The dinghy had drifted, by the time she turned round and swam back to it. She had even whimpered with fear and frustration, clinging on to the side of the dinghy, feeling the strength drain dangerously out of her. And she had hurt herself, scraped a long bleeding weal down her hip when by a superhuman, grunting, undignified effort she had finally heaved herself aboard, panicking in horror that she might pull the wildly cavorting dinghy over on herself. But once she was in the boat and had scrambled into her nightshirt she was alright, although her legs and arms trembled too much for her to row at first. She looked out defiantly for watchers on the bank. They couldn't have known, at such a distance, how complete her abasement had been, so it didn't count. She had had her swim. Her swim had been blissful.

She didn't tell anyone.

Later that afternoon Clare and Opie volunteered to clean the house while the others took the children out. While Opie did the bedrooms upstairs, Clare telephoned David again. She knew she would get him this time, just as she had known for two whole weeks that it was in her power to keep the weather fine. She proposed a date when she could come to London, the soonest date she could manage. She said she would come to his flat.

—Are you on your own, right now? he asked, in an odd low conspiratorial voice.

—Sort of. Bram's sister is upstairs.

—When you come to the flat, then, he said. —I want to fuck you.

She buried her head back among the concealing hot coats hanging in the cloakroom, squeezing her eyes shut. Her hair was scraped back into a plait out of her way, her face was sweaty and gritty with dust, her hands smelled of dishcloths and bleach. Her hurt thigh ached.

—I want to fuck you too, she said.

Then she pressed down the metal rests, and cut him off.

Now she had really crossed the bridge to the other side, to the different place. Although nothing was burning behind her. The image was very precise in her mind, there was no burning bridge behind her, only a wide impassable space of twinkling water, twinkling and dancing and silvery; banal, and shallow, even.

Coming to Grief

A funny thing happened to Marian one Saturday morning when she went round as usual to her father's flat. It was a lapse, a blink of dark in the bright light of ordinary consciousness, like the lapses her father had sometimes when he blanked out something they'd gone through only ten minutes before.

—I have no idea what you're talking about, he would throw out at her exasperatedly, his reproach cold and sharp in his still perfect enunciation.

Euan wasn't senile, he still had his brilliant mind. He was extraordinary considering he was almost ninety years old. But it was as though he saved his brilliance for deeper things now and had cut loose from some of the clutter she had to pester him with: appointments at the eye hospital or at the doctors', money matters, problems with his housekeeper Elaine.

What happened to Marian that morning was that when she arrived at her usual time (she always went round on Saturdays and Sundays to do his food and see everything was alright because Elaine didn't work at weekends), the front door wasn't double locked and the alarm system wasn't switched on. All this really meant was that Euan must have opened the door already that morning, probably to give his usual handful of dried catfood to a visiting cat, and hadn't bothered to redo it all when he went back inside because he knew she was coming. But for some strange reason Marian completely and illogically misinterpreted these signs; she presumed they meant her father had got himself dressed and gone out before she arrived for a walk in the beautiful morning.

This was strange and illogical not only because if he had gone out for a walk he could perfectly well have double locked the door behind him and set the alarm, but because for – how long? eighteen months? two years? three years? one forgot the timings of these stages of regress as one forgot the forward progress of one's babies – for some time now Euan had not been able to walk out into the streets unaided. He could get about the flat, using the route around chair backs and pieces of furniture Marian and Elaine had designed for him and were careful not to disturb; he could even, with the help of his frame which he hated, get himself out into his garden on a nice afternoon, as long as they had put his chair ready for him and beside it on a little stool his straw boater and his plaid blanket and his thick dark glasses to protect his eyes against the glare. Then the neighbourhood cats he gave food to came and repaid him with sinuous and uninvolving cat love. But he was too frail to walk out in the streets alone any more; his legs were too unreliable since a fall a couple of winters ago when he'd cracked his pelvis, and he was prone to spells of dizziness (he had classes for this too, at the hospital, that she had to organise for him).

So it was strange that without in the least examining her idea or its probability, but quite convinced that her father had gone off on a walk on that fine Saturday morning, Marian went on into the flat and began clearing up his breakfast things, running hot water into the sink for the washing up, collecting his night-time glass from the bedroom, putting his porridge bowl to soak (Elaine made him porridge the night before and had taught him how to heat it in the microwave). She watered the plants on the kitchen windowsill, singing. She wouldn't have sung if she'd thought he was there; like her daughter Tamsin he had perfect pitch and they both complained about her tunelessness and her taste in music. She was singing a song whose first line was 'Do you know the way to San José': she couldn't remember whose song it was. It dated her, anyway. She had grown up listening to Jimi Hendrix and Janis Joplin but it seemed to be these poppy middle-of-the-road tunes that had seeped into the deepest layers of her awareness and that made her feel happy now.

The fine day seemed to fill the flat with an unusual light – she usually thought of it as a dark place, dark with his books, dark with the condensed shadow of his intelligence folded in upon itself. It was a University flat; they had always had a University house and he had moved to this flat twenty years ago when Marian's mother died. Like the University it was Victorian gothic, with pointed casement windows and deep stone sills, heavy doors that shut with the deep clunk of finality, and an ancient, vociferous and effective heating system. Euan said – to visitors he said – that it was like waking up inside one of Ruskin's less temperate dreams. To Marian he simply said it was damp and depressing. In her irrational fit she was glad as she washed his breakfast things to think that this morning he had got out from it into the open air, out among all the summer gardens blooming with flowers she had seen on her way over. This thought must have developed in her mind subliminally; if it had bubbled up into full consciousness then she would have woken and known it was not possible.

Afterwards, when she had come out of the fit and was wondering how she had made such a puzzling mistake, she realised that she had felt more than simple gladness at his getting out into the fine day. She had taken the lightness of his step out into the morning so early and spontaneously for a sign, a coded sign from him that she could hang on to however he tried to deny it: a sign of hope, and of his openness still, after all, to pleasure. What easier gesture of acquiescence than to walk out impromptu into a new day? The sky was pale blue and the walls of the back area outside the kitchen window were grown over with white and pink valerian. His going out was like a revelation of easy possibilities they had both been tangling and obfuscating; they had both between them been making everything so difficult and so bitter.

And afterwards when she was thinking about it she also wondered if she hadn't, in fact, been imagining his death. Her fantasy of him released to light and flowers was like a benign fantasy-death, as if she had found a magic bypass round pain and ugliness, and been able to imagine them released from one another, from father and daughter, with a lightness and ease angels might have at parting, not human beings.

That was all it was. It was nothing, really; when Marian tried to tell Tamsin, later, it wasn't even a story, just a moment's blip in consciousness whose power, like the power of dreams, couldn't be carried back into ordinary life. At some point after she tipped the washing-up water away she had heard a sound from the study – a book slammed shut, a chair thrust impatiently back – which in an instant recalled her to herself and filled the flat's emptiness with him and shrivelled into nonsense her fantasy of light.

It wouldn't have seemed strange to Euan that Marian hadn't greeted him as soon as she came in the flat; if he was busy she often didn't bother him. She stopped singing as soon as she realised he was there: probably it was because of the singing that the book was slammed shut. Euan's need for silence while he was working was one of the things he and Elaine fought over most bitterly. He was adamant that with both doors shut and with the volume right down he could still hear her radio in the kitchen; and indeed, put at both their insistence solemnly to the test, it seemed that he could, even though he often failed to hear other much easier things. Elaine joked sceptically at his selective deafness, but Marian believed in it, it would have something to do with his perfect pitch; if he suspected that a false note was sounding somewhere around him then some responsive strained tautness of antipathy in him would thrum and vibrate to it in an effort transcending any disability. He couldn't help it.

Marian made coffee and took a cup in to him. He was writing in the chair she had had made for him, with the sloping desk fitted across its arms, the Anglepoise light aimed at his page from behind his shoulder, his magnifying glass for small print at his left hand, blanket across his knees. Books were piled up, some open, some stuffed with paper markers, on the tables to either side of him. She knew what he was working on, it was a piece about the relations of Dostoevsky's thought to Russian Orthodox theology. Some of the books were in Cyrillic script. Marian could always tell by the way he sat or looked up at her whether it was going well or badly. Her mother, when she and her brother were children, had used to bring reports from the study as if his moods were a weather on which they all depended: if he was stuck she and Francis might be sent off to the cinema for the afternoon. Her father was a big man, he had had the physique – the bulky shoulders and thick neck – of a statesman or an actor or a navvy, not a man of letters. His face had always been complex and as unfinished as a clay maquette, with louring brows and long rugged cheek-plains;

now it was pouched, and purplish and pale in patches. The fine convolutions of inner life and expression had always translated themselves in him into the stubbornnesses and martyrdoms of the flesh. Today he brooded over his page without lifting his head; that might have been her singing.

—It's a lovely day, Daddy.

—Is it?

—Would you like to sit outside?

—No.

—But you know it cheers you up.

—Nothing makes me feel lower than being cheered up.

Setting the coffee down on its mat on the side table, she put her arm around his shoulders.

—Is it Saturday? he asked, which was supposed to mean that he wished it was Elaine and not she who had brought his coffee.

She kissed his head, its baldness blotched with brown age-blemishes, flaky with dry skin. He twisted with irritation and resentment under her kiss, but she told herself that at some deeper level he was fed by it, kept alive, reminded that he was loved. Marian was not, by nature, a kisser or a toucher, but her mother had always done it, and she had taken on the part when her mother died. Possibly what she had taken on was not simply the innocent tending it looked like. Possibly it was instead a part of the subtle fight of the female with the male, of female insisting sweetness against male bitterness, of female blithe confidence against male doubt.

When they were children and their mother came back from the study with her reports, their attitude had been complicated. Everything arranged itself around the father and his work, there was no question about that. They were frightened if he was angry, proud when he did well and was acclaimed. But there was also a subtle kind of triumph in their subjection. They thought it was funny, his moodiness, his weakness, his need for them to surround him with consideration. It was a game they played with their mother, exaggerating their anxieties about him as if he was a ghoul or a troll; and weren't they stronger, she and they, because they didn't need anything so complicated or contingent? When they went off to the cinema or shopping, leaving him to his suffering over books written in languages they didn't understand, didn't they have a kind of swagger, because they could manage ordinary things?

Of course, all the while, it might have been they who suffered, not knowing it, while he pleased himself. Feminists would have said so, and Marian surely was one. Complication upon complication.

Marian didn't like to feel she was playing any part, any longer, in that complicated war of males against females. She had thought she had finished with that forever when her marriage finished: long, long ago. Her marriage – and far behind that, her childhood – seemed ages off, eras ago: like history. Hadn't everything in the world, and especially the things to do with men and women, changed out of all recognition, since then? And hadn't she, Marian, proved it by spending her mostly single life as an independent woman and a teacher?

That morning, after the strange episode of her misinterpretation, the strange half an hour or so of light and flowers, she was stricken with disappointment; she made Euan's bed and tidied his bedroom and prepared his trays of lunch and supper under a cloud of sadness and fatalism, as if something precious had been shown to her and lost.

There was a problem with some money. Marian's mother had

inherited some property; the income from this property was never spent after Marian and her brother left home, it all went into an investment account. Now Euan had withdrawn some of these savings in cash, to avoid death duties; he really had very little interest in money, but he liked to imagine himself as a man of the world, cunning and knowing when it came to material things. He kept the money hidden, despite all Marian's pleadings and warnings, in a space under the floor in the airing cupboard which no one was supposed to know about except Marian and her brother Francis in Toronto. The last time Marian fetched Euan some money from the hiding place she discovered that two hundred pounds were missing. She didn't tell Euan, but crossed out in his little notebook the amount that there should have been, and deducted what she had just taken out, as if nothing was wrong.

At home she confided in Tamsin over supper. Tamsin was her younger daughter, who lived at home with Marian and was unnervingly domesticated. Tamsin had had a very wild youth which had culminated five years before in a dreadful crisis, with a boyfriend who had accidentally overdosed and died, and a stillborn baby. She had shaved her head in those days, and had her nose and tongue pierced; but now, when she was twenty-seven, she had her hair cut neatly short like a boy's, and saved her wages to buy nice designer clothes. She worked in an office for an agency selling theatre and concert tickets, and appalled her father, who had in his youth handed out leaflets outside factories for the Communist Party, by announcing that she had voted Conservative at the last election (the one when nobody else did). She also sang with the city choral society, went out clubbing occasionally with the girls from the office, and, so far as Marian could tell, slept alone every night in her neat, narrow bed.

—Nobody knows where this wretched money is hidden except me and Francis and Daddy, said Marian.

—And me, said Tamsin.

—You don't know.

—I guessed.

—The most likely thing is Daddy's taken some of it out himself and just forgotten to tell me. But what for? Two hundred? And I think he'd find it quite difficult, you really have to get down on your hands and knees. Then there was the man who came to repair the central heating boiler a few weeks ago. Perhaps he had to look around under the floor for pipes, and he found it. But then why only take two hundred, not all of it?

—Maybe to mislead you, so that it wasn't obvious.

—And anyway, I'm sure it wasn't him. This is what's so horrible about the whole thing. He seemed a nice man, we've had him before, and he'd never do anything so stupid, obviously incriminating himself. He was only mending the thermostat, why would he need to look for pipes? Probably the whole thing's just a mistake: I miscounted, or we miscounted right at the beginning, perhaps the building society made a mistake in the first place, and we checked carelessly.

—What does it matter, so long as Grandpa doesn't know?

—Well it does matter: two hundred pounds! Sooner or later he's bound to know; he'll want me to get it all out and count it for him or something.

Marian helped herself to the last slice of quiche. She was always hungry after one of Tamsin's suppers. They took it in turns to cook, although Tamsin didn't really cook, she went to Marks and Spencer's on her way home and bought selections of things in plastic pots that were somehow enticing but not fulfilling. Marian, on her nights, cooked hearty platefuls of rice or pasta which Tamsin picked at. Tamsin's lilac silk blouse

showed off shadowy hollows in her throat and under her collar
bones. Marian had never had those, she had always been tall and
heavy like her father; for a while now she had been aware of a
sort of girdle of packed flesh between her bosom and her hips
that seemed to grasp her tight and make her breathless and
constrained, so that she had to swivel her body in one solid
piece if she wanted to look behind her.

—What about Elaine?

—Oh, Tamsin, no. Of all the people in the world . . . And
anyway, Elaine doesn't know it's there. Unless he's forgotten
she doesn't know, and mentioned it. But wouldn't you trust
Elaine with your life?

—Probably not, said Tamsin. —I wouldn't trust anybody
with my life.

Tamsin often affected this flip cynicism, opening her hazel
eyes wide and blank. Marian didn't know whether it was just
the conversational small change of the girls in the office, or
whether she was supposed to be reminded of that time when
really Tamsin might have imagined her life as a thing thrown
around carelessly by all of the ones who professed to love her,
and dropped, and almost lost. Otherwise they never talked of
that time; Tamsin wouldn't talk.

Elaine stood smoking by the sink in the kitchen with the
window open. Like playing the radio, smoking was forbidden,
but Euan had managed to make her so angry this afternoon
she didn't care, or only cared enough to try to fan the smoke
through the window with her hand. Marian listened with little
groans of sympathy and outrage, calculating anxiously whether
Elaine was actually offended enough this time to go, and leave
her with the dreadful choice between finding a replacement
housekeeper, or facing the necessity of persuading Euan to go

into a home. Before Elaine there had been a quick succession of three perfectly pleasant and competent women who had not been able to put up with Euan's temper and his manner.

Euan had called Elaine a servant again. He had corrected her speech when it was ungrammatical. Also, he objected to her perfume, he said it gave him headaches, although she denied she ever wore any when she came to work. And he insisted on going through all her receipts with her whenever she came back from shopping, even though he had no idea what things cost. Marian thought treacherously of the two hundred pounds. Was it possible Elaine thought herself justified, taking it to make up for all these offences to her pride? Her face heated apologetically for having dreamed of it.

—Sometimes he comes in here after me, when we've been having words about something, Elaine said. —I walk out and he follows me, he can't leave it alone; he comes staggering across the hall without his stick, bellowing at me. 'Elaine, Elaine, you've been touching my papers again, how many times do I have to tell you they are nothing to do with you, my work must not be sacrificed to this mania for tidiness!'

She imitated Euan rather well, in a surprising deep voice, trembling with outrage, his and her outrage at the same time.

—As if I would ever dare touch his precious papers.

That was Marian's mother's phrase exactly, 'his precious papers': contempt and awe at once, and jealousy. Marian thought of women married into some priestly caste, expressing their resentment against augury.

—As if he hates me, really hates me, Elaine said.

Elaine was in her late forties, petite and blonde with plump golden skin whose wrinkles didn't look like weaknesses, but like decisive folds. She had a characteristic, settling, complacent gesture where she drew her head back into a double chin while she tapped the ash off her cigarette; she ran the butt under the tap when she had finished and buried it in the bin. She was the kind of woman who would think less of you for washing your whites with your coloureds or letting the inside of your kettle get furred up when there was a perfectly good device to prevent it: Euan's kitchen was suddenly full of such sensible devices, a splashguard and a meat thermometer, matching oven gloves and panholders, a mug tree. The microwave – which had proved invaluable – had been Elaine's idea.

Marian liked Elaine but rather feared her; she found herself preserving defensively her dignity as a teacher in case Elaine penetrated behind it and caught her out in some careless absent-mindedness. Elaine's son Mark was in Marian's lower-sixth A-level history group: that was not a coincidence, it was through Mark that Marian had arranged eighteen months ago for Elaine to work for Euan.

—What was she shouting about? Euan asked later. —She's got an uncontrollable temper.

It should have been funny, the way each of them imagined the other subject to incontinent rages and was so sure of his or her own calm reasonableness. Marian could never be sure what actually went on when the two of them were alone here, what raw indecorous scenes erupted within the walls of this flat laid out for the deep quiet rhythms of the contemplative life. She knew – at least, she had had reported to her – that once Elaine had slapped Euan, not across the face but across the legs, when he stood over her explaining something while she, on her hands and knees, washed the kitchen floor; and that once when she reached up to tuck in his muffler under his coat collar he had pushed her away so hard she fell and bruised herself against a piece of furniture. Elaine too made it her female mission to kiss and touch Euan, and he hated it.

Their conflict was not the whole story. There were plenty of passages of calm between them. He loved her cooking and mopped up her cream sauces and wine gravies greedily, even though he complained they were too rich; neither his wife nor his daughter had ever cooked decently. And she was very ready to adopt that posture of baffled superstitious mistrust towards the mysteries of his work which suited him better in women than interest or adulation. Days and weeks would pass after one of these big blow-ups where both were abashed and cautious and there was never a squeak out of them.

—Elaine, I'm so sorry, said Marian. —Of course if you really want to go, I can't stop you, I'd even understand, although personally I'll be devastated, I know I'll never find anyone else so able to manage him . . . I know that although he can be so insufferable at least you understand where the frustrations come from.

She was sure that behind her expression of sorely tried forbearance Elaine was not actually thinking over the tragic plight of the brilliant old man, but the convenience of the job, the decent pay, her relative independence. Marian would have thought the same in her place.

—You'll have to tell him, Marian. I won't be talked to like that, though I may not have your education or your lifestyle. (Where had Marian's education come into it, she wondered?) —But he is very good to Mark. I'd be sorry for the boy to lose out on his visits here.

The mention of Mark was a kind of capitulation.

Mark often came to the flat after school, if Elaine was working late. He was an only child, neither he nor Elaine ever mentioned a father. He used to do his homework on the kitchen table, then Euan began to take an interest in him, interrogating him, impressed by his intelligence, appalled by his ignorance, taking it upon himself – grumbling but visibly delighted – to fill up the deficiency. Mark was the cleverest pupil Marian had ever taught. Although her school was an inner city comprehensive school which didn't send many pupils into higher education of any sort, she was encouraging Mark to apply to do history at Cambridge.

When Marian opened the door to the study the old man was balancing a vinyl record delicately on his thick finger ends with his head on one side, looking across the surface for flaws, blowing off the dust. (He didn't approve of the cold sound of compact disc.) The gesture reminded Marian of her excitement when, as a child, she was permitted to breathe the intimate, felty smell of the sanctum inside the gramophone cabinet where she must not touch. The boy smiled round at her from where he sat as he sat in her classes, attentive, obedient, absorbent. Euan was holding forth.

—You know what Dostoevsky says? 'What is given on earth is not final.' Do you believe that? Of course not. But he says it. 'What is given on earth is not final.' Who are we to disagree? And so . . .

He waved irritatedly with his free hand at Marian to leave them alone.

She listened outside the door. Lucia Popp singing Strauss's 'Last Songs'.

Before she married, Marian had been writing a PhD thesis on women in the crowd in the French Revolution. She had been in Paris in 1968; George Rudé, who was on sabbatical leave from Montreal researching a new book, had agreed to meet her and discuss her ideas. She had sat in the window of a cheap hotel near Saint Sulpice writing up her notes from the interview with Rudé and listening to the sounds of the rioting in the streets, which reached her like a kind of mournful thrilling weather carried on the air. It was weirdly like eavesdropping, as she had had unwillingly to do through the plasterboard partitions of her room in residence in her last undergraduate year, on the groans and protests and outrages of lovemaking.

Then the day after she got back to London she met Graham Menges at a party and something happened which overturned all the plans she had had for her life. She found out for herself all about the groans and protests of lovemaking; and involved in that was a whole seismic change of perspective, or so it seemed at the time. Not only the body instead of the mind; also art instead of academic study. Graham's ceramics, whorled and lush with glaze or dragged into brittle lace, represented the wisdom of hands instead of words. Marian thought out quite consciously an analogy between Graham's hands on her shadowy strange-to-herself body under the blankets and his hands turning pots on his wheel. When she thought of herself as whirling wet clay turning under his hands she forgot herself enough to have orgasms. She neglected the writing up of the PhD; it seemed to her to have been overtaken, overtaken by a great culture-quake, after which one could not be sure that any of the same things would matter any more.

It was a time of believing in such overturnings. It was the time when respectable BBC presenters unlearned received pronunciation and tried to say 'yeah' and 'groovy' and talked about pot and psychedelia: all of this wince-making and hilarious in retrospect, but nonetheless a change for ever; the end forever of the imperturbable authority of class and hierarchy. It was the time when the generation of the fathers unbuttoned and undid themselves.

It was also a time of much misinformation for women, Marian thought now. Because of all that pounding, writhing music that purported to be the product of anguished sexual desire – 'Foxy Lady', 'Light my Fire', 'She Belongs to Me' – it was easy to make the mistake of thinking yourself empowered as the object of that desire. Easy not to notice that the object was more or less interchangeable, and that it was to other men, and not to women, that those beautiful young geniuses looked for critical approval when the music was over. Sometimes being the object of that desire was no more empowering than suttee. After Jimi Hendrix died, young girls he'd never known came round to his flat and tried to jump out of the window.

Marian and Graham left London and moved back to live in the provincial city where she had grown up; he got some teaching at the art college, she got pregnant and had babies, and then Graham left her for one of his young students. She had two tiny daughters aged five and three and never considered completing the abandoned PhD. She trained to be a schoolteacher instead, and her second job was at the school where she was now Head of History and in charge of the (small) sixth-form. The school buildings were old-fashioned, nineteen-thirties red brick, with wood- and glass-panelled corridors, white-tiled science labs, and a hall with a stage and draped curtains and a rather skimpily filled honours board. Half of the children at the school were from Muslim families, Pakistanis and Bangladeshis and (toughest) Somalis; the other half were from the local white working-class community. It was a reasonably cheerful, not a horribly deprived or troubled, place. They didn't do very well in government league tables. Marian wouldn't have wanted to teach in any other 'easier' type of school.

A flight of cement stairs for staff use only climbed from the reception foyer to the main corridor; there was a smell there of cleaning fluid, or a trick of the watery light from a high window overlooking the park at the back, which for some reason always, even after twenty years, triggered a gust of sensation in Marian whenever she happened to go that way. Perhaps it had been a sensation of pleasurable pride once, but now it was just like a sudden strong self-awareness in the midst of all her daily preoccupations: this is me, she thought, I am here, I have done this all by myself, this is my place.

Another two hundred pounds went missing. Marian telephoned her brother Francis in Toronto.

—It has to be the housekeeper, he said. —What's her name?

—Elaine. How can you say that, Francis? You don't even know her.

—Are we moving on to one of our 'you're not here doing your share' conversations? Does it help if I'm just abject in advance and we skip that bit?

—And even if it was her, you see, she's so invaluable, I need her so desperately, if she goes I'll have to face up to the idea of a home, and I quake when I try to imagine that. So even if she was taking money, I just can't afford to mention it.

—You're suggesting we just allow her to pay herself a cool extra couple of hundred every week?

—I notice it's suddenly 'we' when it comes to money.

—Our inheritance.

—Oh Francis, don't. It disgusts me that you think of it like that.

—You're such an old romantic. An old hippie.

—Better that than a materialistic vulture. I'm sure it's not Elaine, anyway.

She only phoned up to bother him, really, not because she

thought he would be able to help. She wanted to slop over onto him some small poisonous surplus of her anxieties and put him off his blithe, evasive stroke for a couple of hours.

—It's been such an awful week. He's been on the phone to me every night with some new outrage she's committed. She refused to bathe him, or that's what he said; she said he wouldn't let her. It was all about this aqueous cream she wants him to use in the water for his eczema. He was sure he'd slip. They're both so stubborn. I thought I was going to have to bathe him myself.

—Oh, Marian. Bad for your Electra complex.

—You have to pumice the soles of his feet and dry between his toes. Let alone the other bits.

—God.

—You couldn't.

—I couldn't.

—Actually you could, perfectly well. Anyone can do anything if they have to.

—If you say so.

Francis was an academic like Euan, in literature like him. The women in the family had feared for him in the rivalry with his father – bright and beautiful, slight and fair like his mother – but they needn't have. He had decisively pronounced himself un-great and un-original and taken himself off into safe exile across the Atlantic, specialising in scholarly work in the Henry James archives, taking on a tinge of critical theory when it got fashionable. Euan looked at all his things and wrote him nice notes, complacently. Euan couldn't read James.

—Do you know what Daddy's got sellotaped to the inside of his porch door?

—Go on, surprise me. 'You don't have to be mad to work

95

here but it helps.' 'Go forth gently into the whatever it is.' 'Home sweet home'.

—Shipwreck. Just the word shipwreck. It turns out to be the codeword he's given to the gas company and so on, when they send people round. It's a service for old people, so that they don't let con-men in.

—Sensible.

—But why shipwreck? He's never even been on a ship, not that kind of ship. D'you know what I think? It's what he thinks about old age. Not peaceful or resigned at all. Shipwreck. Black night, a catastrophe that tips you into deep cold water, an undignified dreadful struggle for your life, in vain. No rescue.

—It doesn't have to be like that.

—Oh no? But what if it is?

Marian took the money out from under the floorboards in the airing cupboard and hid it in its biscuit tin at the bottom of an old trunk full of papers and toys in her own home, dreading that she would be burgled. She wrote a note to her father and put it in the space under the floorboards in case he came looking, explaining that she had put the money somewhere it would be completely safe. She didn't seal it, she left it open for the thief to read.

Tamsin and Mark sat reading to Euan. Marian was dealing with letters and bills at Euan's desk.

Marian paid Tamsin to read to her grandfather a couple of evenings a week, to save his eyes for his day work. Euan didn't know she was paid. Marian's older daughter Clare was supposed to help too, but she had young children and moods and didn't regularly manage it; she was in that baffled, lean, wolfish phase of young motherhood Marian dimly remembered, when you feel you may have been cheated of too many pleasures in exchange for the burden of loved children you can't unwish. When Clare read Herzen to Euan she pounced on a remark about 'the summer lightning of personal happiness'.

—Don't be such a glum, Tamsin said. —Herzen was sixty.

Tonight they were reading from a translation of some Russian book on Swedenborg. Tamsin read in a high, flat, sceptical voice, smothering yawns; she was more dressed up than she usually bothered to be for her grandfather, in a green silk top that showed her bra straps and stretch trousers cut off just below the knee: Marian presumed this was for Mark's benefit, even though she had hardly spoken to him since they arrived. She was growing her dark hair, she had it fastened behind her ears in slides, so fine it was like the fall of something liquid. When Mark took over reading she curled up with her head on a cushion on the sofa where they sat together, sucking her thumb, eyes closed.

—This stuff is completely cuckoo, Grandpa, she complained, muffledly. It was the most she ever said about any of the material she read for him; in the same way she never commented on the Bach or Handel or Janáček she rehearsed with the choral society for weeks on end, except to remark on the awful polo necks the conductor wore, or an irritating overweight woman next to her whose elbows impinged on her space. She determinedly got herself moved away from the woman with the elbows.

Marian noticed that Tamsin's bare feet with purple-painted toenails were curled only a fraction of an inch from Mark's thigh, for all she treated him with such disdain. She couldn't tell if Mark was aware of Tamsin's toes so suggestively close. He read with his characteristic half-blush, half-frown, steadily, pausing where he didn't fully understand. His blond hair was cut in a long fringe that hung across his eyes, fashionable with the boys at school (Tamsin had commented – her only comment on him – on its 'naffness'); his skin was reddened over the newly heavy cheekbones and on the jaw where the new beard was coming in. The toes crept imperceptibly across the sofa until they were pushed up against where Mark sat. It could have been mere unconsciousness on Tamsin's part, she could have been simply obliviously making herself comfortable in the space.

Marian felt a pang of regret for the limited, heartwarming, slightly sentimental relationship she had had with Mark, her best pupil, a sweet good nice-looking boy. But such relationships were only possible in school, where things were simpler.

Euan was slumped in his chair. He gave off complex wheezing noises. He often lost concentration and dozed, seeming to wash in and out of awareness of the reading: if they stopped he woke up and complained. But this time the noises grew worse: a grunting, whistling sound, seeming to come not from his mouth but his torso, shaking and tearing it. At the same time – over a period of, say, five minutes while Mark read and Marian wrote cheques – something dreadful began to spread in the room, a smell, a foul stink, unignorable as if it was substantial in the air like a pelt or a thick cloth. Suddenly it was at the forefront of all their attention. Mark stopped reading, Marian put down her pen, Tamsin snapped bolt upright, wide eyes on her grandfather.

—Mum! she commanded furiously.

Marian pushed back her chair. She thought the worst.

—Go and make tea, she told them, —Grandpa's gone to sleep.

They fled, Tamsin with a little involuntary whimper of

release, pulling the door shut fumblingly behind her. Marian stood for a couple of moments listening, breathing: the stink was as strong as a wall across her path.

Distinctly she thought to herself, it's now, it's now.

She was swept under a glistening, prickling, exultant wave of shame, as if some new frontier had been broached which could never be retreated from. She crossed to her father and bent her face down to the racked torso, to where the seamed, purple, chalky neck went under the old yellowed collar of his shirt. She supposed that he had had a stroke or a seizure, and that in a moment she would have to unleash the whole drama of doctors and emergency and last things; she breathed in deep to find what she was sure she would discover, that he had soiled himself, and that they were delivered over to one another through that ultimate lapse at a new level of intimate bondage.

His warmth was against her face; all she breathed in was a sweet, old, felty smell, redolent of her childhood, reminding her of the inside of his gramophone cabinet. Whatever the stink was, it didn't come from Euan.

And then he woke up; with a snort and start, finding her head nestled in his neck. Surprisingly, in that moment of confusion he wasn't angry with her; actually for a second his big hand came up and pressed her head rather clumsily, affectionately, into his shoulder. She was never clear whether he had exactly meant the tenderness of that gesture for her; it had something reflex about it, as if he had been caught out not quite awake enough to be clear which needy woman it was who required his reassurance. But he didn't repudiate it either, or query her waking him. While she began to search under bookshelves and in corners for the source of the terrible smell, he was uncharacteristically subdued and circumspect, making tentative grateful suggestions and remarks.

One of his beloved cats of course had been shut in that afternoon (Elaine remembered it making its getaway when she came in) and had left its little souvenir under a curtain. The smell must have come out as the central heating warmed it up. When Marian went to get newspaper and hot water and disinfectant from the kitchen she rather relished Mark's and Tamsin's excruciated faces and Tamsin's unconvincing preparations for a pot of tea she had thought would never be poured.

Francis had recently told Marian over the telephone things about their mother that she hadn't known: that in the years before her death Jean had left Euan on several occasions, come twice to live with Francis in his flat in London for months on end, actually once even gone as far as renting a flat of her own. This last time she was already sick, she had had the mastectomy, there were already signs of the secondary cancer she would die of.

—But she wasn't off her head, said Francis. —She knew what she wanted.

These were all stories from more than twenty years ago.

Marian's first reaction was characteristic of her relationship with Francis: annoyance at his wrong-footing her, at his having saved up all this time the advantage of this information.

—So what's new? She was always walking out on him. He was impossible. Tell me about it.

—But she never let you know the half of it. This was when you were going through the mill with Graham, remember? And then afterwards you were doing your teacher training . . . We didn't want to add to all your problems.

Marian tried to recover a picture of her mother at that time; but all the pictures from the different ages had been shuffled together since she died, like a fan of cards closed onto itself. The ones that tended to come up when she summoned were of a woman in her early forties, rat-tatting commandingly on high heels the way women did then, blonde hair pinned back in a French pleat neat and glossy as a loaf, and manicured nails with the half moon cuticles she had tried to show Marian how to do. This was the mother – public, charming – who had come to prize-givings at school; Marian in those days would willingly have exchanged all her distinctions and special prizes for adeptness at those more formidable feminine mysteries.

But afterwards, after all, her life had fallen into patterns more like her mother's; there were always babies to restore the common ground amongst women. It had been a relief to both of them that they could, eventually, talk with equal interest about decorating and washing and shopping: Marian remembered this, from when she had brought her little girls visiting at the old house. And she remembered how her father, if he was home from the University, would descend from his study to greet her as if when he crossed the hall he crossed a border-line between domains of life, between the one where women sat and gossiped in a kitchen and the one where he struggled with his books; she remembered how she was slightly disconcerted but not altogether displeased to find herself on the kitchen side of that frontier. Clare and Tamsin had had to be kept quiet so that he could work just as she and Francis had been kept quiet.

Marian had imagined without thinking about it that in caring for her father in his extreme old age she was somehow filling her mother's empty place. It was disconcerting to think of her mother absconding from that place herself, repeatedly delinquent.

—She only went back because he pleaded with her, said Francis. —And the last time she was determined not to, but then of course she got too ill, she couldn't look after herself, she gave up, it was too late . . .

—I'm sure you're exaggerating. I'd have remembered, if she'd ever been away for so long; don't forget I was living fifteen minutes walk away for some of that time. I know she used to come and stay with you sometimes . . .

—You didn't visit them for weeks on end. You had other things on your mind.

—Was it sex, do you think? she asked him warily.

—On your mind?

—No, be serious, on Mummy and Daddy's.

—Christ, it doesn't bear thinking about.

Marian tried to imagine Francis's response when his mother turned up – 'in a state', he said – on his doorstep. He was a young bachelor then, teaching at University College, with a white-painted 'pad' in Islington full of books and paintings by contemporary artists who had not gone on to be famous. (He had really once called it a 'pad'; just as they had really once called him a 'bachelor', until he moved to the States and was suddenly and all-illuminatingly gay.)

—What did she *say*, Francis? Can't you remember?

—It's an age ago. I thought I told you all this before. I probably did: you've forgotten.

—But what did he do?

—Oh, not anything. Not any big thing. He used to turn records up to drown out what she was saying to him. That sort of thing. God knows. He called her a witch. He wouldn't let her wear glasses, though she could hardly see to walk, said they made her look like a tribal fetish. They did, a bit. She said she didn't have any fun. She was bored. He liked books. She liked parties and people.

There was a photograph of Jean in a silver frame on Euan's bedside table. The next time Marian was at the flat, she picked it up and recovered instantaneously the late, last images of her that should have belonged at the top of the successive layers of remembering. What had she been thinking of, imagining sex and all that young kind of desperation to explain her mother's late attempts at escape? This was a funny old lady with a white helmet of permed hair and a bosom like a shapeless cushion stuffed into an inappropriate pink T-shirt with short sleeves tight around the fat of her arms. The skewy mouth that had in the prize-giving days been demurely suggestive was opened like a gash across a face sagged and jowly, not bothering to please, although she smiled – slyly, or derisively – for the camera. A hand held flat for shade like the the peak of a cap cast a dark ledge of shadow down over those terrible – surely deliberately and challengingly terrible – glasses. Whatever Euan had commanded, she was wearing the glasses. And wearing them, what's more, in the one photograph that he had selected from among all the possible others to watch over him.

The photograph had been taken in her garden. It was hard to imagine that Jean had ever wanted to leave her husband enough to want to leave her garden, a big old walled garden with apple trees and vegetable plots and herb-aceous borders where Jean reigned as the only half-benevolent Creator, nurturing plants with tender skilled fingers, dead-heading and pruning, waging war on pests. She used to describe to Marian the remorse she felt, carrying a big slug wrapped in a leaf to her killing pot full of salt water in the shed.

—You can feel its weight in the leaf, a little animal, the weight of a mouse; a living thing.

Jean surely hadn't been all that interested in parties, not in those last years. Marian couldn't be certain that Francis wasn't exaggerating the whole thing, hadn't told her all of it really because he wanted to say, 'she came to me'; to counterbalance Marian's staked claim, now – staked out of the most quotidian necessity – of primacy with their father.

And strangely out of that thought came another, as Marian put the photograph back in its place on the bedside table.

—I'm like him, she thought. —Not like her. I was like him, all the time. We don't like parties. We're neither of us any good at growing things. We're better with people in books or classrooms. We're too ashamed to be tender or merciful.

But then her mother had tipped the slug, in any case, into that dark plastic jug in the shadowy shed, which would develop an unholy smell if she forgot to empty it.

—There was something wrong with that madwoman yesterday, said Euan to Marian. —More than usual. Her time of the month, I suspect. Or else she's menopausal. Said something about Tamsin.

—About Tamsin?

—Complaining about her breaking the lid of the teapot. Ostensibly. But behind that little opening I detected a whole furtive hinterland of disapproval. Her disapprovals are the only extensive thing about her.

—*Did* Tamsin break the teapot lid? What a nuisance. She didn't tell me.

—Of course it's about the boy. You can imagine the sort of dreary petit bourgeois sequence of aspirations Elaine is nurturing on his behalf. I'm quite sure they don't include Tamsin.

He'll have to kick free of his mother, if he genuinely wants to do something. He could soar. He's got the intelligence, but it's not just that.

—Kick free? That's a horrible way of putting it, when Elaine's worked so hard, bringing him up alone. And anyway Tamsin's twenty-five years old, she couldn't possibly be interested in Mark.

—My dear daughter, he said. —Which one of us is blind?

Marian had her apron on, which somehow disadvantaged her. It was Saturday again, she was making him a sandwich to leave for his tea; he was in ebullient mood, there was another pile of manuscript ready to go to the woman who word-processed it for him. He had even asked for a glass of wine with his lunch.

Marian concentrated on slicing tomato. —So did Elaine buy a new teapot?

—I have no idea, he said. —Deliberately, I don't ask. If I'm not careful, she fills every space in my mind with her trivial conversation and I can't think. She does it purposely, whether she knows it or not. Intrinsically, she's opposed to intellectual work. It will be a triumph for her if I never finish the book. Which I won't, anyway. I can feel death coming on – faster than I can keep ahead of it. It lives inside here . . . He pressed his fist against his chest.

—Don't be silly, Marian said. —When you're doing so well.

—And even if I finish it, of course, no one will be interested. I'm writing in a lost language, outmoded, irrelevant, boring. Unforgiveably, I will have omitted to make my obeisances to the new critical gods . . .

—There you are. Your sandwich is in the fridge, Daddy.

—Is she coming tonight?

—Elaine doesn't come in the evenings.

—Not her. Tamsin. That boy doesn't stand a chance. The little cat who always lands on her feet; I like to watch her.

Euan had never been told about the dead boyfriend or the baby.

—It's Saturday, Daddy. I told you Tamsin was singing tonight; and I'm going to hear her. That's why I've put your sandwich in the fridge.

—Singing? What kind of singing?

—With the choral society. 'Missa Solemnis'. I said, if you wanted to come, we could use the wheelchair, it's all fixed up for that now at the concert hall. I could still phone and try for tickets.

—I don't want tickets. What would I want tickets for? I'm too sick to go out, why don't you ever listen to me tell you that? You try to fuss me into things, try to distract me, pretend everything is still alright, as if I was an infant. I accept, you see, he explained with bad-tempered mock patience, as if to a spiritual defective. —I accept this, this doom. I accept it.

—What's given on earth is not final, she offered, rather offhandedly, as consolation.

He turned on her a look white with rage, discovering his precious words in her mouth. —What? he spat out. —What? He screwed up his face, putting his hand to his ear in a derisive pantomime of deafness. His enunciation was icily exact. —I have no idea what you're talking about.

Elaine came to see Marian in school when Marian was busy in her office making last minute adjustments to the invigilation timetable for public examinations. It was four o'clock, the great tide of the children had receded from the site, leaving only the last flotsam and jetsam of individuals in the corridors and rooms, in an air bruised and yielding after the bursting tautness of all day. A greenish summer light came in the high windows of the office, propped open to their full extent, and made it aquarium-like; dapples of light floated across the backs of Marian's hands as she pasted strips of paper across names, wrote in other names in neat black ink.

Elaine had found another job, she would work out her month with Euan, but then Marian would have to find someone else. And then when Marian said she was very sorry to see Elaine go, but she understood that her father wasn't an easy man to work for, Elaine explained that it wasn't simply that, there was something else, there was Marian's daughter.

—Mark's everything I've got, she said. —And I don't want to see him come to grief.

Marian ran her fingers through the liquid-seeming light on the timetable. To grief, she thought. I suppose that's what it is.

—Why? What do you imagine is going on?

Elaine trembled with the intensity of her opposition. —I'm not stupid.

—I suppose I am, said Marian. —Might they not just be friends?

—Bite-marks on his chest, said Elaine, and Marian blushed. —I'm sorry for what happened to your daughter. But Mark's got so much ahead of him. I don't want him to get mixed up in anything.

Marian was afraid that Elaine would see that she didn't want Mark to get mixed up in anything either; it didn't seem supportive of Tamsin. —I'll talk to her, she said. —I'll try and find out what's happening.

—Just so long as you're aware of my views, said Elaine. —I'd rather they didn't meet, so I won't be bringing Mark to Euan's any more, for these last weeks.

—Fair enough. Although my father will miss him.

Elaine gave a very qualified grunt of assent, tucking in her double chin; she was thinking perhaps that she and her son would be better rid of the whole dangerous family of them.

When Elaine had gone – neat heels tapping smartly in the empty corridor – Marian had her timetable to think about; and behind that the worry about Euan, and whether she could face the idea of his going into a home, or whether she had to go through trying to find another housekeeper. She hardly had time to consider the bother of Tamsin and Mark; and then when she walked to get her car, the last one parked in the concrete area behind the labs, there were two dogs mating, embarrassingly and absurdly stuck together. The male – she couldn't tell which it was – must have slipped off and somehow couldn't disengage; they stood side by side, shamedly ignoring one another, pretending they weren't attached at their rear ends so that wherever one stepped the other had to shuffle dejectedly alongside. Both gave out little whimpers of pain when they moved. Marian felt responsible; was one supposed to throw cold water? But she would have to walk a long way back to get water; and what if it was cruel? She also felt slightly disgusted and humiliated; she hoped no one was around to see her seeing this and not knowing what to do. She was supposed to be so sensible and unsqueamish.

Then from nowhere came the thought of 'bite-marks' like a wave of heat, making her wet under the arms; avoiding the pantomime-horse-dogs' pleading looks she got quickly into her car, drove off and left them. Nature ought to have its own cure for such a wretched mess; it wasn't any of her business. How problematic, how foolish, it all was. Thank goodness she was well out of it (twenty years out of it, although she didn't confess that to anyone in case they thought she was sick, or deprived): the abjectness, the pairing up, the whimpering, the wet and sucking flesh. Something for dogs and teenagers.

Marian often came in from school to find Tamsin and Mark in the house. She wondered at the amount of time off from work Tamsin seemed to be taking. More, she worried about Mark's school work: he used to spend all his free time in the library. They weren't exactly furtive when she came in; they weren't even always in Tamsin's room; sometimes they were drinking coffee on the sofa, or beer on the patio. They didn't blush, or look resentful at being interrupted. Mark would stand up politely; he still called her Mrs Menges.

He had his hair cut differently. What a handsome pair they made; you couldn't help thinking that, the tall fair boy with his attentive ironic watchfulness, ready to joke, the slight dark fey girl leading him after her by the invisible silken cord. If Mark began talking to Marian about work and school then Tamsin tugged. A raised eyebrow, a low-voiced word left behind her as she exited through a door; with an apologetic glance to Marian as though he knew she appreciated it couldn't be any other way, Mark was pulled after. Neither Mark nor Tamsin ever offered any explanation for their suddenly keeping such constant company, or any name for their relationship. Their languorous circumnavigations from TV to hi-fi to garden to bedroom and round again filled up Marian's house when they were there and she found herself skulking in the kitchen or going into her own bedroom to be out of their way.

She dutifully told Mark that his mother was worried and wasn't happy at him spending all his time with Tamsin. He reassured her kindly that he was working as hard as ever but she wasn't any more convinced than Elaine would have been; there was a distracted dry glitter in his eye that suggested to her the phase of the overturning of goals and idols, the phase of the discovery of secret possibilities so all-altering that in pursuit of them any loyalties could be sacrificed and any assurances could be given. When school started up again after the summer holidays Mark resumed attending his A level classes diligently, but while he was listening to her he was sometimes unconsciously smiling at something else.

One day there was a flash of crimson across the landing at the top of the stairs as Marian came in at the front door: Tamsin running out of Marian's bedroom (the only room with a full length mirror) in a crimson dress, a stunning full length dress in clinging satin cut on the cross over her hips, long black beads (Marian's?) whipping after her. A whirl of Tamsin like a paparazzo's snatch of film star, loud laughter cut off, a door (Tamsin's bedroom door) pulled shut with a bang. Left for Marian on the wrong side of the door was the not-quite-quiet of the shut out. From behind the door came warm and thick as dove-song or slow-cooking, the burbling of silly talk, the up and down crooning of pleasure: not sex-noises, just pleasurable intimacy. For the first time, something was being deliberately hidden from her. She couldn't exactly stride up and throw open the door upon them, though. There wasn't even any possible sense in which they weren't allowed to do whatever they might choose to do in there.

Instead, something else dawned on her. She went to the old toy chest in the TV room and dug out the biscuit tin from the bottom. It had never occurred to her to check the money since she had moved it here; she had only feared a burglary. Now she suddenly thought with puzzlement about what she had been distracted from these last few weeks, worrying about Euan, advertising for and interviewing the new housekeeper. Tamsin had flickered distractingly on her horizon in a succession of splendid outfits: trouser-suits, jeans with skinny T-shirts, a velvet pinafore, a beaded blouse, a short chiffon dress with satin appliqué. Now it occurred to Marian for the first time to ask how she had possibly been able to afford these – and her share of rent and bills and food money – when she only seemed to be working half her usual hours? It had seemed a sort of conjuring trick, or a sort of genius, something beautiful youth could do and that it wasn't for dingy middle age to question.

She knelt on the carpet in the TV room and opened her father's slightly rusted old biscuit tin, breaking a fingernail on it. She tipped the money out. More money had gone, much much more; Marian's hands were so sweaty and shaking so nervously and her thoughts were racing so fast that she couldn't focus to count it properly, she kept on making piles of notes and then forgetting how much was in each pile and having to recount them. Perhaps a thousand pounds were gone altogether, a whole thousand pounds: only, because she was so upset, she didn't trust herself to have done her sums properly, she had better start again. When she started counting again she began to cry, rather loudly and excessively, as if there was a point to this crying and it was not quite for herself alone; and after a while the crying took over and she gave up counting. She wiped her soaking face and runny nose on an old blouse of hers that had been folded on top of her workbasket, waiting to have its button sewn on and a rip mended.

Someone put a hand on her arm.

Crouched on her haunches opposite where Marian had collapsed was Tamsin, changed out of the crimson dress into leggings and baggy T-shirt; Tamsin was peering at her with a mixture of dismay and, ready close behind it, annoyance.

—Mum: for God's sake! It's only money.

But it wasn't only money. It was the flash of a crimson dress, and the door banged shut.

Marian had a dream. It was such a blessed dream; she tried to explain it to her father. They had a morning's respite from his pains and his troubles (his eyes were too bad, he had had to give up writing the Dostoevsky book). They seemed to have found a live-in housekeeper who was suitable, although Marian could already see the fault lines along which the arrangement would fracture: Dana filled the flat with expensive bunches of flowers (like a funeral, Euan said) and called him sweetheart and poppet. She had pretty eyes and a strong jaw and favoured pastel dresses; Marian suspected she might be a transsexual and wondered if Euan suspected it too, and whether he'd mind.

It was Saturday, Dana's day off: Marian made them both coffee.

—I was in a meadow – I know in the dream that's what I called it, though I also thought *pré*, like the French. Anyway, it was a lovely meadow full of long grass, all different species of grass, and hundreds of kinds of flowers, sloping away out of sight in the sunlight, and everywhere you looked there were butterflies, hundreds and thousands of them, beautiful ones, rare ones, going from flower to flower collecting nectar, and then when you looked closer there were little animals too, all kinds of species mixed together, hares and field mice and these little black fox-like things with big ears – that was because someone at school was talking about seeing fennec foxes at the zoo. And then I saw there was something dangling in the grass, there'd been some sort of fall – if you can imagine that on a perfectly fine day – like an ice-storm, and hanging in the long grass were these ice-medallions, perfect and transparent like glass, but formed in the shape of pictures, perfect tiny pictures, of deer and castles and dogs and trees. And I knew it was a paradox – I knew the really amazing thing was that they had been accidentally arrived at, in nature, these perfect representations. I knew that once I'd seen these, it had to change everything I believed about the world, and about what was possible.

But Euan looked at her confusedly, and she had to give up her attempt to explain how it had charmed her, and had made her happy when she woke up, and how it was still with her now, like a dispensation, a sign of reassurance whose explicit meaning lay just out of reach.

He was very vague this morning.

—Where was this? he asked her irritatedly. —Where did you say you'd been?

Twisted

Clare thought about Helly, her best friend.

She was cooking fish fingers for the children's lunch; Helly didn't have any children. It was raining outside. There was another week before Coco and Lily went back to school and Rose to nursery. That morning Rose had woken them at six o'clock and Clare, whose turn it was to get up, had sat resentfully downstairs watching Rose play for an hour and a half before the others got up, drinking tea and listening to farming programmes on the radio, wrapping her cold feet in the hem of an old pinkish grey nightgown that had once belonged to Bram's grandmother. In fact it still had a label with Bram's grandmother's name on, stitched into the neck, from when she had ended up in an old people's home where all their washing was done together and things got mixed up and lost.

Bram got up and went to work. Since then Clare had made breakfast for the children, washed up the dishes, got them all dressed, tidied the beds. She had sorted out a wash for the machine, and hung it out when it was finished on one of the two drooping wooden clothes horses she had to use to dry the clothes in a corner of the kitchen when it wasn't fine enough to hang them outdoors: their rungs were permanently blackened with wet and left marks on pale clothes if you weren't careful.

The children had mostly watched television (Clare had bought it for them at the beginning of the summer and they hadn't fallen out of love with it yet). Rose had managed to step on the Tintin comic Coco was meticulously drawing with a ruler and pencil crayons; she crumpled and tore it and left a dirty bare footmark. Coco, understandably but unpicturesquely, went berserk, trying to pound his baby sister with his fists and baring his teeth and squeezing out from between them a kind of growling scream. Clare thought helplessly of different, better children somewhere sometime else who played adventurous games together away from the adults, and had been taught self-control and discipline and that you didn't hit girls or anyone younger than yourself. She sagged with the sense of a lost civilisation, and was nagged by a guilty idea that she ought to be doing something creative with them. But she knew what it was if you began creative things without conviction, how quickly you were found out, how shamingly your temper would fasten on their ingratitude.

And anyway, there were all these other uncreative things she had to do, taking up an impossible space, swelling to stuff out every corner of her time and to smother any chinks she had fondly imagined she was keeping for a grown-up coffee and a read of the paper. Now it was lunchtime; the children must be fed. One felt as if one invented this stuff, in some kind of crazy conspiracy of martyrdom; surely other better mothers had found sweeter, lighter ways of passing their days than this? She must be producing this impasse, this stickily inflating burden of routine, out of sheer spite: it must be oozing from her own smothered vengefulness. But if she tried to come clean and step out of it, she was confronted with real unanswerable problems. What would happen if she didn't feed them? Didn't dress them? Didn't tidy the house and wash the dishes and wash the clothes and shop and cook? It wouldn't be liberation, they would just all drown deeper and more miserably in their sticky mire. This domestic machine required her drudgery, implacably; the hours of her life were the fuel it needed just to tick over.

She had a pain, somewhere: was it in her heart? In her spleen, more like; or no, between her ears, arced like one of those rigid Alice bands she had once worn to school. Or a dim poisonous fog connecting and attacking all the organs of her body.

She thought about Helly.

She imagined a morning for Helly, a parallel place in the world where Helly moved with lightness between free choices, taking a long shower, picking out clothes from her wardrobe, drinking filter coffee, eating a croissant and then a peach from a shallow ceramic fruit bowl on a glass table, looking over a script for a rehearsal she was going to in the afternoon. She knew enough about Helly's life, of course, to picture the flat accurately and fill in some authenticating detail. The flat was not tidy – Helly was notoriously slovenly – there were clothes dropped over the backs of chairs and on the floor, the duvet in its yellow cover with red poppies was heaped on the bed where she'd climbed out from under it, and Sunday supplements and magazines were strewn all over the place. But it was clean, she could afford a cleaner these days, after the ice cream contract and now the work for the TV series about a special needs teacher (Helly was not the special needs teacher but the French teacher the special needs teacher's partner was having an affair with). Sunlight struck in through its open sash windows across the polished wood floor, there were flowers in a vase drinking up the light, unusual cut flowers, delphiniums or something that you could only buy in good florists in London. Blue delphiniums and yellow goldenrod. Not in season: but Clare allowed herself this one little cheat.

David, Helly's boyfriend, was not part of Clare's picture.

Partly, it was precisely the singleness of Helly's life that Clare most envied. She and David kept their separate flats and didn't see one another for days at a time. The idea of such empty acres of solitude was a cooling balm against the promiscuous itch of Clare and Bram's crowded little house where every surface was greasy with touching and there was no lock on the toilet door and at night the children wandered from bed to bed.

Partly, it was better not to think about David's life with Helly, because there was something going on between him and Clare. Not an affair, exactly, yet, but some kind of promise of one. This promise occupied a very particular space in Clare's thoughts at the moment. It was buried deep under all the casual daily material of her life and the deliberate thought of it was mostly avoided by her; and yet at the same time she was never for a single fraction of a moment unconscious of it wrapping her around and changing her like an alien skin fitted indistinguishably over her real one.

David and Clare had slept together once before, years and years ago when they were teenagers, long before either of them belonged in any couple, at a party so drunken and drugged that neither of them had any very clear memory of it. Neither Bram nor Helly knew this.

Now she was going to meet him in London in ten days.

For a long time Clare Menges hadn't distinguished Helly Parkin from the alien crowd at school. Helly didn't practise the moody dark withdrawal that was standard for those who chose not to belong: she was even good at netball, and loud and exuberant, with fair hair braided onto her head like Angie in *EastEnders*, protuberant ears, a husky voice, a grin so wide her laughter was a red gulf. Clare inclined towards the ones who wore their hair like Annie Lennox, short and spiky, and didn't grin.

One lunch break towards the end of their second year, when the PE and double maths to come was casting its deep shadow across the sunshine and the crowds of green-clad girls in it foolishly-innocently French skipping across knotted elastic bands, Helly claimed her. Clare was sitting on the grass with her back to the wall of the biology lab, devouring a book, holding it open with her elbows, with her hands over her ears and her forehead screwed up in what was meant to be an all-excluding frown. She and a couple of friends were in a phase of passing round dreadful historical novels: in irony, knowing they would be disappoved of, but also genuinely addicted to the ripe lurid matter inside which fed some hunger left over by the long, pale school days. (She never had any trouble later in life remembering the marriages and adulteries and sticky ends of the royal families of Europe.)

Helly, who as far as Clare could remember had never talked to her before, crouched on the grass in front of her, forcing her to look up from the book, and speaking in an absurdly portentous artificial voice.

—Come forth with me to witness the secret sacrifice. Speak to none else of it.

Clare was dizzy from being dragged out of her story in too much of a rush: Ferdinand and Isabella had just made a messenger who brought unfortunate news eat his own boiled shoe leather. Helly's words seemed a left-over bright end from her book, improbably trailing in the thin real air: otherwise she might simply have ignored her. She certainly felt embarrassed for her: by the end of the second year it was not the thing to play imaginary games, you were supposed to have graduated to games with rules.

—I don't want to, I'm reading.

Helly put a finger to her lips in convincingly real dismay. —Speak not: 'tis deadly dangerous, if they but knew. Come forth at once, utter no further word.

With a darting surreptitious glance around at the crowds of tranquilly idling girls she walked off. After an exasperated moment's hesitation, Clare followed. They wound through the knot garden beside Old House, through the door onto the terrace, then down the terrace steps and past the tennis courts and around the huge trunk of the old cedar to a gap in the tall thick shrubs that grew around the boundary wall. Clare felt apologetic and ridiculous, following – she shrugged at an enquiring friend who passed going the other way – but at the same time she was half excited, susceptible to the suggestion that under the banal surface of school life there must be reserves of possibility, untapped.

Behind the gap in the shrubs was a space big enough for a den; Clare had been in there before. The earth was worn shiny, the bushes in their interior were twiggy and dusty and leafless; you could sit on the wide top of the wall. The wall overlooked a suburban street whose empty ordinariness was mysterious and desirable because it was outside and free. Helly had a couple of acolytes squeezed already into the space, girls Clare didn't know well. They couldn't keep up the unfaltering seriousness Helly managed, they giggled and looked as if they felt exposed in foolishness when Clare joined them.

—What's all this about?

Helly closed her eyes, waited for silence.

—Clare Menges, you have been chosen.

—For what, exactly?

—To join the sacred sisterhood of the stump.

There was a sawn-off stump of some kind of shrub at the back of the den, beside the wall: when Clare looked closely at it she could see it was studded with drawing pins and that there were hairgrips and scraps of cloth and bits of jewellery stuffed behind its bark and into its crevices. They all looked wet and dirty and rather dismal.

—You have to give something, Helly said. —In return for our sacrifices the guardian of the stump protects us with his powers and brings misfortune to our enemies.

—The drawing pins are the curses, one of the others said. —They really work.

—I don't know if I want to belong to the sisterhood of the stump, said Clare.

—Too late, intoned Helly, who could sustain her portentous intonation without collapse or irony. —You've seen his mysteries. If you betray them, may you rot in torment.

—But anyone could see them. And anyway, why does the guardian of the stump have to be a he? (Clare's stepmother was a regular at the Greenham Common women's protest against Cruise missiles).

Helly frowned. —He just is. Don't you want his powers?

—I just thought it would make more sense to sacrifice to a female thingy, that's all. As it's a sisterhood.

—But the powers that control this school are female: haven't you thought of that? We need him to combat them, the great guardian of the stump: let his name be ever sacred, and his mystery deep.

—If you say so.

Clare considered: she was slightly in awe of Helly and her absolute seriousness. She found a button in her purse which the others said would do as a sacrifice, to begin with.

—Close your eyes, said Helly. Keep them shut. Then she took hold of Clare's hand, painfully tightly, squeezing it until Clare protested, although still with her eyes obediently shut. Helly held on, pressing her fingers down inside something wet, mossy, splintery. It was only when Clare thought of slippery creatures that might be lurking in the stump that she had the strength to pull violently away, letting go of the button.

—Well done, said Helly, smiling into her eyes.

Clare's heart was actually thumping, and all afternoon she could smell moss and rotten wood on her fingers. The details of the cult seemed to her gauche and embarrassing. But she somehow didn't mind it getting around that she was Helly Parkin's friend now. She even helped Helly steal bits of stuff from certain girls in the class – scraps of notes, bits of the ties from their science overalls, even name tapes cut out of their gym blouses in the locker room – which they then pinned to the stump with drawing pins, to bring bad luck: or 'evil chance', as Helly called it. Whenever something unfortunate really happened to one of these girls, the four cult members were drawn together in an exhilarating uneasy mixture of guilt and scepticism.

Clare and Helly fell in love with one another's houses.

At weekends Clare and her sister Tamsin lived with their mother; during the week they lived in a big chaotic house in Kingsmile with their father, who was a ceramicist, and their stepmother and half-brother. There were four flights of echoing stairs and rooms at the top they didn't even properly use. There were striking things everywhere: Graham's ceramics and paintings, an Indian embroidered canopy over the fireplace in the sitting room, a copper vase full of unusual flower heads Naomi had dried, old jewel-coloured Turkish rugs on the stripped wood floor, bookcases built of stained planks piled on bricks, a crumbling antique rattan settee. In the kitchen there was a vast stripped-pine table round which any number of family and friends might be assembled to eat Naomi's vegetarian curries and wholemeal crumbles. There was always a mattress and a sleeping bag for anyone passing through or temporarily homeless, or for the girls' friends, or Toby's. In the evenings the adults would sit round the big table drinking wine and rolling up, and the smell of marijuana, thin with just an undertone of acrid nastiness, would rise through the house.

—Be sensible girls, said Graham. —You know what not to mention, and where not to mention it.

Helly loved the house in Kingsmile. Its emptiness and air of casual improvisation made her wild. She raced up the bare stairs three at a time, she lay on her back on the floor in the sitting room in the dusk so that Graham and Naomi fell over her, she climbed out of the attic windows and sat with her feet in the old lead-lined gutter looking down to the faraway street over the parapet. She would pretend she got high, leaning over the banisters on the top landing and breathing in the smell of the marijuana. She staggered about and fell on Clare's bed, describing her visions, the room swaying like seaweed in a pool, rainbow colours, something cold and scary touching her.

—It's the guardian of the stump, said Clare, and Helly screamed and then they wrestled together on the bed and Helly tried to make her beg forgiveness for her sacrilege.

For Clare there was something unsatisfactorily unfinished about the house. Because there were no carpets anywhere it was filled with noise. Doors didn't shut properly and the stairs were half stripped and then abandoned and one wall in the sitting room was half painted red. In the cinders in the big fireplace in the morning there were orange peels and cigarette packets; no one did much dusting or sweeping, and when she thought of the house when she wasn't there she thought of cold, bare feet on gritty floors. It was always difficult to get comfortable to read, except in bed: the chairs were all unusual – an old green chenille chair with a broken mechanism for folding out and supporting your legs, a circular nineteen-fifties basket chair in an iron frame – but there were none that you could snuggle down in. She did her homework at a beautiful fragile little walnut desk in her bedroom whose drawers had lost all their knobs and which was never quite big enough for her books.

She knew her father sometimes felt the unsatisfactory unfinishedness too. She and Tamsin were very finely attuned to his moods, they called him 'the honeypot' and catalogued his behaviour with a mixture of derision and devotion, smug at having their place in his favours without trying. He sometimes as good as admitted to them how the trying wore him out: Naomi's anxious efforts to please him especially, although they suspected that their mother's sensible phone calls about practicalities and money (the girls needed new shoes; Tamsin wanted to start clarinet lessons) were in a hidden way a kind of trying too.

—What a burden it is, Tamsin pretended to sigh when he wasn't there. —What a mess these women make when they fall at my feet and I have to walk all over them.

They knew that their mother still wanted to know about him; they saved up fragments of his dissatisfaction with the house like trophies to compensate her. He suffered with backache, he asked why they couldn't buy a decent sofa. There was always money for special little finds in junk shops but there was never the kind of money that bought decent sofas. Naomi anyway preferred to sit cross legged on the floor.

—But I'm nearly fifty, he said, with a little grim laugh. (His 'at least someone round here has a grasp on reality' laugh, the girls agreed.) Naomi (who wasn't thirty yet) looked frightened: it was one of her superstitions, that she didn't like anyone to mention their age difference.

In spite of his dissatisfactions, the girls knew that the little remarks he made when they went off for their weekends at Marian's weren't really complimentary. He said that 'it must all seem terribly sensible and organised and quiet compared with living here' (that meant dull). He took an amused interest in Marian's decorating – 'she must have been longing for a fitted kitchen all along' – and was delighted when the girls let slip that she didn't allow them to use a mug without a saucer in case of drips. When she had a burglar alarm installed he started calling her house Fort Knox. They didn't report these jokes to Marian.

Clare would have liked to live in Helly's house in Poynton. Poynton was a little village that had been blotted up at the edge of the city's advance; Helly had a long bus ride to school every day. (She didn't mind: the same bus collected up boys for the grammar school too, there was always some fantasised romance on the go, someone to swoon over if he brushed obliviously past you.) The Parkins lived in an estate of new houses, her father had a management position with British Gas, her mother was a primary school teacher. There was a younger brother who played the guitar and wanted to be in a group. Everything in the house was new and clean and comfortable and worked. The walls between the rooms were so thin that when they lay whispering in Helly's bed at night her father lying in his bed next door hardly had to raise his voice to tell them to be quiet: you felt you slept with the whole family, the partitions were merely polite. Helly's father, whom she quarrelled with bitterly – luxuriously, Clare thought: somehow she and Tamsin just couldn't afford to quarrel with Graham – was short and dapper and satirical, he was good at crosswords and puzzles and competitions. Helly was good at them too; before she was a teenager and turned against him they had won things together, a holiday and a freezer and a diamond ring. Mostly they quarrelled about politics: he was an enthusiastic supporter of Mrs Thatcher, and exaggerated his enthusiasm to goad her.

At Poynton Clare met boys. Helly belonged, improbably, to the Methodist youth club, which seemed to have nothing to do with religion but was a sort of cover operation for disaffected youth. There was an intimate core of girls who ran things and then a number of boys moving more loosely on the periphery, like planets, exerting their huge gravitational pull all unconsciously upon the centre. Some of them, like Helly, were bussed into the selective schools in the city. But most of them went to the local school and it was with these boys Clare fell in love: cocky, teasing, irreverent, dangerous. The grammar school boys kept apart in a different set and were too superior and sophisticated to bother with Clare and Helly; also, there was a kind of embarrassment of recognition, the clever girls and boys looked at one another and knew they had all bought in to the same system, and did not particularly want to be reminded of this outside of school where they were pretending to be something else.

Helly and Clare would spend an hour or more in Helly's bedroom dressing up and putting on make-up, then they walked self-consciously along to the church hall, without coats to spoil their effect, however cold it was. There they played table tennis or badminton, or hung around in the kitchen making powdered coffee and taking part in some repartee which was usually sexual teasing. The boys outdid one another in outrageous suggestions and boasts, often involving sexual disgust at the exploits of some girl not present.

—She's a fucking slapper, she was all over me.

—Man, she was gasping for it: and she's a fucking size, I was suffocating, her big tits were in my face, I wanted air.

The girls responded as required with a certain kind of fending off, a demure immunity of slow-burning smiles, avoiding eye-contact with the boys, glancing blazingly at one another then down again, as if they moved flexibly and slowly inside a sexual shape of the boys' words' making, thrilling and dangerously capable of shaming them. Clare found it felt very womanly to be spooning out coffee and boiling kettles of water, capable and impatient ('Wait! That one's not got sugar in it yet!'). And there was a certain kind of dry, bold, loud, derisive remark which made you strong in your resistance and which the boys particularly admired: Helly was good at these.

—David Taton, you were so keen to get your trousers down you didn't care who it was!

—So what do you expect if you suffer from wandering hands trouble, Stuart Hopkin!

Clare wondered at their complex ironic other selves suddenly insignificant and tiny: none of the languages they had used before had ever seemed as powerful as this coarse one. She was not quite sure quite what reality it represented: were these boys really doing half, or any, of the things they boasted of? Where did such things happen, how did they begin? Sometimes couples disappeared round the back of the church hall, but they were never left alone long enough – surely? – to be having intercourse. Helly was evasive, she wasn't sure, things happened at parties.

The boys would break off from time to time into scuffling fights, more or less serious, flares of violence raging out of nowhere. The girls split up into factional gossip; Clare feared some of these girls more than any of the boys; the boys mostly ignored her, the girls smelt out right away that she was an outsider. Two of them, two short, fat girls with blue eye make-up whose names were often invoked in the slapper stories, took Helly outside to talk about her. Was she pregnant? (That was something to do with the way she stood and the dress she was wearing.) 'Pregnant' was a sexual word in their talk, like other ordinary words suddenly electrified: 'fancy', and 'talent', and 'touching up', and 'sucking' and 'hard' and 'coming', all these words revealed other, explosive selves. That it could be thought she might be pregnant! She was excited and humiliated.

Helly and Clare walked home; sometimes some of the boys walked part of the way with them. A different mood would settle on them all. The walk from the youth club back to the estate could make you think you really were in the country: there were dark fields and trees with birds rustling in them, a few cottages with televisions flickering in rooms with turned off lights. Their voices were quiet and intimate under the high starry spaces of night, dreamy because they were invisible to one another. A kind of gallantry came out in the boys; they confessed their ambitions, which turned out to be rather honourable and stirring: one wanted to be an air-force pilot, one wanted to work relieving poverty in Africa, one of them wanted to draw cartoons. All of these seemed improbable to Clare; the parents of these boys were car mechanics or worked in supermarkets or the local meat processing plant, and she had in those days, for all her socialism, a rather fixed idea of who got to be pilots and artists. (She was wrong, about the pilot at any rate.)

But the improbability made the boys' ambitions all the more poignant; afterwards, upstairs in Helly's bedroom, the girls talked about them tenderly.

—Imagine, said Clare, —if it was like the First World War. Imagine if they had to go off and fight, and we were going to say goodbye to them at the station. Imagine how they'd look, in their uniforms, all brave and solemn. We'd be so desperate to stop them, they'd be so sort of fatalistic and stubborn. Stuart Hopkin: although he's so small, he's so sweet, he's really intense; imagine the look he'd give you, just as the train began to leave . . .

She had real tears in her eyes, real pain in her heart.

—Imagine how we'd kiss them, said Helly. —Because they might not come back.

The idea of kissing hovered over those walks home, the sensation of the possibility of it brushed them for moments with its panting heat, unspoken. They might kiss where the boys turned off to go a different way. Mostly it didn't happen. Once or twice when Clare was there it happened to Helly. There was a movement with which a boy chose you, separated you off; even the rehearsal of that movement in her mind could make Clare melt, its astonishing predatory decisiveness: that he could be so sure he wanted that, and from you! She could only imagine the total acquiescence of the flesh at such a tribute. Then he bent over you and put his arms around you and the kiss was taken while others watched and jeered, long and slow, and there were names for this too – 'snogging', and 'French kissing'; techniques you were afraid you might not know.

—It's weird, said Helly. —Not exactly nice, having some-one else's tongue in your mouth.

—Like what? said Clare.

Clare and Helly in their bedrooms tried out kissing on each other, and sex. 'Imagine if he did this,' they said: 'and this.' They took it in turns to be Mr Garrick the French teacher (the only male teacher at school), or David Taton from the youth club, or Elvis Costello. Sometimes it was into this trying out that Helly's father's voice intruded through the wall, telling them to be quiet and go to sleep. It never occurred to them to wonder what he thought they were doing, rustling and murmuring and squealing with giggles in the same bed together. Clare was astonished sometimes, thinking about it afterwards, that they had no shame, nor any adequate sense of how they should conceal what they were up to. Partly they simply assumed that their teenage secrecy was impenetrably dark and deep; it was unimaginable that adults could know anything about their lives. Also, Helly had a friend in the village whose father had subscribed to a sex encyclopedia in weekly issues; everything they read in there – and avidly, of course, devouring its initiations, such as that you might pass out with the pleasure of orgasm, or that the male organ when erect could be twelve inches long – seemed peculiarly preoccupied with reassuring them that there was nothing they could do that they need feel ashamed of. They took the encyclopedia's word for it; blithely and with no burden of embarrassment they did what they liked.

What they did together seemed uncomplicated. What they longed for were complications; for that barbed curdling male-ness which would drag down and darken and make real at last their little lightweight floating clouds of pleasure.

Now Clare was slicing peppers for supper with her Sabatier knife, cutting away the pith and picking out stray pips on its point. Tomato sauce bubbled splashily in the frying pan, the stove was speckled with orange: pasta again.

Bram was pressing Coco's crumpled picture flat with a hot iron. Coco had brought it straight to him when he came in, trusting that he would have solutions; Clare had only said it didn't matter, and not to make a fuss. Bram even thought he might be able to get Rose's footprint off with a rubber. He was tall, he stooped over the ironing board, he looked tired but he had been brought up never to complain. Clare felt sorry for his thin strong back and jutting shoulder blades under his saggy T-shirt.

—I've been so fed up, said Clare. —I've not stopped for a single second all day, and yet I've achieved precisely nothing. The kids have been hideous, bickering and whining.

This wasn't what she'd meant to say, and wasn't even strictly true – after lunch she'd fallen asleep in the armchair, then she'd sat down and watched television peaceably with the children for an hour in the afternoon. She had meant to commiserate with Bram; often this happened, that the kind thing she'd meant to say turned in his actual presence into an unstoppable spurt of protest, grey and shaming.

The shoulder blades winced. —Poor old thing, he said with effort, coldly.

—How was your day?

—Oh: depressing. Meetings.

—But that always sounds so jolly! Sitting round in a nice clean room with grown-ups drinking coffee and arguing about real things.

—Real enough. The exchange we were promised by the development people – new wetlands reserved as SSI in exchange for wetlands lost – turns out not to be quite so straightforward. They're trying to back down from it, saying

130

it won't make any difference to bird populations if we end up with an area half what we'll have lost. I can't tell you how much I'd rather have spent the day talking to Coco and the girls.

—You're always making it sound as if you prefer children to adults.

—You ought to hear the adults.

—It's the same thing as preferring animals to humans. Sentimental in the same way.

—How's it the same thing? Why ever are you suddenly picking on this?

She didn't want to quarrel, really. For a moment she could imagine a reconciliation, her invisible soul stepping over to where he was turned away, concentrating dutifully, using his skill and good sense to make something right for the children that had been spoiled. She could imagine her soul-self putting its arms around him from behind in contrition, putting its face against his shoulder blades: she saw them consoling one another.

But he turned his face to her, the too-well-known handsome tanned face, whose almost girlish sweetness was not for her, indifferent to its own effect, closed with lack of sympathy. And she heard her voice pick up the quarrel, as if she was sprightly and jubilant.

—It just interests me. It makes you safe, really – doesn't it? I don't mean you, I mean anyone who thinks like that. To have made up your mind from the beginning that everything people do is spoiled and bad and ugly. Really, I can't separate it from someone who believes in original sin. It's the new doctrine of original sin, environmentalism: the sins of the technological revolutions shall be visited upon the children until the nth generation. You believe the worst, so you never have to be disappointed. It's so cowardly, really.

131

—How would you have any idea of what I believe?

—Well, I don't know. Perhaps I don't. Why don't you tell me?

He folded up the ironing board, she tore open the pasta bag.

—Some other time perhaps.

—And anyway: your 'nature'; how much regret does she feel? When she makes earthquakes, spews lava out of volcanoes, covers up thousands of square miles of land and its precious unique flora and fauna in ice or sea when there's some climate change of a few degrees? She's a rotten conservationist, isn't she?

When he came back from putting the ironing board away he said gently, —I expect things will be better for you once the children are back at school, and you're able to get back to your own work. I know it's really hard for you, stuck all day in the house with them, I do appreciate that.

She said, —Yes. I'm looking forward to my day in London, getting down to work in the library.

As she spoke she took off with her sharp knife the two ends of a clove of garlic, slit down its skin and peeled it. Slipping off the papery skin she was thinking about what she had hidden under her jumpers at the back of her drawer upstairs, wrapped in tissue paper from the shop: new underwear for her London trip, satin and lace écru underwear such as she had never worn before, and which had cost more than – almost twice as much as – their weekly supermarket bill. She was ashamed – really, at that moment her face felt hot at the thought – at how much it had cost, which they couldn't afford.

That was the only thing she felt ashamed for. The other things that should have shamed her, the careless sacrifice of her husband and children and friend: she felt as if these things spoke to her through glass, they were mute, they had lost their voices. She was not like a heroine in a nineteenth-century novel realised through her adultery, because there was no counterweight to justify her, no repression to break out from, no self-accusation to expiate her, no fear of punishment or burden of guilt and suffering to hang over her and earn her forgiveness. Where these counterweights should have been to make her sacrifices meaningful there was emptiness.

There was just the sense of want in her like a tiger, a great rapacious cat; want not need; want like a reflex, the strong tension of slack muscles collecting themselves to spring: unmoralised. And she rejoiced in this rapacious cat in herself, shamelessly, as if might was right.

There was a whole history to Clare's betrayal of Helly, a history of entangled teenage love affairs.

First, there was the piano player, Alistair, who played for the Methodist church services in Poynton. He was one of the grammar school boys who got the bus into the city with Helly, and Helly loved him first. She began to sit through the humble services in plain man's language in the little bare white church where they used Ribena for wine and Ryvita for bread. The congregation consisted of a handful of old people and a few of the teenagers from the youth club. The cheerful bachelor minister who was such an enthusiast for youth was well known for touching up the girls at youth club parties and outings, so something riotous and crazy was always bubbling underneath the respectable church surface, and the teenagers teetered dangerously on the verge of contempt and blasphemy as if the back pews were the back row of desks in a classroom.

Alistair said he believed in something, but not in the cheap cheerfulness of the Methodist hymns he had to play. His skin was golden, his hair was blond with dark streaks like dark honey, he was not tall but compact, his blue eyes were narrow and slanted, his glance was oblique. His mouth was loose and feminine, he pouted and sulked and delivered his verdicts with a bitchiness that entranced the girls. He believed in a force in the universe, an energy you could tap into if you didn't let yourself be dragged down by negativity. He came closest to feeling this energy when he was playing the piano, not the hymns whose clichés he parodied to make them laugh, but the other things he played, classical music and songs he wrote himself. He wanted to be a singer-songwriter.

Helly said she didn't believe in anything. She thought life was just a cruel accident, a freak of chemicals in an empty universe. (This was what her father thought, too.) Clare said that she thought you couldn't know what the meaning of things was and that she didn't believe in anything 'out there', but that you ought to plunge yourself into life and taste every kind of experience you possibly could. Helly loved Alistair first and then he loved Helly. But as soon as he did Helly was suspicious and bored, so it was Clare he first kissed and for a while 'went out with', and then later, after he'd finished with her, Clare discovered that Helly had all the time resented her taking Alistair away, and then Helly and Alistair got back together and it was obvious he had wanted Helly all along.

Then there was Danny. Danny was the older brother of one of Tamsin's friends from the comprehensive, and Clare loved him from the first moment she saw him, as people do in books; only this was probably the straightest, purest desire she ever felt, absolutely unmuddied by literature, coming straight in at the eye. He was tall, lean, olive-skinned, with a narrow mouth that smiled at the corners, and a face rapt in a kind of deliberate, sleepy, sensual attentiveness. Tamsin knew Danny because she bought weed and other things from a friend of his; he was friends with some of the motorbikers too. But he was a talented boy; he was staying on at school to do art in the sixth form. He lived off and on with his divorced mother in a flat on the twenty-first floor of a tower block in Churchtown, circled at its foot by great, orange-lit dual carriageways like broad rivers, eerie in the dark, uncrossable. After the vandalised lift and the shadowy urine-smelling concrete stairwell, the flat was brilliant like the crystal interior of a stone struck open: flock wallpaper, gilt lamp brackets, a lit fish tank, a leather sofa and a zebra-skin rug. Clare loved the flat with her strong inverted snobbery of that period; although she rather feared Danny's mother, who had his fine bones but was ironic and haggard with black-dyed hair. When Danny gave his jeans to his mother to mend Clare envied her.

Clare loved Danny: desperately. Through her he met Helly and he loved Helly, and Helly went out with him for a while, only always holding something in reserve, an implication that while he was very sweet he just slightly bored her. This gave her an advantage in relation to Clare, who was abject. Then Helly finished with Danny to go out with somebody else (her Italian – which was another story), and a couple of times after parties or when parents were away for the weekend Clare and Danny ended up together, and she overflowed with blessedness. She lay beside him, ran her finger ends across his narrow hairless chest, dark-olive skin stretched across bone like the ribs of some beautiful boat, a coracle; and underneath his heart beating.

She said, —I'm so lucky.

He said, —I'm not doing so badly either, am I?

And she was grateful, for that.

But the last time it happened, he and Helly were already supposed to be back together again, and Clare found out months afterwards that Helly knew what had happened between her and Danny, and it was another tangle between them, in which both of them claimed to feel betrayed, although in the end surely whatever justice one claimed was only straw in the blast of the jungle law of sex attraction that had nothing to do with justice.

Always, in that teenage time, Clare had to submit to this cruel law that poured all the kingdoms of the earth, it seemed, into the already overflowing laps of the beautiful ones. Helly found herself tall and blonde and slender and golden-skinned, with a wide astonishing red mouth and Clare found herself short and round-shouldered with black hair that wasn't sleek but muzzy: and from those accidents all their lives unfolded. The inexorable operation of that law was a thing almost too terrible to directly contemplate, so there was always a muffled hopefulness one lived in, and then certain long nights of searing recognition that in fact worse than the worst one had dreaded was true. Once in an elaborate solitary ceremony Clare, dressed in the Victorian cotton nightdress Naomi had given her for Christmas, burned in a candle a list of the names of the boys she had loved (and a couple of men, including the French teacher still), renouncing all hopes of them and of any imaginable lover. She kept the ashes in a little silver pill box. It was a long list, for seventeen. She had had a gift for loving boys. It was Helly who had had the gift for being loved.

You didn't get both gifts at once, it seemed.

It was Helly (in spite of her belief in the guardian of the stump) who seemed to keep a perpetual reserve of irony and disdain in relation to male qualities. Clare (in spite of having Greenham Common in her background) loved the expertise and seriousness of boys, their deep real interest in other things, vehicles, politics, machines, music, drugs even. You knew when girls weren't there boys felt relieved at being able to talk undistractedly. Male seriousness was authentic, Clare believed then, in a way female seriousness wasn't. Most interests girls had seemed to be pretences put on and off to attract boys; their abject fascination with sex relationships sapped the truth from every other subject. Her own passionate love for books did not count for freedom, it was too muddled with her life, she was searching too feverishly in her reading to learn how to live and what to be: things boys just knew without searching. The best you could hope for was to be able to break in on male objectivity and bathe in it cleansingly: what you desired was that the authenticating look of male seriousness would actually come to rest on all you were, and make you real.

And now, because adulthood turned out to offer all kinds of redress to the inexorable teenage law, Clare was arriving on the train at Paddington. Inside her carefully chosen adulterous costume – her loose black crepe jacket, charity shop pink silky shirt, and baggy black trousers – her new underwear slithered strangely. When she shifted on the seat she smelled her own warmed body and wafts of the orangey perfume she had sprayed on her wrists and her neck in the bedroom at home that morning. She had sat as far away as she could from any families with small children; she had unpacked her book from her briefcase – she was rereading *L'Education Sentimentale* – and then couldn't concentrate on her reading, but looked out of the window all the way. She had thought about Rosannette telling Frederic as they drove in the forests of Fontainebleau how she was first sold to a man when she was fifteen; she had thought about Flaubert telling Louise Colet in a letter that he had just finished writing the 'Big Fuck' between Emma and Rodolphe in *Madame Bovary*, among the trees while their horses waited. She had fallen asleep once. The sky outside the train window was powder blue with faint drifts of cloud as though it had milk stirred in; she filled with the imagined embraces of lovers all the woody dells, tipped with the first bronzes of autumn, of the resplendent sunlit England that rolled to the horizon on either side from where the train divided it, straight and speeding as an arrow. She had sat deliberately at a table of men – a student and a businessman with a laptop – because she didn't want to be drawn into the kind of conversation friendly women had, offering little hostages from family and home in an exchange of decencies, flying the safe white flag.

This time there could be no mistake between her and David. They had said too much on the telephone for either of them to understand what she had come for any other way. The train stopped outside the station for five minutes; the passengers looked onto a blackened wall patterned with a relief of arches, draped with thick ropes of black cables, painted at intervals with numbers in old white paint. Pale buddleias had taken root in the mortar between the bricks. Then the train eased, groaning, alongside the platform.

David was waiting for her where they had arranged, near the foreshortened little statue of Brunel: she saw him before he saw her. He was wearing a shirt she immediately didn't like, with short sleeves and a fifties retro motif of trellis and grapes in black brushstrokes against yellow and green; it tipped the strong planes of his face, the carved prominent cheekbones and jaw, almost into foolishness. He had his shades pushed up, too, into his thick brush of dark hair. She wondered at once, of course, why it was him she had chosen. But then she had prepared exactly for all this, gone over and over the sequence of emotions she must expect: doubt and distance, panic and regret. She was quite prepared even to feel at moments the absolute conviction that she was making a most terrible mistake. None of this must confuse her into forfeiting her chance.

—Hey, babe, he said.

It was alright: he stepped towards her, his expression lit up, he took her in, she looked good (she had starved herself, to be thin, she was hungry now).

—Hey, she said.

She knew they mustn't wait to kiss; she slid herself into his arms with a movement she had imagined at home, but had not been quite sure she would execute with this sureness, this gliding feeling of two fluid pieces locking into their fitted place against one another. He was scorchingly warm where they pressed together.

—Clare, he said, stroking her hair: not asking her anything, but as if he weighed her name. That was very gratifying. She thought, he must have dwelled on my name, and sometimes used it deliberately: just as I've used his.

He had kissed her before, so she was prepared for the wetness of his mouth and the salmony taste of cigarettes. They stood and kissed for several minutes; he was about her height (Bram was taller). She hung with both arms around his neck; he held her with one hand cupped behind her head and the other, with spread fingers, around her waist, squeezing and pressing, working down until he was moulding and pressing her bottom. They began to forget where they were. He pulled his mouth away from her with a gasp.

—Shall we go back to my place? he said. —You know Helly's away? Shall we go now? Why don't we? We'll get a cab.

She looked up at the pigeons flying under the roof; Brunel's vault was turning, swooping rhythmically down past her as if she was drunk.

—There's no hurry, she laughed, exulting. —We can wait just one more hour. I'm so hungry, I'll fall over if we don't have lunch.

She couldn't quite have named the pleasure it was, to stretch out to its utmost the last hour before she had what she came for.

Helly arrived at the house just as Bram was packing up the few things for his trip. He had been pulling out the tent from the back of the cupboard in the spare room; when the doorbell rang he sat back, banging his head painfully against the shelf above, and cursed, and almost decided not to answer it.

Helly was the last person on earth he was expecting to see.

She was so far from his thoughts that for a moment he hardly recognised her; also, she wasn't dressed up in one of her usual spectacular outfits; she was wearing some big shapeless dark jumper and her face wasn't made up. Her usual beauty – which he thought of, if he thought of it at all, as a kind of remote and dazzling performance in a genre that was of no interest to him – was quenched. She looked ordinary: ordinary and, in some indefinite way that rang a vague alarm, perhaps unhappy or ill.

—Hello Bram.

—God: Helly, why didn't you phone? Clare's not here. She's away for the weekend.

She couldn't have come at a worse time; he was all ready, he wanted to get going. He had an exasperated sinking intimation that he would be obliged to go through the sociable motions with her, invite her in, talk with her, perhaps even feed her; and all the while he would be raging inwardly, longing to be alone, stricken with visions of the little sandy field with rowan trees behind the dunes at Ogmore where he planned to put up his tent the first night. Although he already knew he would submit to those wretched laws of sociability – not his laws, but laws whose authority he conceded in the world of Clare and Clare's friends – he didn't yet move from his position at the door.

—So what are you doing down here?

—Oh. Oh, she said. —So Clare's not here. And she executed a funny little turn on her feet, looking behind her, twisting her long mouth in a stricken way that put him on his guard: she was portentous with something, with trouble, with scenes, with confidences.

—I'm so sorry. She's staying at a B and B in London tonight, so she can get lots of work in at the library. You should have phoned. I'm just on my way out. I've got to go.

—So you're here with the kids?

—No: the kids are at Clare's Mum's.

—That's such a shame: I really wanted to see them.

—Why don't you go round to Marian's? She'd love to see you; and she'd be delighted at a bit of adult solidarity, I should think. He hoped he didn't sound too relieved as this solution to her appearance presented itself; he even stepped back slightly into the hall and opened the door wider, as if to distract her attention from how eager he was for her to go.

—Can't I come in?

He sighed; he submitted.

The house looked strange to him as they walked through it: empty of all the presences whose signs still filled it with mute clamour, the usual litter of the children's toys and drawings, Clare's desk with its piles of library books built up like walls around her sacrosanct working space.

Helly sat cross-legged and straight-backed in the armchair in the living room and lit a cigarette: he hated smoking, he had to find a saucer for her to use as an ashtray. She talked to him while he made her tea. She always talked as if she was in public, laughing and finding startling and original things to say. Bram's role was to react as if he was slightly perplexedly amused by her, but he wasn't sure if he really thought her amusing. She said she was down visiting her parents at Poynton for the weekend: she described to him the effect she had in the Close when she arrived in her leathers on her motorbike. —My mother said she wished I would invest in a nice little Nissan.

—Milk? Sugar?

—Black, please. No: actually, why not, I feel like sugar, milk and sugar, make it really sweet, put two. Three. So: Bram. Where are you so eager to be off to? You can't wait to get rid of me. Where are you going? Are all these piles of macho-looking outdoor equipment yours? Have you got a thing for getting the stones out of horses' hooves?

He felt a visceral reluctance to part with the information: his field, his rowan trees, his deep covering night, pregnant with his absence, awaiting him.

—Work. A field trip.

—D'you mean lots of sweaty biologists with worms in jars singing folk songs in a Centre?

—One sweaty biologist in a tent, in fact. The worms and the folk songs are my secret.

—Let me come with you, she said in a suddenly completely different voice.

He stopped still, slopping the tea he was carrying in for her. —Don't be ridiculous.

—Let me come, she said.

142

—Under no circumstances can you come. Or – he remembered to be courteous, —could you possibly want to come,
where I'm going.

—Please let me come. I can't be alone, not tonight. Otherwise I'll die. Are you really so oblivious? It doesn't occur to
you: if Clare's in London, why isn't she visiting me? What
am I doing here? Of course it does. I know it does. I know
you know what I know about what Clare's doing in London
this weekend.

He felt a kind of rage against her that made his hands shake.
Wasn't this just the sort of thing her set thrived on?

—I'd really rather not talk about this, he said. He handed
her the mug of tea, she took a mouthful of it and wiped her
eyes on the sleeve of her jumper.

—But for God's sake! Don't you care? Don't you want to
do something? If your wife is fucking my fucking boyfriend?

—I really don't want to talk about this with you.

—Then I won't talk about it. I swear to God I won't talk
about it, I won't say another word, if you don't want. But let
me come with you, wherever you're going. I'm not up to
anything, honestly. I'll sleep in the car. I'm not trying to get
my own back or anything you might think. I know you don't
like me much. It's just, if I'm alone I'll die, I'll really die.

—How do you expect anyone to take you seriously when
you talk like that?

He sat down on the sofa with his head between his hands,
fingertips against the temples where he had a headache coming.

—She's done this to me before, Helly said. —A long time
ago. I didn't dream that it could happen again. I thought she
was so happy, with you and the children.

She held the mug of hot tea in her laced fingers as if she
was frozen, the usually pale skin of her cheeks was blotched

with red and her big mouth was ugly as it slipped loose with weepy protest.

—I don't want you to come, he said. —I'm sorry. I really want to be alone.

—But let me.

David took Clare to a Polish restaurant and they drank cold, sweet beer while they waited for their food. She felt the alcohol thud into action instantly around her system, because she had an empty stomach: she told herself to be careful, to drink just enough to unbind her for what was to come, not so much that she made a mess of it, or lost any of it in a drunken fog.

Under the table they pressed their knees together. Over the table they smiled at one another with slow-burning smiles, and he took her hand from where she was playing with the packets of sugar, and kissed it.

—Very Eastern European, she said. —Shall we throw our glasses into the fireplace too?

—Not till we've finished our beer.

—When did you remember me? I mean, that we'd known each other before, at that party?

—'Known', in the biblical sense.

—In the biblical sense. So, when? I didn't recognise you at all, when Helly first brought you to the house. I'd never have remembered.

—I remembered. Not straight away, though there was something nagging away at me. Maybe when you changed into that dress. 'Something in the way she moves', as the song says.

—But for God's sake! I was seventeen and probably dressed as a vampire! I'd have hoped I'd have changed beyond recognition.

—You were nice then, he said. You were a nice vampire. Now, you're better than nice. I love that little edge that thirty brings. Seventeen's too bland and formless.

—I'm not thirty, she said. —Not quite yet.

—But you've got that edge.

It was very exciting to Clare, that he met her with his frank sexual interest in her. Men were supposed to approach you like this, always wanting one thing, but in her experience they mostly did not: you had to pretend to be talking about books, or politics, or telling each other your life stories, so that the sex could seem to happen inadvertently when you had drunk enough.

While they were eating their blinis with sour cream, someone came into the restaurant who knew David. David jumped up to shake hands with him and punch his arm, saying it was great to see him, inviting him to sit down with them. Clare guessed from this that the man – Nick – knew Helly too, and that David was embarrassed that he had found them together.

Nick gave Clare a qualified careful smile as he sat down.

—This is our friend Clare, said David. —She's an old friend of Helly's. She's up to work at the British Library; I'm entertaining her to lunch. This is Nick: the video whizz-kid, worked on Helly's ice cream contract and he's done some shows with me, the one with the band in Vienna.

—Nice to meet you, said Nick, more unreservedly.

—And you, smiled Clare warmly.

Inwardly she was appalled. What was David doing? He had given away too much, too eagerly. And he had invited this stranger to sit down with them, to spoil their delicious flirtation: she felt as if she had been dragged out from a snug secret sensual cocoon into cold hostile air, to stand on her own two uncertain feet. How long might it take to get rid of him? Hot tears welled up in her eyes, she had to pretend to wipe her nose with her paper napkin. She realised she was drunker than she had thought she was.

Nick was nice-looking and softly spoken, with self-deprecating public school know-how. He ordered beer and a sausage and sauerkraut; he ate it while they drank their coffee and plum brandy. Clare wanted to get up when she had finished her coffee and say that she must get back to the library now, but she was afraid David wouldn't find the right way of explaining that he was coming with her, so she sat paralysed, painfully conscious of the time spilling away and soaked up in conversation. Her alibi was less plausible, too, for every five minutes she sat on.

—I've edited those sequences we shot on the river, said Nick to David. —There's some excellent stuff; the water in that weird light lapping at the piers of the old iron bridge looks completely abstract. Why don't you come now and have a look at it? My place is only round the corner. If you're not doing anything else.

David stood up, his thighs rather thick between the bench and the table, and frowned and hummed as if in a dilemma, biting his lip and running his hands up through his thick brush of hair. She saw something about him that she hadn't seen before; she was reminded that she hardly knew him. He wasn't just being over-friendly to try and put this man off the scent, he actually found it hard to resist his suggestion, he really wanted to have all these pleasures that offered themselves, wanted to fit in being the man's friend as well as the other things he had planned for that afternoon. Helly had said that he could never turn down an invitation, that they hardly ever went out on their own. He was like a friendly dog, she had also said, wanting to lay his head on everyone's knee.

—We could, I suppose, he said, pleading to Clare. —Just for half an hour. We could just have a look.

—Well, as I've finished at the library now, said Clare stiffly, not looking at the other man.

—Exactly.

—Although we were going to go to that exhibition at the ICA.

—But just half an hour, said David.

—OK, she said, putting her head on one side and smiling hard at him, to communicate her resistance.

Nick's flat was further away than she had expected. David carried her heavy briefcase, which held her night things and her toothbrush as well as her notebooks and papers, but her new shoes began to hurt. David and Nick walked ahead, talking. The long London streets seemed implacable; a hot wind blew up dust and litter and smells of dogshit and rank vegetation from the locked gardens in the squares.

Inside, the flat was stylish, and made her feel that her clothes and her hair were provincial; she sat on a long cream and chrome sofa afloat on a sea of waxy boards and slipped off her shoes and was suddenly overwhelmingly sleepy after the beer and food and the walk. Nick laid out papers and tobacco and grass wrapped in a twist of newspaper on a table of thick green glass, and told David to skin up while he made more coffee. While he was out of the room David took the opportunity to reach over and stroke one fingertip down her cheek and promise they would only be half an hour.

—I just didn't want to make it too obvious, he said.

The doorbell rang and someone else arrived, a friend of Nick's David didn't know, a fattish man with a shaved head and a thick, short neck in folds and little gold-rimmed glasses, the producer for a music video Nick was working on. They all three became very absorbed in watching the material Nick had shot for David on a huge television screen. The picture was mostly rippling water, black and white. It was going to be the back projection for a cross-over concert at the Queen Elizabeth Hall. They talked about what cameras Nick had used.

The fat man hardly said hello to Clare. She imagined how archetypal a situation this probably was, the three men excitedly involved together over some project or other while a bored, unidentified girl dozed on the sofa, put down by one or other of them on the way in to be picked up again later when they had finished. It seemed astonishing that she, who believed her life so important, should be that girl. An hour passed. Dutifully, every time the spliff went round one of them brought it back to the sofa to offer to her, and she smoked it because otherwise they might forget about her altogether. She noticed that the two other men treated David as just slightly their junior in status, leaving some of his remarks unanswered, their enthusiasms cooler and more measured than his. She judged that they were cleverer than he was.

The grass made her feel sick and she went to find Nick's bathroom. It was all white-tiled with a line of crimson tiles at waist height and a crimson shower curtain. She threw up in the toilet and then had to borrow Nick's bristle toothbrush and his specialist bicarbonate toothpaste to freshen her mouth, guiltily washing the brush over and over for him afterwards in case she had tainted it. In the mirror over the sink she saw that she had a clown's face now, white and staring with black pits of smudged eye make-up. Eros and farce were always very close together, and now the switch had been thrown between them: everything that had been blissful was now ridiculous.

148

There would be some image in Eastern philosophy to express how these two worlds were packed together, folded inside one another: one world taut, alight, numinous, so that you stepped out and were borne up on the insubstantial rainbow; the other grey and deflated, in which the deepest desire was for a safe, dark hole in which to hide yourself.

On her way back to the room with the sofa — someone had put music on, trancey electronic music — Clare saw her coat and briefcase on a chair by the front door. She imagined going to her B and B after all, burying herself in anonymous clean sheets, drinking tea and nursing her hangover, watching television all alone. It seemed to her a desperate and dreadful eventuality, an absolute defeat for ever and ever; but it was also all she had it in her to desire now, now her gods had abandoned her, and she suddenly longed for it. She was sick and shivery and her head pounded. She slipped on her coat, picked up her briefcase, and let herself quietly out of the front door.

Helly had insisted on stopping at an off-licence and putting a paper-wrapped bottle in the car boot which Bram presumed was wine but turned out to be Armagnac. They didn't drink enough of it to get drunk — he never did — but after he had put the tent up they poured out some into the plastic beaker he had in his kit and shared it. It was early evening.

—It lowers your body temperature, he said. —It only makes you feel warm.

—I'm happy with feel warm, she said, although she seemed cold all the time. She kept wrapping herself up further and further in the big jumper she had on under Clare's borrowed kagoul, pulling the jumper up over her chin and down over her hands. He offered to take her to the pub for supper but she shook her head.

149

—I like it here. Do what you would do if you were alone.

—Well, I'd probably go for a walk, look for some birds before the light goes. Then I'd come back and make tea, eat some bread and cheese.

—Go for your walk. I'll stay here.

—I think you'll get very cold. You ought to come with me.

—OK. If you don't mind.

—I don't mind.

They went down the track through a wood where a flock of goldfinches was feeding on the rowanberries, then out on the sandy road which led past the closed tea shops to where they could see the sea. The sky was overcast with thick clouds like grey wool, the sea was grey and whipped by the wind into little dirty waves; they walked on the beach and Helly picked up stones, making a collection of white quartz. He saw redshank and dunlin, she was quite interested; she told him that her brother used to be a birdwatcher. He was surprised how he really didn't mind having her there. He had nursed the idea of his solitude, and when he finally gave in to her he had driven down full of furious resentment (and with a pounding headache). But probably he had been fooling himself. You dreamed of these precious spaces – the rowan trees, the dry stone wall, the hillocky field – but when you arrived at them you still weren't where you'd dreamed of; no matter how close you got they didn't let you finally inside. Before they left the beach Helly threw all her pieces of quartz back into the sea one by one, with a good throw like a boy's.

Back at the tent in the sheltered field, he got the spirit stove going and they drank tea and ate bread and cheese and chocolate companionably. Helly put brandy in their tea. He noticed that his headache had gone, blown out of him beside the sea. Now the wind dropped. The light drained out of the field until it was just twiggy, bushy silhouettes against a still luminous blue sky, noisy with the rustling of animals and the liquid whistles of birds settling for the night.

—So what would you do now? she asked. —If you were alone? Time for worms and folksongs?

—Turn in, he said. —Nothing much else to do, in the dark.

—I'm sorry for spoiling your weekend, she said. —I was very selfish. Now I'm here I can imagine you here by yourself, and what you get out of it. It's a lovely, healing sort of place. I don't get enough of this, the way I live.

—You haven't spoiled it, he said. —I was just thinking how glad I was you came. I'm not sure being by myself was really a very good idea.

—Oh, thank you, she said, sounding surprised and pleased. —But I never think you like me.

—I feel such a fool, he said. —About this business.

—I suppose that's what we are. The fools, the rejected ones.

—It's painful.

—Did you guess all about it?

—More or less. I didn't know you knew.

—What will you do?

—I don't know. What will you do?

—I don't know either.

An owl hooted and a few moments later they saw his shape glide over from a copse of trees in the next field.

—It's nice in the dark, said Helly. —It's amazing. But I don't know how you could manage here all on your own. I'd die.

—But then you die rather often. From the sound of it.

—You're teasing me. But it's the truth.

They couldn't see each other's faces any longer; Bram switched on the torch and crawled into the tent to sort out the sleeping bags.

—I'll sleep in the car if you like, offered Helly quaveringly: the car was parked two dark fields away.

—But you might die.

—I might.

—And that would be awkward. So you might as well stay here. It makes no difference to me.

They took off their kagouls, kept on most of their clothes, climbed into their separate sleeping bags, and said goodnight lying decorously side by side. Bram turned his back on her and fell asleep easily, not troubled by Helly's presence beside him, even soothed by it – he dreamed of something from childhood, a boat and a river and a long ago innocent excitement.

But in the night she was cold, and woke up shivering and couldn't fall asleep again. And although she tried not to wake him, awareness must have reached him – even in the deep chambers of his sleep – of her consciousness, active, close to him: and he surfaced. She was shuddering, her teeth were actually chattering together. He reached out an arm from his sleeping bag, touched the canvas of the tent above his face, found her huddled shape.

—Are you cold?

—Bram, I'm so cold, she said, muffled, from her clenched jaws. —I can't get warm, what's the matter with me?

—I don't know. It could be shock, perhaps, because you're upset.

—I'm so sorry.

He half sat up. —I could unzip these sleeping bags and zip them up together. If you'd like. If you think that would help.

For a minute she didn't say anything. —You don't think I set this up deliberately, do you? I know how you might think I'm using this, to get my way.

—I don't.

—OK then.

He found the torch and by its light he sorted out the sleeping bags into one double one, and then climbed back in beside her: before he switched the torch off the beam picked out a tangle of fair hair and a triangle of creamy skin behind her ear: her face was buried against the rough sleeve of her jumper. In the dark he pressed himself against her where she was turned away from him and put his arms around her. It was strange that she could be cold; she felt like a flood of warmth against him which he then poured back into her; gradually as he held her her shuddering eased off and her rigid limbs relaxed. They didn't speak another word. After a while she turned around in his arms and they found each other's faces in the dark by kissing.

It should have been awkward making love through all the layers of their clothes, but perhaps because he'd wakened out of deep sleep and was still half dreaming, he seemed to find his way through them with supreme ease, parting them and pushing them aside: they seemed in his dream organic layers through which he was penetrating to the hot centre of her.

Accidents in the Home

Toby booked a flight home from Kathmandu on what turned out to be a *bandh*, a holy day when all wheeled vehicles are forbidden on pain of being set alight or stoned. He could not find anyone willing to take him to the airport. So at dawn he climbed over the wall of the compound where he was staying, walked with his pack for about a mile, then managed to hail a stray *tempo* which was prepared to risk it before the six a.m. *bandh* deadline. The airport was shut when he got there; he leaned his pack against the concrete guard post at the entrance, sat down beside it, and waited. After a while they opened up and let him inside. It was evening before he got on a flight to Delhi. From Delhi – after a night spent asleep in a hard plastic waiting room seat, embracing his pack – he flew to Rome, where there were more delays; and from Rome to Heathrow. He arrived at Heathrow at eleven o'clock at night, the second night of his journey home.

From Heathrow he telephoned his mother. Angie, her friend, answered the phone.

—Could I speak to Naomi, please? he asked.

Her voice was gruff and terse. —Who wants Naomi?

Toby cleared his throat, he was embarrassed to say; he and his mother's friend hadn't parted on particularly good

154

terms when he left to go on his travels three months before.

—Naomi doesn't live here. Naomi's over. Naomi's dead, said the voice, not bothering to wait for him to go on.

Then she hung up.

Toby frowned. He gave up the phone booth to a girl backpacker waiting behind him, went to an empty seat and carefully counted over the English notes in his purse. There was not enough for a coach ticket home; he would have to hitch. He did not really believe that his mother was dead; if she had been dead, her friend would have listed those three things differently, surely: death would have come first. If someone was dead, you did not begin with other things about them. But none the less, an anxiety about his mother like a little hard ugly mannikin took up its old place in his chest.

After waiting for about an hour at an intersection he got a lift with an all-night lorry driver going west who took him to the nearest motorway junction to home; then he had to walk for three or four miles through the sleeping outskirts of the city, hoping he'd see a bus or a taxi or a phone booth. When he did find a phone he discovered that all the coins left in his pocket were rupees. He decided to go to the house in Benteaston where his half-sister Tamsin lived with her mother; his father's house was another long walk across the city in Kingsmile. Benteaston was on his way in from the motorway, Victorian and Edwardian terraces crawling up and down the hills; always respectable, now even desirable, and professional.

He didn't want to wake Tamsin's mother by ringing the doorbell, so he left his pack in the front porch and went round to the back lane, then climbed the wall into the garden. Tamsin's room was upstairs at the back. He couldn't

find any gravel – it was very dark, it was three in the morning
– so he had to scoop up a handful of earth to throw at her
window; it hit the glass with a soft spattering thud. On the
third attempt Tamsin came to the window in pale pyjamas
and opened it.

—Fuck off! she hissed loudly into the garden. —Whoever
you are, fuck off, you stupid bastard, or I'll come down there
and blow your fucking head off with my shotgun!

—Tamsin! It's me! It's Toby! I didn't want to wake your
mum, but I've just come home.

—Toby! You dickhead, you complete dickhead. Why
didn't you phone like normal people do? Wait there!

Lights went on: a few moments later she was opening the
back door for him, then he was inside the kitchen, blinking
and grinning while Tamsin kissed and hugged him, and not
quite able to believe it was possible to wander so very far
away on such a long leash and then wind it in again and
find oneself back precisely here in the same small familiar
place, the neat fitted kitchen with matching ovengloves and
tea-towels, fresh herbs growing on the windowsill. He saw
Tamsin with the surprise of sameness too, as everything
familiar began to overlay everything he had come from. He
had managed somehow to forget while he was away her aura
like a groomed fastidious cat; even woken in the middle of
the night in pyjamas she was neat and self-possessed and her
straight dark shoulder-length hair looked brushed. She had
long hazel eyes full of cat-scorn, too, and eyebrows that met
in the middle: an Aztec, their father called her.

—Have you really got a shotgun?

—Oh yes, Toby, really I keep a shotgun under my bed;
didn't you notice all the holes in the wall where I've
been practising? Idiot; what do you think? And I suppose

you've had all your luggage stolen, have you? That would be so typical!

—It's in the front porch.

—So go and get it! And you probably want me to make you a cup of tea. Although I ought to warn you before you touch meat or drink in this house that it seems to have become some weird sort of women's refuge. Seething with evening primrose oil and female angst and synchronised menstruation and all that. We have refugees. First Naomi moved in with us, then Clare.

—So Naomi's here! And she's alright?

There was a sulky downturn of the mouth whose edge was as exact as if it was outlined in pencil. —Alright?

—I mean, alive. And well. Reasonably well.

—Oh, we're all alright, if that's what you mean by alright.

—Good. That's good.

—As far as it goes.

Marian – tall and heavy and grey-haired, belted into an old-fashioned man's dressing-gown – came downstairs, woken up by the noise; then Clare – pale and serious, with her hair in a plait. They stood sleepily round him in the kitchen in their nightclothes with puffy faces and muzzy hair, giving off the warmth and the yeasty smell of bed, exclaiming and smiling and touching and kissing him. Marian put the kettle on.

—Oh Toby dear, she said, —your mother will be so delighted to have you back.

—Shall I wake her? asked Clare.

—I don't know. Maybe. Has Tamsin told you, Toby, that Naomi's staying with us for a while?

—I did phone the Leigh Mills number and spoke to Angie, but she was pretty weird.

—You didn't mention that she might be here?

—I didn't say anything. She hung up.

—It's better if she doesn't know Naomi's here for the moment.

—Shouldn't I wake her? said Clare. —Wouldn't she want us to?

Marian shrugged. —You can try. I'll make a pot of tea.

Toby followed Clare up the stairs. Halfway up, on the little landing, she turned on him and clutched his arms and looked desperately into his face.

—Oh Toby, my life's such a mess – has Tamsin told you? Bram and I have separated, and I'm living here, and I go there to look after the children at weekends. I haven't managed to sort out anything else yet, because I'm so miserable, everything's more hideous and horrible than I ever could have imagined.

—Separated? Toby felt himself blushing: he wasn't used to Clare's taking much notice of him, she could be condescending and overbearing. —I don't believe it.

Her face distorted in a silent ugly spasm, her nose and eyes reddened and her cheeks were wet with tears.

—I know. But I can't talk about it now.

—But you and Bram . . .

—No, she said, wiping her face on her sleeve resolutely and carrying on up the stairs. —Not now. We've got to go and wake up Naomi.

He stepped through the spare-room door into the thick, familiar soup of his mother's smells; incense and aromatherapy oils and sweat and drink, the warning smell of drink, rich as Christmas pudding. Naomi was snoring, she was a mound under a duvet with only a swirl of black hair showing on the pillow: when Clare switched on a bedside lamp whose shade was swathed in a purple silk shawl the mound snorted and protested and a hand tweaked the duvet protectively over her oblivion. He would have known it was his mother's room even if she hadn't been in it because every surface of Marian's sensible spare-room furniture was laden with Naomi's intimate clutter: bangles and rainbow candles and perfume bottles and scarves; a stone painted with Inuit designs; a Victorian coffee cup with a gold rim and no saucer; paperback books with pages furry and splayed and turned down.

Clare sat down on the bed beside the mound.

—Naomi, she called. —Wake up! Look who's here, who's come back. It's Toby!

The mound didn't stir. Clare looked round at Toby. —She's been drinking a lot, she whispered. —There've been terrible things with Angie. It's like the other times. She picked up an empty wine bottle from the floor. —She brought this up to bed half full. And she'd already had most of another bottle.

Toby nodded. He crouched down beside where the mound's head must be. —Mum? Are you in there? It's me.

—Toby? There was a disturbance under the duvet, and then came the thickened, false, wooden voice that always seemed to him to be the counterpart in his mother of the ugly little anxiety mannikin that sat in his chest. —What are you doing here?

—I've come home.

—Where've you been?

—Oh, you know, all round India, and then Nepal. I flew from Nepal the day before yesterday.

Naomi pushed back the duvet and then heaved herself round and up onto her pillows, frowning in concentration as if she was balancing something heavy and slippery that rolled inside her. Her make-up was smeared under her eyes like ashes, her skin had erupted across her cheekbones in a hectic-looking brick-coloured rash. She had gone to sleep in dangling earrings, one of which was twisted back to front, and a black satiny petticoat whose border cut like a band across one bulging breast exposed almost to the dark nipple. Clare tugged up her petticoat strap until she was decent.

—Did they tell you I wasn't feeling too good tonight? Do you know about what happened with Angie?

—They told me something.

—I fouled up again.

—It wasn't you, Mum.

—Marian's so kind. I'm such a nuisance.

—That's not what anybody thinks, said Clare.

—I've let everybody down again. I've let Toby down. I didn't want him to come back to this.

When his mother had been drinking, Toby always felt as if he was in contact with a simulacrum, a mere unsatisfactory representative of her real self. She didn't look quite like the real Naomi, she sounded louder, as though her volume control knob had been cavalierly twisted up at some interior party. Her thoughts were pretend thoughts, her emotions were ones an impersonator might have guessed at and acted. This simulacrum must be soothed and propitiated but at the same time ruthlessly shut out; he was expert at this deception.

—Now I'm home, he said, —everything'll be fine. I'll be able to look after you.

—Clare's got troubles of her own, she said. —She doesn't want to be bothered with me.

—Don't be silly, said Clare. —We're both in the same boat.

—I've got a good son, haven't I? He's a good boy. I must have done something right.

160

—You haven't done anything wrong, said Toby.

Marian, in dressing gown and slippers, made up a bed for Toby in the dawn light.

Clare had offered to sleep on the mattress in Tamsin's room so that Toby could have the sofa bed in the study.

—No fear, said Tamsin. —I'd never get any sleep, holed up next to the fountain of eternal sorrow. Toby can come in with me. It'll be like the old days. We can pin up a turning-off-the-light rota.

—I suppose it's alright, said Marian.

—Oh, for God's sake, Mum.

When Tamsin and Toby were little they had shared a bedroom for several years in the house in Kingsmile where their father lived then with Naomi. Tamsin's and Toby's room was a wild place at the very top of the four-storey skinny Georgian house: painted white, bare of furniture except their mattresses on the floor, out of earshot of the adult life that washed around in the rooms downstairs. They developed an elaborate ritual of games and magics and taboos which no one outside the room knew much about: invisible uncrossable lines on the floor divided up their space; in the ceiling that came down at odd angles under the roof there were lucky cracks to touch, there was a cursed corner with a dirty broken skirting board they must not even look into. Whatever lived and groaned up behind the ornate cast iron flap that closed off the chimney from the little empty fireplace, must be propitiated with offerings stolen from downstairs; currants, dry pasta, lentils, salt. Certain games must be played at certain times of day or year or on particular occasions. They had a torture game where one of them thought of a secret and the other one had to try and persuade them to tell, by rubbing strong toothpaste onto their tongue, say, or giving Chinese burns, or eating chocolate in front of their face without offering any. Clare was sometimes allowed to join in this one but she went too fast and hurt too much too quickly, not appreciating the point of the long drawn out exquisite contest and endurance. There were games that were self-consciously childlike, too young for them, commemorative of previous phases of their lives: like choo-choo trains for the day of a guest's departure.

There was a game for when there was a grown-up dinner-party on downstairs. Tamsin and Toby would get into the same bed, sitting up in it with the sheet draped over their heads like a tent, and in a mixture of telling and acting and urgent *sotto voce* planning, they went through adventures featuring Han Solo and Luke Skywalker against the evil amphibian, Mr Beale, who led an army of seals. Tamsin and Toby were not Han Solo or Luke Skywalker themselves, they were only involved with them; Tamsin tended and consoled them when they were injured, crooning to them and stroking their invisible faces. If the party downstairs was a full-blown party then things got mad; Clare joined in too and any other children staying. They would barricade off the top floor altogether with mattresses across the top of the stairs; they sent foraging parties down to spy on the grown-ups, to return with reports on who was drunk, who was dancing, who was kissing, who was quarrelling or crying. They brought back stolen food and drink. They kept guard, with a system of Red Alerts to warn of any adults advancing too far up the stairs. The sense of immediate, infinite possibilities snatched the breath out of their lungs, infected them with a heady energy they didn't know what to do with, so they screamed and ran about and threw themselves onto the beds and on top of each other, panting;

they stole make-up and clothes and dressed up, boys and girls, and danced and sang in lurid mockery of their parents down below, waggling their hips and rolling their eyes. Children from nice quiet homes whose parents didn't let them do things went maddest. It was they who dragged mattresses, who drank vodka. Clare and Tamsin and Toby would watch them (there was no need to encourage them) with a certain satisfaction, as if this wildness that lay just under the calm surface of life was something all children ought to be initiated into, for their own safety.

In his dreams he was afloat on those sheets; laundered, and ironed into neat rectangles, wafting their perfume of washing powder. They flew out under him as they had flown out across the room under Marian's proficient hands, like big birds balanced on currents of air.

He woke up hungry, to the smell of cooking.

For the first few days in the house at Benteaston the ordinary sensations of physical comfort – the sheets, the hot shower, the clean clothes, the central heating, the home-cooked food – were almost too much, as if his capacity for them had shrunk while he was on his travels: they made him drunk and muddled.

Tamsin wandered into the room wearing the ginger cat round her neck like a boa and eating a toasted sandwich; she sat cross-legged on her bed, which was neatly made even though she was still in her pyjamas. (The whole room was neat, apart from him on his mattress: Tamsin, whose teenage floor had been uncrossably deep in dirty clothes and overflowing ashtrays and coffee cups growing mould, had had a Damascus road conversion to cleanliness a few years ago, when she came back to Marian from living in her squat.)

—So what happened? she said.

—How do you mean, what happened?

—In India, stupid. On second thoughts don't tell me. It'll be all the predictable spirituality-materialism, roadside-pickles, music and flowers, poverty-dysentery stuff.

—I didn't get dysentery.

—That's one thing then.

—I've taken loads of photos.

—Predictably. Luckily you won't be able to afford to develop them. 'This is an American girl I met, standing in front of a Hindu temple. This was Sanjay, our guide round the ruins of the Ranee's tomb.'

—Actually something did happen.

Tamsin had just taken a big bite of sandwich; she narrowed her eyes suspiciously at him while she finished her mouthful. —Oh no. You found a guru. You saw through to the meaning of life.

—Not that kind of thing. I don't know if I should tell you. I don't want Mum to know. I don't want anyone else to know, really. Just because there's no point in anyone worrying about it.

—You've got AIDS.

He shook his head. —An accident.

—What kind of accident?

—In a car.

—What were you doing in a car?

—We hired one. We were going to do some trekking in the Annapurnas.

—Who's we?

—Me and some girls I met at the hostel in Kathmandu. Three girls, Dutch girls. I'd only met them the day before, they had the whole trip planned out, they had food and maps and toilet paper and everything. Actually, toilet paper's not much use, it's better just to use snow. They said I could come along, there was a space in the car.

—Did you sleep with any of them?

Toby blushed deeply scarlet. —It's not that.

—Too ugly?

—No. I mean, not particularly, that wasn't the reason why. They weren't those kind of girls.

—You bet, said Tamsin. —They're always those kind of girls, only you don't notice. So, go on.

—We hired a car, Toby said. —It looked alright. You couldn't hire a car without a Nepalese driver. I think hiring a car was a mistake: most people get the buses, but one of the girls had sort of fixed on this, this girl called Bregje. She was mad enough that they wouldn't let her drive. We'd hardly gone any way, we were about twenty miles outside the city, on the Pokhara road where it's quite flat and runs beside a river. The car hit something in the road, a stone or something, which was ironic considering it was the only road in Nepal I ever went on that was tarmacked, and didn't have too many potholes. But the car just – well, the axle snapped, I think. That's what the man said, the one who was driving. Except his English wasn't very good. The girls said it was his fault, they were going to try to prosecute him, they said the vehicle was unfit and all this stuff, they got kind of obsessed with getting justice, they kept arguing with the police and everything, and the Dutch Consulate, and they got involved with this dodgy lawyer. But you know, the car looked alright but it didn't look that good, they just don't have the kind of checks we have over here, or the regulations, everything's just different.

—So was anyone hurt?

—There was this big crunch when we hit the stone, then the car skidded along and hit a post at the side of the road – maybe it had been a roadsign once but now it was just a grey painted metal post, doing nothing – and it spun round and stopped. And you could see one of the wheels rolling off in another direction. It wasn't really all that terrible, we weren't going very fast, there wasn't much other traffic. The girls were screaming, but I thought we'd be OK. One of the ones in the back next to me hurt her shoulder, the other one cut her lip where she hit the seat in front. I was alright. I thought the girl in the front passenger seat must have been concussed. I wanted to get her out of the way because the car had sort of slewed across and the front of it was sticking out into the road, and the driver had jumped out and was trying to open the bonnet, for some reason. I managed to get her out of the car and carry her to the side of the road, she opened her eyes, I sort of laid her down and kept holding her hand and told her she was going to be alright. The other girls were trying to call somebody on their mobile, one of them was crying because her shoulder hurt, the driver was climbing under the front of the car, where it was propped up on one wheel. While the others were still calling – they couldn't get a signal – she just died.

—Just like that?

—Just like that. She was gripping my hand and then she just let go. It was so strange; it really hadn't been such a terrible accident. It all seemed quite ordinary and calm, the others didn't even realise what was going on, they were still trying to get through on their phone. It turned out she had broken her neck, but I still don't know how. You try and remember what happened, but it all seemed quite sedate, the other girls were screaming but until the last minute she was still trying to grab the steering wheel from the driver and pull it round, I remember her shouting something angrily in Dutch, probably swearing, and the driver was probably swearing in Nepali too. It was quite funny really.

—Next minute she was dead.

—The trouble was I didn't particularly like her. Out of the three of them she was the one I didn't like. She was bossy, kind of unfriendly in the way she said things, I don't think she'd really wanted me to come along. She was a big girl; there was something about her that sort of spilled over as if she was unhappy with herself. She had a really pale face and her writing was huge. You know those people who do circles to dot their 'i's and take up two lines for a single line of writing? She was the one who'd made all the lists for the trekking.

—Ugly people die too.

—She'd made some big scene the night before, sulking and stomping off to bed early, because the others thought she was planning for them to walk too far every day. That's what she was like; you could tell she put everything into planning some great future project all the time, and always overdid it, and then she'd be the first to be groaning and complaining when things went wrong.

—Only not this time. Sounds like good riddance to me. One less fat monster abroad, making everyone's lives miserable.

—So it was strange that it was my hand she was holding, when it happened.

—Her personality was already over. That was just physiology. Bio-chemistry.

In the mornings Clare went out early to go home and help

her husband get their children ready for school, and Marian went to work. Naomi had a new job at the box office in the theatre. She didn't have to start until ten o'clock, and she wasn't drinking every night, especially now Toby was home. Even after a bad night she could still just about manage to pull herself back together in the morning. She showered and washed her hair and appeared downstairs looking fragile and pretty and with only – as Tamsin put it – a faintly piquant aura of abuse, the purple crescents under the eyes, the etched lines beside the nostrils, a patch of angry skin between her eyebrows, hands that shook as she reached out for her mug of coffee.

—You can be sure, Tamsin also said, —that the next sadist has already sniffed her out and is halfway to convincing her he's the one to save her from herself. Let's just hope he's a *man*, for God's sake, and heterosexual. At least then we'll know where we are. I loathe lesbians. I'm praying she doesn't try to start anything with Mum.

—Don't be ridiculous, said Toby. —You are ridiculous.

—You know how she works. 'I'm such a failure! Everything I touch comes to no good! I'm just too trustful, the people I get involved with always seem so sweet at first, I'm so hopeless at seeing through them.' I mean, she's so right: but Mum's a complete sucker for that stuff. And now we've got Clare too: 'I've made such a mess! I'm such a failure! I'm so selfish: I wrecked my relationship, I've damaged my children.'

Toby didn't take offence when Tamsin insulted Naomi. All his earliest memories had Tamsin in them. He seemed to have always known that Naomi was his mother and that the girls had a separate mother somewhere else, but in his family memories from childhood it was Tamsin Naomi was mostly preoccupied with: Tamsin screaming and kicking and (her speciality) banging her head against the floor; Tamsin refusing to go to the play park, Tamsin refusing to eat anything except cream crackers and peanut butter, Tamsin waking up with nightmares, Tamsin cutting vengeful slits in the sitting-room curtains with scissors after she was told off for something, Tamsin wetting the bed. He remembered that during these scenes Clare would frown and put her fingers in her ears and read her book; he wondered what he'd done. Perhaps he watched. He had somehow known from his mother that they must put up with this; that they must hold off from one another because they owed something to the girls, something they couldn't do enough to make up for.

—Because, you see, I have Daddy, she had explained to him once; so that he understood what a weighty counterbalance Daddy was to all the difficulties she struggled with. (He visualised this very literally: Graham's six foot three to Naomi's five foot two.) And then, when Toby was twelve, Graham left Naomi and went to live with the woman who became his third wife, Linda: so there was no counterbalance any more.

Tamsin had given up her job at a ticket agency, so in the mornings once Naomi had gone out Tamsin and Toby had the run of the house together. They got up late and cooked themselves extravagant breakfasts: curried scrambled eggs on toast and fruit salad with crème fraîche; fresh rolls filled with bacon and mushrooms cooked with garlic and parsley. When they finished eating Tamsin took laxative powders; she explained to Toby that she needed to stay slim.

—Everybody does it, she said. —And I might get a job modelling, like Helly.

—I thought Marian said you were thinking of doing A levels and going to college?

—Oh, that's just to keep stalling her so she doesn't hassle

me about the rent and bills. No way am I going back to studying at twenty-seven. What I want is a job that will earn me lots and lots of money and be really piss-easy. Like lying around having photographs taken of me.

It was easy to imagine that someone might want to take photographs of Tamsin. Toby could see there was something formidable in her looks which made people stare. She didn't have boyfriends though; or rather, there had been one boyfriend, years ago, when Tamsin was at her teenage wildest. He had died of a drugs overdose, and she had had a baby that was stillborn; that was when she had come home from the squat they had lived in to be with Marian.

—And what are *you* going to do, Toby?

—Oh, I'm going to go up to London and look around. Make some contacts, find a place to live, find some work to pay the bills, volunteer as a runner for some film project or other on my days off . . .

But for a few weeks he made no move to go. This list of achievements he had set for himself sounded improbably difficult; he was not quite sure what sequence they would need to be attacked in, and in the meantime it was so comfortable in Marian's house, where he and Tamsin watched television in the afternoons and then Marian or Naomi or Clare came in and cooked them supper.

In the evenings the house filled up with some or all of its women. They took it in turns to cook, and Toby ate. Tamsin often refused to eat with them, Clare if she was there had no appetite, Naomi never ate much, Marian was afraid to put on weight: so Toby who had come back from India even skinnier than he had gone away demolished plateful after plateful to their immense gratification.

—He sings a little song while he's eating if he's really enjoying it, said Naomi. —He doesn't know he's doing it. I always listen out for that.

After supper when the dishwasher was gurgling, Marian and Clare, if Clare wasn't spending the evening with her children, would sometimes sit together at the kitchen table round the big pink-shaded lamp. Marian marked schoolbooks, Clare was working on her thesis on George Sand, reading and making notes and looking things up in the dictionary. Sometimes Naomi sat with them too, doing her needlepoint. Tamsin watched television; if she came through the kitchen to fetch herself a Diet Coke, the cat draped contentedly across her shoulders, she cast a look of withering disapproval at the congregation round the table. Sometimes she went out to choir practice. Sometimes someone – a male someone – telephoned for her, but she told Marian to say she was not in, and Marian sighed, and lied, obediently and unconvincingly.

One night Toby brought his video camera downstairs and filmed the three women sitting round the table. They all protested – Marian who was normally so calm was flurried with dismay at the thought of having her picture taken – and then for a while held their faces self-consciously before they forgot about him. They weren't talking much. Naomi, with her head bent to count the holes, pulled her thread with a soothing rasp through her canvas stretched taut across a frame. Marian went patiently over and over a routine of ticking and correcting, and the pile of books on her right hand grew taller while the pile on her left diminished. Clare read with a willed absorption, frowning and moving restlessly in her chair as if she wanted to surround the book or get inside it.

—Why don't you find somewhere more comfortable to read, darling? asked Marian.

—I like it here by you.

You could catch a sort of circling of glances and gestures and smiles around the table. Marian squeezed Clare's hand, or lent her a tissue, or a pen; they passed round Naomi's sewing to admire it. Naomi made coffee and they took a break. Marian talked about a friend at school who had had a mastectomy and was trying to persuade her to come to yoga classes. Naomi told them about a jacket she'd seen in Monsoon and was tempted by. She also mentioned a flat she'd heard about through a friend at work, which might be possible for her.

—Which friend was that? asked Clare.

—Oh, just the bloke who runs the cellar, really nice actually. He's just come out of a gay relationship like me, and he's trying to decide what it was all about. We've been comparing notes.

—Naomi, said Clare, —don't get involved with renting a flat or anything, from a friend. You know how these things end up.

—Oh, it's OK, nothing like that, said Naomi, blushing. —Anyway, he's about fifteen years younger than me.

Clare talked about George Sand coming to stay at Flaubert's house, and how she got on with his mother. Then she mentioned that Rose, her youngest daughter, who was four, had been in trouble at nursery that day.

—Mrs Worral in her designer tracksuit couldn't wait to tell me. She's so ghastly. She gives them pictures of policemen to colour in and tells them off if they don't use blue: believe me. We don't like her but we like the school, so we think it's worth keeping Rosie on there. Apparently Rose had offered a sweetie to this little boy which turned out to be a bead from a game, or something. So I'm supposed to give Rose a serious talk on the dangers of choking. But the trouble is . . .

Then Clare suddenly couldn't go on; she pressed her mouth with her fist, her nose went red, her eyes filled with tears and her voice changed register. —The trouble is I don't want to say anything negative to them at all. I only want to say nice things. I feel so guilty I can't tell them off. It's so pathetic.

—Of course you can't, darling, said Marian.

—Why should you? said Naomi. —She was only playing.

—Oh no, said Clare, recovering herself. —Rose actually has a thing against that particular boy. I'm sure she knew it was a bead. I'm sure she meant to choke him, in fact.

When he ran the pictures through on the viewfinder Toby thought for a moment he could actually see something flowing round the table, like a slight distortion in the tape: a stream flowing between the three women, a stream of kindness, of sympathetic intuition, of wishing one another well.

It was strange, Marian thought, how during that time the three of them could sit around the table so peacefully in the evenings. The peace was real: although of course she was always worried about Clare and her situation, it was sometimes nonetheless real, and blissful, for half an hour, an hour at a time. In her imagination it even lapped away from where they sat with their heads bent over their work at the table, to wash around and include Toby and Tamsin, whether they wanted it or not: Toby hovering neutrally in that slightly exasperating way he had, as though he imagined he was invisible, all gangling six foot two of him; Tamsin fortified in her hostility next door in front of the television. Banally as a mother hen, she was still warmed by the sensation of her chickens safe under her wings. And just like a dumb imposed-upon hen her warm sensation of family seemed to have adjusted itself to accommodate even these two others, these intelopers, these ones she had not asked for.

Sometimes, suddenly, like a dark flash exploding on her inner eye right in the middle of all the peace and the pink-shaded light, there came a picture. She remembered Naomi sitting at another table in another kitchen: this was the kitchen in the house where, almost a quarter of a century before, Graham had been in the process of leaving Marian. She could not imagine what Naomi had been doing in that house. She could certainly only have come there once, or twice, in all that terrible time which Marian thought of, if she ever thought of it at all now, as a kind of melting down, a shaming reduction to mush and pulp of all the substance of her flesh and self and personality. It was the only time in her life she had ever tasted anything like that self-abandonment; it was the only way she knew she had inside her – buried deep now under the concrete of everything steadying that had happened since – such a howling thrashing screeching frightful creature.

She remembered what Naomi had been wearing, knew the exact words which had come into her head, then, to describe it: it was a dress worthy of a princess. She thought that to herself, she didn't say it. The dress was made in India, when fantastical things were still coming out of India, out of several different brilliant red patterned prints; the skirt, tied with a sash round her diminutive waist, was vast and long with bands of braid and embroidery at the hem; the bodice and the cuffs of the long sleeves were thickly embroidered. Naomi sat on a tall stool at Marian's kitchen table. The skirt of the dress fell like a scarlet wing to the floor behind her; she put her long black hair back from her pale face, clasped her hands in her lap and stared desperately ahead. She looked like a suffering saint. It was an ordeal which she must have put herself through as some sort of penance. She couldn't meet Marian's eyes: perhaps Marian was howling at her. Graham must have been there but Marian couldn't remember him; Clare and Tamsin must have been upstairs in bed (in bed but surely not asleep, surely listening to their mother losing herself).

Naomi had looked perfect. Marian could see that, that was exactly what she saw. She looked like a princess, an impossible prize, she glowed with helpless involuntary youth and beauty, the clean sharp jawline, the skin like cream, the tiny waist like a stem that could be broken, the small cuppable breasts swelling under her bodice. She must have been twenty. The envy Marian felt was like a hunger, it was like a sexual desire, it was as though she was feeling by proxy what her husband must feel, the baffled devouring need to press this perfection to your breast, to penetrate it, to break it open, to find its explanation.

Instead Marian had picked up the heavy chrome pasta-making machine Graham had given her for Christmas and thrown it at Naomi's head as hard as she could. Naomi screamed and dodged and the pasta machine crashed into some china on the table and then onto the floor where it broke. She hadn't wanted it for Christmas anyway – how could she, with two small children, possibly want to make her own spaghetti? She had wondered when it was given what message it could have for her, this unwanted, unuseful thing that took up so much space. And, oh yes, at this point Graham came bounding back into the picture from wherever he'd been lurking, consoling and anxious and raising his voice in insufferable protective indignation. Of course it was true that if she hadn't thrown so clumsily, if the pasta machine hadn't been quite so awkward to take hold of, she could have killed Naomi. Of course. That was the whole point.

But now she and Naomi, who was not killed, sat at peace at the same table together: what did that mean? What had once mattered so terribly didn't matter any more. And now Naomi had ropes of tendon in her neck, her flesh was loosening from under her jaw, she had deeply incised lines under her eyes and beside her nose, she had a little pot belly that showed when she wore tight trousers. She was still sometimes pretty: but the other day Marian had noticed, standing behind her, that on the crown of her head you could see her scalp through her thinning hair. And Naomi feared Tamsin. Tamsin was rude and unfriendly but it wasn't simply that: Naomi flinched if she had to speak to her or hand her anything, as if the contrast between them − her worn face and hand and Tamsin's glossy presumptuous youth − was scalding, something Naomi could not forgive herself.

Marian had always known the story of the lovely lady who shared a body with the old crone (she had imagined a fat sprawled dame with dabs of red and blue marking out a face on shapeless flesh, and wattles in her throat). She had always understood the point of it: as you are, so was I once; as I am, so will you be. Like mother-in-law jokes: the mother-in-law dreaded and ridiculed because she is what the wife will become. But she used to think that there were a thousand years, a lifetime, between the two kinds of women. Probably, when she threw the pasta maker, she thought there were a thousand years between the imperturbable beauty of her husband's student and herself, overweight, sagging, lapsed into a fug of maternity, her hair already turning grey. These days she saw things in a different time scale. She knew that for the crone to change places with the lovely lady took almost no time at all, although you never saw it: it happened while you looked the other way.

One night Naomi was ill. She had been drinking – she had stayed on at the theatre bar after her shift at work. She was sick in her bed and Marian had to change her sheets while she retched in the bathroom.

—It must be something I've eaten, she insisted woodenly. She kept on retching long after there was anything to bring up except a dark slime. Toby wiped her face with a flannel. Tamsin banged on the bathroom door and insisted she wanted a bath, could they please hurry up.

When, finally, Naomi was asleep Toby sat cross-legged on his bed in Tamsin's room and skinned up. Primly Tamsin, cross-legged on her own bed, frowned at him tearing Rizlas and sprinkling gear.

—I need to relax, he said.

—I disapprove.

—I keep having these dreams.

—What dreams?

—Well, not exactly dreams. That is, I'm not asleep, exactly. Sometimes it just happens when I'm walking upstairs.

—For God's sake, Toby, what do you need chemical stimulants for if you're already off your trolley? What kind of dreams?

—I'm carrying that girl: the one who died in the accident.

—Carrying her?

—Just carrying her. I can feel the weight of her in my arms. Her head's sort of lolling down one side: she's all wrapped up in something, I can't see her face.

—And where are you carrying her to?

—I'm just carrying her. And then I'm up at the top of the

177

stairs and it fades out, only there's a sort of flickering light and I'm all pouring with sweat.

—You complete idiot.

—I suppose it's because I probably did cause her death.

—What are you talking about?

—Two separate possibilities. I was sitting behind her. I was thrown forward when we hit the post. I probably broke her neck then. And then I moved her from the car, not thinking. You shouldn't move spinal injuries. Perhaps if I hadn't moved her, she'd have had a chance.

—Have you talked about this to anybody?

—Just to you.

—No, I mean these medical things: do you know for certain how she broke her neck, for instance? Or whether she should have been moved?

—It wasn't really like that. Everything was so mixed up. Nobody seemed interested in how it had happened. I think maybe one of the other girls thought it, about me being thrown forward, she said something about it, maybe, in Dutch, to the others. That's all.

—But it wasn't your fault, anyway: even if it was true. And you don't understand Dutch.

—No, of course not.

—So you shouldn't have those dreams.

—No.

Tamsin sat thinking while Toby lit up and smoked.

—I know a way, she said. —We have to put our pyjamas on. And clean your teeth. I can't stand the smell of smoke.

When he came back from the bathroom she was sitting on her sheet with the duvet draped over her head like a tent. —Come in here, she said. —It's like the games we used to have.

—You're ridiculous, he said. —I'm six foot two.

—Come on. Trust me. Put the light out, I've got my bike light.

Toby didn't really have pyjamas, he put on some old tracksuit bottoms; then he climbed in under the duvet with Tamsin, bending his back and stooping his head so that he didn't wreck the tent. The bike light lit her up improbably: she held it under her chin so that her face was a leering mask, then buried it in the duvet so they were in the dark. She put her arms round his neck and her mouth close to his ear; her flesh was as he remembered it, it was cool and firm and smelled of something like fruit.

—I've got a secret too, she whispered. —Do you know I can't do sex? Since Lu and the baby died. I've tried but I can't. I just sort of seize up, my muscles clamp together. It's got a medical name, I looked it up.

—No. No, he said. —I didn't know that.

—Nobody knows. I just thought I'd tell you. That boy who calls; that's why I have to put him off. He just thinks I've gone off him.

—You could get help.

—Can you imagine? Some hairy doctor. The idea makes me sick.

—Shouldn't you talk to your mum, or Clare?

—Marian and Clare? What do they know? Look at the mess they've made of everything. Everything anyone in this family's ever done is shite, it disgusts me, it all makes me sick. The past makes me sick.

—So what are you going to do?

—I invented this magic.

—How do you mean, magic?

—Don't be scared.

She picked up the bike light and reached a battered leather wallet from under her pillow.

—Lu's wallet, she said.

From the pouch she took out something wrapped in tissue: a small blade, the kind that comes with a craft kit. She slipped her pyjama top down from her shoulders. —Hold the light. Here. She showed him where to shine it. On her arm just below the round ball of her shoulder was a row of five precise cuts, each about four centimetres long, one under the other. The top cut was a healed pale line; the ones below looked successively newer, the last one was puffy with an ugly red scab.

—It's a sacrifice. Like the Aztecs.

—But what's it supposed to do?

—It makes you strong. It stops bad things happening.

—Does it work?

She shrugged exasperatedly. —Toby, it's just a game.

—I really don't think that it's a very good idea.

—If you tell I'll kill you. I don't do it very often. You have to use it with care, or it works against you. I'm doing this one specially for you. Keep the light steady. She pressed the blade into position to make a new cut underneath the last one; then with only a sharp suck of breath, she pulled it smartly across, slitting the skin. Beads of blood brimmed out of the cut and ran down her arm; she blotted them up with a handful of tissues she had ready, then pressed the tissues against the cut and held them there, hissing slightly through her teeth.

—Now give me the light. It's your turn.

She gave him a new, clean blade out of her wallet, then put the bike light under her face again and grimaced, making a leering mask.

—Do you dare?

Toby took the blade. Something in the hot, shifting space with its careering shadows and its intense focus on the ritual act made his heart pound: he felt again as he hadn't felt since they were children the old exhilarating liberating power of play. He put the blade against the top of his bare arm, and when she had the light steady he held his breath, and cut.

Breakdown

Clare asked Bram if she could have the car to take the children away for the weekend. She had a chance to borrow a cottage in the country that belonged to a friend of her mother's. She and Bram had been there together with the children a couple of times.

Bram had fixed up to take the car in for a service that Saturday.

Clare said surely it wouldn't matter, it could wait another week. Couldn't he rearrange it?

Of course he could.

Then on Friday night on her way down to the cottage the timing belt went, and one half of the engine stopped still while the other half kept going and the second half mashed right into the first half and wrecked her pistons. This was how the man at the garage explained it to her later. All she knew at the time was that there was suddenly no power; she pressed the accelerator to the floor but got nothing. The car slowed and stopped. There was no crunch or bang, although from the garage man's description of what had happened one might have expected it. They sat for a few moments in the sound of the rain. When she tried to restart the engine, though, there was an awful, decisive, clangour. She tried a couple of times more but she knew from this sound that the engine was injured, probably mortally: probably dead under its tin lid. She didn't even entertain the idea of taking a look at it.

There was no way she was to blame for this. Bram really hadn't put up any objections to her borrowing the car. He hadn't suggested for one moment that it was rash and irresponsible of her to postpone the service, or that she was taking any risks in putting off an essential check.

Everything had been going so well. She had wondered what it would be like coming away all on her own with the children for a whole weekend. Family experiences were distorted at the moment, because of the separation; she alternated between passionate, desperate love for the children, and then a sort of astonishment that, after all, when she spent time with them it was all absorbed in the old, ordinary tedious things: eating, cleaning up, squabbles.

They had been playing Wally Whyton on the car stereo; they were all singing along to 'Everybody Likes Saturday Night' and 'I'm Gonna Mail Myself To You'. Clare had always had a superstitious anxiety about the feelgood exhilaration of music on the car stereo; when she first learned to drive she had vividly imagined how after an accident the music might play on in a kitsch irony over tangled metal and bodies. But this moment of family togetherness had caught her out and she had forgotten to fear it. Also, she was concentrating as well as singing: it was dark and it was raining hard, she had the windscreen wipers going at full speed and she was leaning forward over the wheel, frowning ahead to make out the road, a winding country road she had only driven once or twice before. They had not met any other traffic but if they did she would have to reverse, the road was too narrow for two cars to pass. She was thinking that this was an adventure, an adventure they would remember.

The silence after the timing belt went and the car died was an absolute transformation. The girls in the back waited untroubled for her to start up again; but Coco in the front passenger seat suspected disaster at once, and after she turned the ignition to restart and got that dreadful snarled-up grinding noise he was quite certain. He turned his head – which was otherwise always straining in slightly tense eagerness to look ahead, even in the dark – in a quick assessing glance at her, gauging her reaction, probably her competence.

—Hazards on? he suggested lightly.

Clare put her hazard lights on.

—Jesus Christ, she said. —I have no idea where we are.

They were nowhere. They were still a long way from the cottage. They had been driving for something like ten minutes since they went through the last village. (Or was it five? Or fifteen?) She hadn't been aware of any houses at the side of the road since then, she didn't even really know what landscape she was driving through, only that the road had wound up and then down again, and that the tunnel of her headlights on main beam had swung at the turns in the road onto the slick grey trunks of the beech hedges, sometimes overgrown into trees. Now she couldn't see anything beyond the little cell of blinking light around the car, which was filled with slanting pewter-coloured needles of rain. They had stopped on a gentle slope, pointing downwards.

—We'll have to call someone, she said. —We'll have to use the mobile. We'll call the AA, or maybe the police. I hope it works here.

Lily, catching on, moaned softly at the idea of the police.

—Lo Batt, Coco said. (She could hear that he said it in

the spelling in which it appeared on the little screen of the phone.) —Low batteries. I tried to call Granny earlier.

—Now why do you *waste* it? she spat at him. —I told you not to use it precisely because it's supposed to be for an emergency like this. This is what I keep it for, not for messing about making unnecessary calls.

—I didn't. It was Lo Batt before I tried to make the call. I couldn't make it. It needs recharging. You forgot to recharge it.

—It's always my fucking fault, she said, as if he was a grown-up.

He was adjusting position nervously inside his seat belt, shuffling skinny legs so that he could sit on his hands inserted flat from the sides, staring out ahead through the windscreen again although there was only the long tunnel of rain-splinters to see.

—I'm sorry. I'm just panicking. Trying to think of the sensible thing to do.

They tried the mobile but the batteries were down of course. She tried the engine again. Horrible.

—You could put it into gear, Coco suggested. —Then let it freewheel down without the engine. We might see a house. We could look out on either side for lights while you steered.

Clare considered this. It sounded like a good idea: it sounded like something that Bram might have tried. —I can't, she said. —I don't dare. I don't know if it would be alright. What if I couldn't stop it?

He shrugged. —Why wouldn't you be able to stop it? Your brakes wouldn't stop working, just because you didn't have the engine on.

—I don't know. I don't dare. What if a car came the other way and couldn't hear us, or I couldn't stop?

—What if we hit an animal because it didn't hear us coming? Lily said, panicking. —A deer or something?

Coco dropped his head back on the rest and raised his eyes in exasperated incredulity. —Oh Lord! I suppose the woods round here are just packed full of deaf deer.

Clare imagined leaving them in the car while she went to look for a house. She imagined herself killed on a road, and her body buffeted around by oblivious traffic in the dark like a sodden doll while the children waited patiently, bravely, passing the hours. (Long ago she had read somewhere about this really happening to someone, and had stored it in her archive of horrors.) She imagined coming back to the car with help and as she turned the corner seeing a door torn open, the car empty. She imagined how if they all stayed huddled under their duvets waiting for morning in the car, some swift vehicle might come upon them out of the dark without warning and have no time to stop. (In the last moments as the engine died she had managed to steer onto a little verge against a hedge, but more than half of the car still stuck out into the narrow road, and there probably was not room for anything to pass.)

She decided that they must all get out of the car and walk back to the village she thought she remembered driving through: at least she found a good torch (Bram's) in the glove compartment. It was better opening the car door and standing up in the windy, wet night than sitting inside thinking about it. In the few moments while she fished out waterproofs, hats, and gloves from the boot, her hair went into soaked quills, piping water down her cheeks; water spattered across the protesting girls when she climbed into the back seat to force Rose's resistant arms into the sleeves of her mac. She

stuffed sweets and drinks into their pockets, found her purse
and chequebook, ordered the children out onto the road,
locked the car, left the hazard lights on. Already Lily and
Rose were crying at the dark and the rain. Looking behind
as they set out, she felt a kind of outrage at herself on behalf
of righteous motorists: at her car blocking the road, flashing
its orange lights (how long would they last?). She felt as if
she had fled the scene of some error, irresponsibly; as if there
must be some superior sane solution to this which she was
incapable of seeing.

Coco went first with the torch, Lily stumbled after, Clare
carried Rose. Water was running in a little stream down
the edge of the road where they walked; the night was
full of the noise of rushing water. Soon Clare felt the
water in her socks inside her boots. It was dark, but once
their eyes adjusted they could just make out each other's
shapes, and the bulk of the hedge against the sky: perhaps
there was a moon behind the clouds. Coco and Lily trudged
ahead in a mute stoicism. Wet, leafy trailers from the hedge
smacked across them: a bramble ripped Clare's cheek and then
snagged on Rose's tights. As soon as they were round a bend
in the road and out of sight of the lights of the car, Clare
was convinced the whole expedition was insane: the village
might be five miles away, might be ten. There might be a
house five hundred yards the other way down the road, its
lights hidden by a dip in the land. Rose was so heavy. Clare
wondered how long she would be able to carry her: another
five minutes, or ten?

She stopped. —Oh God, she said. —Are we doing the
right thing?

Pale blobs of faces turned to look towards her.

—We could have just waited in the car for someone to come along and help us, said Coco.

—But perhaps no one would have come.

—Surely someone would.

—Then they'll pass us now. We can wave and stop them.

—But we'll have to be careful. We're not wearing anything white, we won't show up much.

Lily without a word pressed her chin in Clare's coat and stretched up her arms pleadingly: it was her baby gesture, meaning she wanted to be picked up.

—Can't you see? How can I? Do you seriously think I can carry two of you? Actually, I can't even carry one. She unpicked Rose's wet woollen mittens from where they were clasped at the back of her neck and slithered her down to the ground. —There. We all have to walk. We just have to walk. I'm not going back to sit in that car and wait, like a sitting target. This is England, not Russia or somewhere. There'll be a house soon. When we get to the top of the hill we'll see lights. Then we can telephone.

She held Rose's hand and they trudged on. They were splashing through such deep water on the road it was like walking upstream. Then Rose tripped and although she dangled from Clare's hand and didn't go down completely, her legs and skirt got soaked. Clare picked her up and carried her again, and felt the wet soaking through her own coat to her skin.

Rose moaned and shivered.

—Shut up, said Clare. —Stop it.

Clare was reading Tolstoy's *Resurrection*. (It was packed in one of the bags in the boot of the car.) She thought there were two ways you could read it, either with your defences up, or your defences down. If you read it with your defences up then you could cleverly perceive all the ways it was unbalanced and twisted by certain sex obsessions. For instance, the portraits of the wealthy women in the novel are so distorted and uncompassionate, loaded with Tolstoy's disgust at how he desires them, their flattering flirtations and their naked shoulders.

But she was wondering about that now. What if the cleverness to see those twisted things was just another kind of complacency, to defend oneself against the truth in the book? A privileged wealthy man sees a prostitute tried for murder; he recognises her as a girl he once seduced, he understands the falsity in his own life and the inequity in his society, he gives up everything to follow the girl to Siberia. He offers to marry her, not because he desires her again (apparently he does not) but to redeem himself, to do right.

He changes his life.

What if this expresses a true possibility?

Clare thought while she was reading this novel that perhaps in her life she was wrong, she was perverted, she was, in her foolishness and vanity, sacrificing something precious. What if she was leaving a good man and breaking up a family, not even for love, but just for curiosity, out of dissatisfaction? What if she was doing this not, as she had believed, out of deep inner need, but in fact because she was following a pattern, a seductive and flattering and false suggestion that flowed at her on all sides from novels and films and advertising, about the importance, the paramount and endless intricate intriguing importance, of her own fulfilment?

The wind dropped and the rain eased off. The night dripped

and rustled; there were stinks of rank vegetation and dung. They reached the top of the road where they had left the car, and turned left, and then right, Clare trying to remember their route when they'd come the other way. They must have reached the top of a slope because they found themselves climbing down again; but they hadn't seen any lights. For a while, Clare found, you could achieve a kind of mechanical equilibrium, where your body repeated the round of movements that produced a forward motion, while your mind floated detached somewhere outside: presumably this was what soldiers did when they marched. But the moment that she was aware she had achieved this equilibrium, it was spoiled by consciousness; she became painfully aware of how difficult each effort was, and then her movement disintegrated; she stepped onto something awkward underfoot, a branch or a stone, Rose slid down her hip, her back ached, her restraining hands parted under Rose's weight, she simply couldn't move forward any further. She had to let Rose slither to the ground again.

They heard the sound of a car, then saw its lights. Partly Clare was concerned to press them all back safely into the hedge, partly she was trying to think how to stop the car and ask for help. It took a while to reach them, dipping out of sight, winding behind a hill and then re-emerging; and then when it was close its lights and speed and the roar of its noise were bewildering. Clare, waving her hat at the car and pointlessly shouting, felt a strong embarrassment: who would these people be, what would they think of her, wandering with her little vulnerable brood astray in the wild night?

Somehow in the disorientation of the approaching din and glare Rose slipped Clare's hand. She was well beyond the age of darting heedlessly into traffic: she might have been trying to attract the car's attention because she was fed up with walking, or she might have panicked at its oncoming noise and been unable to escape in any direction except right at what she feared. The slick blue of her waterproof was suddenly illumined in the car's lights. Clare screamed: her hands flew to block her mouth as if to stop what was going to happen coming out from there. Coco threw himself at Rose and snatched her back out of the way of the car as it passed in a waist-high spew of water: she landed on her face at the side of the road with Coco half fallen on top of her. He smacked her once heavily across the bottom in the wake of the drama of the receding car.

—You naughty naughty little girl, he shouted.

There was no way of ever being quite sure, in the reconstructions afterwards, whether the car would have hit Rose or not, if Coco hadn't snatched her back. The car didn't stop. Probably the driver never even saw them; or he shook his head at such irresponsible pedestrians.

Clare knelt on the road beside her. —Is she alright? Rose didn't move. They shone the torch on her: sou'wester elastic up under her nose, mud smear on her creamy cheek, a trickle of blood, big eyes staring into a tangle of muddy roots in the hedge.

—Course I'm alright, she said, willing there to be nothing dangerous or dreadful that had happened, that could touch her. She sat up.

Coco rocked on his haunches, shivering and chattering his teeth. —I saved her life, he remarked experimentally.

—You ran into the road, Rosie, reproached Lily. —How many times have you been told?

Clare sat in a pool of water. The rain began to fall again, the sound of the first drops sharp as a handful of thrown gravel, then the successive sweeps of it like a rustle of fine cloth through the trees, pressing, hastening.

—I can't go on, she said. —You go on without me. I just want to stay here and die.

The children peered into her face incredulously.

—Mum, don't be stupid, said Coco, embarrassed for her.

—Mum's stupid, said Rose, glad to distract attention from her own mistake.

Lily slipped her bare hand inside Clare's sodden knitted glove and squeezed her fingers. —Come on Mummy darling, she said. —We have to be brave.

—I don't want to be brave, said Clare. She held up her face in the dark to the rain, taking her punishment. —I can't. I give up. It's all my fault.

That same morning at eleven o'clock she had felt very differently about things. She had had a meeting with Tony Kieslowski, her supervisor for her PhD. Tony was in his thirties, single, American, plump with soft eyes in a bruise-coloured, pouchy face, shoulder-length dark hair curling onto his collar: his appearance faintly reminiscent of the Romantic poets he was a specialist in. Clare had noticed this tendency of literary specialists towards a physical rapprochement with their subjects: modernists in crumpled linen suits and James Joyce glasses, Jamesians with paunches and waistcoats and pocket watches, Plath fanatics with Alpha-grade bright faces and long, gathered skirts. She hadn't liked Tony at first. He was always phoning to cancel meetings they had arranged – sometimes he even forgot they had arranged them and didn't turn up – and she had thought him self-important, probably because he didn't register the bright gift of intelligence she brought to unwrap at his feet and impress him. He was abrasive and opinionated; she heard from the other students how he was resented and disliked.

Recently, though, she'd found herself taking pleasure in how genuinely distracted and disorganised he was: it made her imagine a life so different to her life with the children, where thought had to be fitted into little discrete spaces inside her routine. She imagined the slow ripening of Tony's ideas in a rich vegetable chaos, uninterrupted by the petty necessities of mealtimes and housework. When she came to his office he would clear a space for her to sit by moving a heap of papers from a chair, and then wouldn't know where to put them down among the dead plants and cold coffee cups and mountains of other papers, so he'd stand holding onto them while he started to talk. He loved to talk. She loved it too: especially about these abstract subjects, about genius (he scoffed and deconstructed the idea of genius, she defended it), about wilderness (he was susceptible to the idea of wilderness, she was sceptical), about the sublime. It was true that occasionally her mind wandered when he went on for a long time, and she impatiently waited to get her chance to speak. But she supposed that his eagerness to talk to her must mean he had begun to intuit her responsive intelligence, worthily matched with his.

It had been raining this morning while she was in his office, rain was running down the big window overlooking the smeary grey-washed city and overflowing a gutter splashily in some courtyard four storeys below. The screen-saver on Tony's computer was an underwater scene too, with little fishes and big sharks slipping in and out of the weeds. When he offered to telephone her with the title of a book he couldn't find, she gave him her new number, told him she was separating from her partner. She had waited for the right moment so that she could drop this information offhandedly and ironically, making herself and her life sound colourful and dangerous.

—Oh, he'd said in concern, and put down the pile of papers unheedingly onto an apple core on his desk. —I'm sorry. Am I sorry? I don't know why one feels obliged to say that. Maybe this is good news. Is it what you want?

He was quaintly disconcerted, as if he doubted his competence as an academic to make adequate responses to this lick of trouble from out of real life.

—What I want? she said. —Isn't that the oldest riddle? If we knew what women wanted . . .

And she had laughed as if she had said something poignant and plucky and at the same time faintly suggestive.

Out on the road in the dark and the rain she was remembering this moment: the cosiness of the underwater light in the little room; the open poetry books; the sense of their being marooned there together amidst the waters, outside the world; the warm curl of possibility that a flirtation had begun, no more than that, nothing that needed to be thought through or faced, just a wriggle of pleasuring possibility that could swim in and out of stern realities irresponsibly as a fish. The memory seemed to her as vivid yet remote as if an aristocrat in a filthy torn shift on her way to the guillotine were to remember drinking chocolate out of fine porcelain among satin pillows: she thought of it not only with regret and incredulity, but with accusation too. There might be some causal connection between the oblivious prodigal pleasures of that luxury, and this punishment now.

A few minutes walk further on from where Clare sat in the road and wanted to give up, Coco found a gate and a rough track and a sign advertising Bed and Breakfast, 50 yards. The house must have been hidden behind trees in a little hollow; halfway along the stony track they could suddenly see all its lights, pink velvety light through drapes behind diamond-paned leaded windows, a carriage lamp beside a front door between clipped dwarf cypresses. It looked like a house people had retired to, not a working farm.

A man opened the door before they'd even reached it: he must have heard them coming and been mystified to hear children's voices with no car at such a time of night.

—I'm so sorry to bother you, called out Clare. She was astonished at how out of near-disintegration it was possible to summon such a sensible-sounding, ringingly middle-class, confidence-inspiring self. —Our car broke down. I was afraid to leave the children. My mobile batteries were low. Could I possibly use your phone, to call the AA?

He let them advance closer before he responded; wondering whether to shut the door on them and activate the alarms, Clare thought, in case they were some kind of trickery, the softening advance party of something sinister and criminal concealed in the bushes.

—How many of you are there?

—Just me and the three little ones.

—You'd better come in then.

—We're so wet. I'm embarrassed to drip all over your floor.

—It's alright. The porch is tiled.

They crowded in to the tiny little entrance porch and both the girls began to cry quietly, probably with relief at the light and warmth. The man shut the door rather hastily behind them. He was short with the springy slimness of someone who exercised: his face was tanned and crinkled, his hair was slicked back from a receding hairline, he was wearing check slippers. He smelled faintly of whisky, and there was jazz music – Glenn Miller? – playing in the house behind.

He looked at them in perplexity. They must be a dismal sight: water was already making pools on the porch floor. His house, to judge by the porch, was probably immaculately clean and tidy: coats were hung by their loops on a zig-zag rail, the tongue and groove walls were ornamented with painted horseshoes and dried flower pictures, there was pot pourri in a miniature basket tied with ribbon.

—My wife's not here, he said. —She's away for a few days. How long have you been out in this?

—Oh, not that long. It's just that kind of rain, it soaks you through.

Clare tried to explain where they'd left the car and the way they'd come.

—It took about twenty-five minutes, Coco said. I checked.

—Rose ran out in front of a car, said Lily.

—I saved her life, added Coco casually.

Clare wished she'd arranged with the children in advance not to give her away; she prayed they wouldn't tell how she'd sworn at them and cried and lain in the road. She needed the man to have faith that she was adult and competent.

—All I have to do is to phone the AA, she said brightly and optimistically. —I'll give you the money for the phone. Then maybe we could just wait in your porch till they come.

—Perhaps if you take off your shoes and hang up your coat, he said. —The phone's in the hall. He looked at the children and sighed. —I suppose you'd all better take off your things. It's going to take time before the AA get here. You'd better come in and get dry.

★　　★　　★

The children sat in a row at the pine breakfast bar in the kitchen drinking tea with sugar in, looking like the bedraggled survivors of the wreck of some ship from exotic lands: their eyes were huge and dark-ringed, their hair was plastered to their heads or drying in wild curls, they seemed to be wearing particularly gaudy and unsuitable clothes. Rose at some point before they left home must have exchanged her sensible top for a pink sleeveless sequined T-shirt: around her neck was the filthy last scrap of her Superman cape.

The AA were going to take an hour at least.

—It did say Bed and Breakfast on the gate, said Clare. —I've got my chequebook and card. There isn't any way that we can stay, officially? I mean, otherwise, I feel too embarrassed about this.

—My wife does the bed and breakfasts, said the man gloomily. Actually, there's a 'No Vacancies' sign. I don't know. I wouldn't be able to do you a cooked breakfast. Or make up the beds.

—We don't even like cooked breakfast! Clare exclaimed. —And I can make the beds. But we'll pay you the full price. You don't have to do anything. I'll clear up after us. If you showed us the bedroom we could just keep out of your way.

—Won't they want to eat? he asked.

—Oh no, we've eaten, Clare lied. She thought of the chocolate and sweets they could share out once they had their room, and willed the children not to protest, or ask for anything. They seemed intuitively to know how to perform the submissive and needy children required for her act as responsible adult: Rose's head was even drooping pathetically forward onto the table in sleep.

He capitulated, not terribly graciously, to the inevitable.

—Well, there is a family room you could have, I suppose, although I've no idea what state it's in, I don't go in there. Probably it's alright. She keeps everything very clean.

Unmistakeably he was a man adrift in a woman's house: he picked things up warily, opened the cupboards and used the kettle and found the milk with a frown of irritated unusedness, surprised at finding himself going through these motions of service. If he had grandchildren – he was the sort of age where you expect grandchildren – he had certainly never looked after them: he poured scalding hot tea the same for everyone, in china cups. Clare had surreptitiously to top them up under the cold tap.

The house was old and rambling, but done up, overdone: a thick tide of fitted carpet and knick-knacks had overflowed into every nook and twisty corner. Going upstairs they had to pick their way past nests of tables, lamps with pleated fringed shades, displays of horse brasses, baby-sized wicker chairs, a collection of miniature sillhouettes, a cabinet of china thimbles, vases of silk flowers. Lily yearned towards a display of collectable teddies in an alcove. Up under the roof was a big low-beamed pink room with a double bed, two single beds, a Teasmade, a television, and a scatter of those worn-out ornaments people put in a room they never use themselves. The man brought Clare a pile of flowery sheets, irritably flustered as to whether they were singles or doubles. She fiddled with unfolding them, pretending she could tell.

—Is your wife away somewhere nice? she asked. The woman's presence in her house was as overwhelming as if she'd stood large and loud among the ornaments in the corner of each landing. —Staying with friends?

—Friends of hers. What are you going to do about your things?

—The kids will be delighted with a night off from tooth-brushing. And we'll just sleep in our underclothes. She suddenly blushed. —I mean they can. I'll get my bag when I go with the AA man.

He came back in a few minutes with something else for her: a nightdress to match the house, layered and florid with a huge tulip pattern in pink and blue and a blue satin ribbon threaded through broderie anglaise at the neck.

—You could get inside that twice over, he said. —But I suppose it'll be better than nothing, so to speak.

He was very deadpan; Clare didn't know quite how much she was supposed to acknowledge the risqué joke, if it was a joke.

She sat with him in the sitting room while she was waiting for the AA, and she decided he might be quite drunk, quietly drunk. She and her disaster had intruded on a solitary pleasure-ritual, with his whisky and his jazz; perhaps he did this every night while his wife was away.

—Actually she's left me, he told her. —Again.

—Again?

—She goes every six months or so. It makes for a funny kind of marriage. She's not my first wife. Or my second for that matter. I've no objection to her going off. But there is a down side to the arrangement.

—Well, I should think so: it must be very emotionally draining.

—Which is that she comes back.

—Oh, I see.

Clare could see he might have been a charmer, to have several wives. He had the crinkled up eyes of someone habitually, socially humorous, and one of those dark quick faces that might have been as appealing as an alert little bird: she thought of a charm formed in an era when men murmured dangerous, sharp things into the ears of women with bare shoulders and dangling earrings whose role it was to be shocked and excited. He had no illusions that it would work with her, nor any interest in her beyond the most perfunctory. He didn't even offer her a whisky.

The sitting room was done in gold, with gold and pink upholstery and pink velvet curtains; a contemporary landscape in oils hung above the teak fireplace, lit from above by a brass striplight as if it was in an exhibition. Clare worried in case her wet jeans left a stain on the cushions of the sofa. She was curious about how the man accommodated himself inside the shell of his absent wife's taste. He was submissive to her arrangements, using her coasters for his glass, fetching the dustpan for some ash that fell from the end of his slim panatella: obedient but perhaps vengeful. The music (not Glenn Miller but Duke Ellington: Clare read the CD cover) coiled out of the hi-fi system like a snake of dissent, a last word unanswerable because spoken in an unknown language. His privacy merely used the convenience of the place so lovingly-smotheringly put together.

—Do you like jazz? he asked her.

—I don't know much about it. I like John Coltrane, and Miles Davis.

She had said the wrong thing: or the right thing. He gave her a smile from behind his smoke that made her know she had given herself away somehow, that he had set her a test of taste which he was pleased that she had failed.

Clare didn't need to go out with the AA man. He found the car, looked at the engine, arranged for it to be towed away, gave her a telephone number for the garage. She phoned her mother and arranged for her to come and collect them from the bed and breakfast in the morning; they'd drive on to the cottage and Marian would stay with them for the weekend.

—Do you want me to come and get you now? Marian asked.

—Oh no, it's much too late, we're fine here for the night.

But when she put the phone down she felt a pain of childish homesickness and fear of the strange place. The house made her breathless and hot, as if it was hermetically sealed. There was no lock on the inside of the door of the family room. She undressed hastily, and, overcoming an instinctive distaste, pulled the other woman's nightdress over her head. It was huge on her: ludicrous and demeaning, changing her from herself, as she verified in the mirror in the tiny, damp-smelling en-suite bathroom. There was also a streak of mud on her cheek, which must have been there all the time she sat downstairs. She would far rather have slept in her T-shirt and pants; but she submitted to the humiliation of the nightdress as if the man exacted it as a price for how she had inconvenienced him. She spread out her clothes alongside the children's on the radiators, rubbed at her teeth with a finger wet under the tap. Her hair was drying in frizzy chunks and she had no brush.

The children's heads on their pillows were cast about in exaggerated abandonment to sleep, they snored and groaned; at the low casement window where she had forgotten to draw the curtains a huge nursery rhyme moon rolled out of the clouds. She pushed at the window but couldn't work out how to unfasten the catch, and didn't want to make a noise; if she pressed her face to the cool glass she could hear the rain which dripped off the trees and was swallowed up by the soft earth.

Behind her, outside the door of the room, a floorboard creaked. She didn't ever seriously, really, think the man was coming for her, but she held her breath long enough for the whole spectrum of possibilities to reel through her awareness: the unlikeliness of his trying anything with all the children in the room; his having drunk so much that such a rational consideration wouldn't deter him; the reassurance that her mother knew where she was; that compromising nightdress, as if he might mistake her having put it on for an invitation. As for his disdain for her, that could work either way: could make him not want to touch her with a barge-pole, or could make him need to punish her for being – what? – young, ugly, indifferent to him? Or simply for being female.

Needless to say, at one far end of the spectrum of possibilities there flashed out the irresistibly lurid vision of him standing out there with a shining machete and a homicidal light in his eyes, intending to hack them all to pieces.

She felt – not in her heart exactly, but in the pit of her chest where lungs and heart, the aerial organs, transpire out of the material base of the guts – the clench of that inward gesture that must be the beginning of praying for those who pray. She wished she could pray. There was a movement outwards from inside her, a beseeching, like a sick-making flutter of trapped wings.

—Help me, she tried, silently. —The hills from whence cometh my help. I'm making such a mess of things. Yet will I fear no evil, thy rod and staff still comfort me . . .

There was only that one giveaway creak from outside the door. If the man was ever there, he went away again.

Prayer addressed itself involuntarily, it seemed, to a male auditor: 'rod and staff' gave the game away. Whatever goddesses she knew – Isis, Artemis, Aphrodite, Kali – she only knew vaguely from books, she couldn't talk to them: and anyway, capricious, ruthless, vain, requiring flattering propitiations, they weren't the ones she sought, she wanted a moralising *good* God. There was the Blessed Virgin, but she was on the side of the salt of the earth, the ignorant and the weak, and would surely disapprove of Clare's sophisticated, modern problems. To her surprise (what kind of feminist was she?) Clare was overcome by a passionate longing to lie down in the bosom of a wisdom different to her own, deep-resonanced and subtle and fatherly.

She should go back to Bram.

Standing watching the door in that ugly inimical pink room (it was a pink that tried for roses but instead hit something medical, like adhesive dressings) she was visited by a vision of herself going back. The vision was vague but sweet, involving some highly improbable gestures such as her kneeling and pressing Bram's hand to her cheek, his touching her head with his hand in a kind of absolution, her burying her face in his shirt as he drew her to him so that she didn't have to meet his eyes (that last one was from literature somewhere). In the vision as in reality she was wearing the blue tulip nightdress.

—Look at our precious beautiful children, she imagined herself saying to Bram. —I've made such a mistake. It disgusts me now: following what I wanted, as if that was something to live by, want after want.

The vision was highly ridiculous. Not only had she never in reality dreamed of asking Bram to forgive her, it had never occurred to her that there was anything she needed to be forgiven for. Everything the break-up had actually been like – the impossible, convoluted ferreting out of blames and causations, the twisting round of their old knowledge of one another to use in hostilities, the sheer meanness of their unleashed dislike of one another – all that was cleared aside in this vision as if it was finished with, when of course it wasn't.

But then ridiculous was just what one ought to expect revelation to be, that was the whole point. By definition it couldn't show you anything you could deduce or arrive at by yourself. It didn't follow on from anything that had come before, and it changed everything.

She could really do this. Perhaps not in the tulip nightdress, and perhaps not actually kneeling: but she could really go to Bram and offer herself, and – even though he might turn her down, even though it might turn out he already loved Helly instead – to do it might be in itself a kind of solution, a blissful simplification, whatever happened. It would be restful to submit to its outcome. Clare already felt its strange bliss in her limbs as she went round the room, picking up the last clothes from the floor, covering the children with their duvets, kissing their sleeping faces. Everything that had been rigid and willed in her movements was now suddenly free and fluid, she thought.

Rose was wrapped up in her bottom sheet like a cocoon and had to be unwound from it, protesting sleepily. In her eagerness not to be a nuisance, Clare had taken all single sheets from the man, too small to tuck in on the double bed: she and Rose spent the night with the sheets wrapped sweatily around their arms and legs or wrinkled in clumps underneath them. All night long in light uneasy sleep Clare dreamed she was driving. The road wound down a forlorn hillside, muffled in a sort of thick grey rain which then became shrubby furry wet undergrowth and was somehow inside as well as outside the car. Or she was driving on a causeway across an inlet with shallow tepid salt water full of seaweed washing about to either side of her, suddenly realising she'd forgotten to check the safe times for crossing on the notice-boards.

The first thought her mind reoccupied as she came to consciousness in the morning was this plan for her reconciliation with Bram. It seemed to her instantly factitious and false, sickening; a scene out of a novel, not out of her real life. She felt ashamed at her capacity for this kind of fantasy and at the danger she was always in of acting upon her fantasies and living by them. In contrast what she felt that morning, waking before any of the children in the strange room, was the welcome abrasiveness of the real. It was bright outside. Pools and glimmers of pink light came and went on the walls. Under her bare feet the carpet was hairy and greasy; all their clothes on the radiators were still soaked, as the central heating had never been turned on. She wet one of the little handtowels in the bathroom to wash herself, then pulled on stiff wet socks, cold pants, heavy jeans, relishing the resistance the clothes offered to her wincing warm flesh. Of course she was not going back, of course not. This was what she had left for, to have adventures in strange houses, to wake up by herself in rooms that weren't snugly and safely moulded to her shape, ugly rooms like dead shells inside which she would know herself more sharply alive.

—I was hopeless last night, she confessed to her mother later. —I didn't know what to do. I got the children out on the road in the dark, and in all that rain. Rose ran in front of a car, it was Coco who grabbed her.

—I'm sure you did the right thing, said Marian, surprised. —You brought them where they could be dry and warm, in a house where you could phone.

—But what if there hadn't been a house? Or if the man had been dangerous or something?

—Well there was a house. And the man seemed perfectly pleasant.

—What if Rose . . . ?

—But she didn't. Good for Jacob. I'll have to give him a special life-saving medal.

They found the garage and picked up Clare's bags and arranged for her to collect the car later in the week, then drove on to the cottage. Clare was making up beds and Marian was cooking supper when the phone rang. Clare thought it must be Bram. She'd left him her number; perhaps he'd found out somehow about the car. She began to run downstairs but Marian got there first. There was a low crooked window on the landing where she paused to see if the call was indeed for her; she had to drop to her haunches to see through the distorting old panes thick as bottles to where the children were playing in the garden on a climbing frame and a swing. Coco was walking along the top of the frame with his nose screwed up to hold his glasses and his arms outstretched either side for balance, like wings. He was pale because he wasn't a natural but he moved in a swift true line because he believed he could do it. Lily was mothering Rose, wrapping her arms around her to hold her safely on the swing and singing to her in an exaggeratedly encouraging baby voice; there was a protesting scowl on Rose's blunt little face and she was pulling busily at Lily's hands to dig herself out from under the embrace.

—Someone for you, called Marian, grimacing to communicate she didn't recognise the voice. —American? she added in an undertone.

Clare saw air bubbles in the greenish glass between her and the happy scene outside, as if the glass was suddenly more opaque: as if she was looking through it at something which had in those seconds already changed.

So Tony had phoned her.

Had bothered to phone her, in fact, twice: he must have tried her at home or at Marian's first, and got the cottage number from Bram, or from her sister. He would be phoning to give her the name of that book. But she also knew, with a flash of that passional-intuition nineteenth-century writers make so much of, that by the end of the conversation he would casually suggest that they should meet for a drink sometime. She would of course say yes. And that would be the beginning of something between them. This was a thrill, a bliss, flattering her, opening up infinite new possibilities, shoring her up. There was never any chance of her refusing it.

But in the split seconds before she stood up and ran down the stairs to talk to him – they were like those elastic seconds that are supposed to be given to the drowning, to review their lives – she was sorry. Was this all the freedom she had meant, pulling on her wet jeans that morning? Love, again? All those emotional entanglements poised ready to fall into place: the jubilations and the raptures, the tugs and rendings and abasements, all quite outside the jurisdiction of her suspicious separate self. It would be good to refuse, to choose instead like George Sand retiring to Nohant after all those lovers the sounder happiness of gardening, cooking, children, books. It would be good to set out on the road like the old Tolstoy trying to leave the fraudulent fantasies of lust behind. Not going back to Bram, but not changing him for another man either.

But that would have to wait, she thought. After all, she was only thirty.

Absurd, anyway, absurd. Probably he was only phoning to give her the name of the book.

She picked up the phone, spoke warily as if to the unknown.

—Yes?

The Cartwheel Hat

Graham met his third wife, Linda, at a party.

He hadn't even wanted to go to the party, he was too old for parties. It had been Naomi, his second wife, who wanted to go, and because he worried sometimes that his middle age must weigh inhibitingly on her youthful need for a social life (she was twenty years younger), he braced himself to accompany her uncomplainingly. Then in the afternoon of the day of the party Naomi started to get a sore throat and a headache. He could remember standing in their kitchen while she made herself a Lemsip and dithered, with genuine disappointment, over whether she felt well enough to go.

—The one time I manage to get a babysitter on a Saturday . . . !

The kitchen door stood open onto the brick-paved herb garden and from outside came something – at this distance in time he'd lost the specificity of what it was, it might have been a trill of birdsong, or a finger of breeze that slipped under his shirt, or a smell of green things – something that as he ran his eye down the *Radio Times* to see if there was anything to watch on television instead made him make up his mind, to his own surprise, to go to the party anyway, whether she was sick or not. Naomi was surprised at him too, and of course he registered although he studiously pretended not to register the little hard gleam of anxious jealousy that kindled instantly in her stare at him.

—Of course I don't mind. I just didn't think you were that keen. You hardly know them . . .

But he was suddenly subject to an unexpected stir of that restless ennui he thought he had forgotten.

He took it for granted that he would be disappointed; that his ennui would be just as *ennuyé* out as it might have been at home. He had found himself at parties recently taking on the role of someone avuncular who stood back and watched and considered and approved (or, worse, disapproved). It went with his height, and his curling grey beard, and – most of all, he supposed – with his age, his fifty-plus years; but it had happened without his altogether meaning it or quite liking it – one said and did the same things as one always had, and they were taken differently. The stream had flowed past him, and was leaving him behind. Of course, some people usually knew he was 'the potter' (that was the name he had always made a point of, eschewing the phony professionalism of 'ceramicist' – which probably also dated him). That helped out with the problematic dignity of the avuncular role. But these days he had to mount careful guard against a pleased vanity when he was recognised and shyly admired or loudly lionised. There had been a time he'd hated to talk about his work; now he was afraid he liked talking about it too much.

He didn't, indeed, know many people at the party that night; and they were mostly much younger than he was. If Naomi had been with him these things might have been the source of a patiently controlled irritation; as it was, alone, he found himself rather enjoying his alcohol-fuelled prowl around the rooms, the fragments of vivid irresponsible contact with strangers, the cat-pee thin trace of pot woven in and out of an air thick with spiced food and incense. His hosts were the couple who owned the shop Naomi worked in, businesslike ex-hippies who travelled in India and North Africa and the Far East buying goods to sell: she had henna-ed hair cut to hang across her eyes, and he had a skin so tanned it looked smoked, with a dark stubble set in it like inkdots, and finely incised laughter lines: when hippies made money they didn't exactly change their look, but it aquired a high gloss and a new coherence around the edges. The inside of their stolid Victorian semi was rich with curiosities, hangings and paintings and dishes and glassware, much better things than ever went into the shop. It was a fine night: the windows and doors of the house were thrown open as far as they would go, the party had spilled out into the garden and clumps of guests drew talking close together as the dark came down, louder and more animated and warmly intimate as they lost the precision of one another's faces. Their host lit big torches stuck into the earth of the flower-beds; they burned smokily with coloured flames, illuminating shocked-pale bushes of rose and clematis.

From the room where people were dancing to what sounded like South African township music (so the craze for that had come round again, had it?) there came a crash, a scream, voices raised in laughter, consternation, reassurance. Graham was in the garden talking to a young colleague from the College of Art he'd bumped into unexpectedly. Mark Elstree was a painter whose work Graham particularly disliked. He had been holding forth only the other day to someone about the defeat for visual meaning in an art that depended upon explanations in words, and about a generation of painters who couldn't draw: so it was strange that meeting him at the party Graham had been pleased to see him and to be seen there. Mark stood out rather stylishly against the background of ethnic dresses and collarless shirts; he had his hair shaved close to his well shaped skull (because it was receding, Graham suspected), and was dressed in a suit with narrow lapels and a tie whose knot he had pulled half undone. Tentatively he offered Graham a share of his toke.

—I don't know if you're interested in this . . .

Graham inhaling under the night sky could smell – mingled with the pot and the smoking torches – green things again, earth.

—So how do you know the Marshalls?

—My wife works for them, as a matter of fact.

—But she's not here?

—No, she didn't feel well this afternoon, she seems to be developing a sore throat.

—They've got some incredible stuff. Not exactly my style, though.

—Not exactly my style either. For all their impeccable political correctness, there's an unmistakable aura of heaped up booty, isn't there?

Mark laughed delightedly at the sky. —Plunder.

He seemed genuinely respectfully interested in what Graham thought; although it was perfectly possible that out of earshot in another conversation he might have condemned him as an old dinosaur, or lightly dismissed his work as catering for the craft fair end of the market.

—Caftans and Cabernet Sauvignon . . .

A woman in a white dress and bare feet stepped out through the French doors and came towards them, carrying something with concentration in her two hands. Graham guessed she was drunk from how she stepped out across the gravelly path and the flowerbed as unfalteringly as if they were carpet. A few people crowded watching in the door behind her. He thought she must be coming for Mark, and he moved himself just very slightly out of her trajectory, smiling the avuncular smile.

She didn't smile.

She was dressed to attract attention: her white dress was unbuttoned down to between her breasts and slit up to her thighs, pinched in at the waist with a wide elastic belt. Her hair was piled up on top of her head in a tangled bird's nest of curls: it was too dark to see its colour, which was bright orange. But probably other things you could see – skin of that slightly blemished luminous paleness, long complicated ears, knobbly boyish shoulders and big hands – suggested the type and the orange hair along with it. You could see even in the dark that she wasn't exactly beautiful. She wasn't curvaceous enough, really, for the revealing dress; but on the other hand she carried it off with confidence, she walked in it as though she was a priestess involved in a rite, or had a part in a play. She was actually – this is probably what Graham thought, that first look – scary, formidable. He would probably have avoided her if she hadn't been heading straight for him: not for Mark, it turned out, but for him.

She held out to him whatever it was that she had in her hands.

—Apparently I've broken one of your bowls. They tell me it was yours.

Her voice was drunken, too; not slurred, but challenging.

She was carefully carrying a pile of five or six huge jagged pieces of thin, pale, glazed pot. Graham felt Mark glance quickly at him, perhaps to see how he took the loss of his work. He didn't recognise the broken pieces in the slightest, had had no idea the Marshalls owned anything of his. (Should he have been more polite about their taste?) He took the pieces from her in dismay.

—Never mind about the bowl. You shouldn't be carrying these nasty things around. You'll cut your hands to ribbons.

—I'm an idiot. Forgive me. It was nice. You won't believe me, but really I had looked at it and thought, there's one real, good, pure, true thing. You'll think I made that up, though.

—Thank you. Thank you retrospectively for the bowl that's gone. And believe me, I had forgotten it existed, until you put an end to it. Let's see your hands.

He was pulling out his handkerchief to wipe her hands if she was bleeding: suitably avuncular, he thought (though she was his wife's age). She sank to her knees on the grass in front of him and embraced his legs, resting her face against his thigh so that he was looking down into the bird's nest of hair.

—I've come to do penance, she said. —What can I give you to make up for what I've done?

There were cheers from the people crowded in the French windows. Mark laughed, pushing his hands boyishly in his trouser pockets with the unmistakeable slight excitement and bravado of sexual envy. —I don't get women breaking my pictures, he said.

—This is the one great advantage of ceramics, said Graham.

—Now he tells me.

—I could sleep with you tonight, she said. —I've had a row with my husband anyway. He's gone home to his mother. That's the kind of marriage we have.

—Well, said Graham, looking down at her bemusedly. —It was only one bowl. Though I'd have to say, it looks as though it might have been a good one. I'm sure we could come to an arrangement.

An idea that he would like to see that tangle of hair nestled against his thigh under different circumstances stirred in some deep chamber of his thoughts.

—Or I could dance with you, she said muffledly. —For starters. I'm Linda, by the way.

—Don't mind me, old man, said Mark. —I'd hate to get between you and a lady's penance.

Graham flattered himself he did a passable township jive. He helped Linda up and wiped her hands, which were indeed bloody from one long but shallow cut across the ball of her left thumb which he tried to tie with his handkerchief (afterwards he found her blood on his trousers where she had embraced him, and he tried to soak them, which was how Naomi got suspicious and the whole thing came out). He followed her into the room where people were dancing, slightly apprehensive that he might be expected to jump around a lot; but she hung herself languorously around his neck so that they moved in a slow waltz-like counterpoint to the poignant happy-time music.

He was very discreet. These were his wife's friends. He made his courteous farewells and left the party early; but Linda followed him out twenty minutes later as he had suggested she should, and he drove her to her home where they had sex in her marital bed under a reproduction of a Robert Doisneau photograph of adolescents kissing beside the Seine. (He had had in the years since then – discreetly, again, discreetly – to gradually filter out the worst of the pictures and things she brought to the house they moved into together.)

He remembered distinctly the twenty minutes he waited for her in his car. He nearly drove off without waiting – he was sure anyway she wouldn't come. He sobered up in the presence of so many reminders of his real life: the petrol smell from the leak in the fuel pipe he had to take in for mending tomorrow; Naomi's incorrigible clutter of tissues and beads and apple core and headache pills on the dashboard; the girls' perfumes still lingering from when he'd given them and their friends a lift into town earlier (all dressed up, as he had put it to them, like a parcel of whores); the dried mud lozenges fallen off Toby's football boots. His middle age was rich and flavoursome and sustaining as a mulch; he couldn't quite believe in himself sitting there still hoping for this quite other thing which ought to belong to youth: dicey, raw, stupid, intoxicating. He felt as if he had just discovered in himself – after all the reassurance of the sober years – an addiction dangerous as gambling or alcohol.

After the sex, when he was trying out for the first time the orange of her hair against the muddy skin of his arm and noting the incipient vulnerable sore at the edge of the lips he had sucked on, he asked Linda what she did for a living. She told him she was headmistress of the adolescent unit at the psychiatric hospital. At every turn she was powerful, more powerful than he would ever have chosen for himself, she was not the sort of woman he would ever have approached. Again he was scared, and felt he was in deep water.

And he was. She was deeper water than he had ever entered, and she closed over his head. Now, when they had been together for years and looked as settled as any other married couple (their oldest daughter was ten), he was still in a state of perpetual exhilarated anxiety about her. He feared so many things.

He feared of course that she would go off with another man. She was not really beautiful. Filled out by a lesser spirit, her face and figure could have been merely freckled and worthy and worn and proletarian: she sometimes made him think of Walker Evans's photographs of farmers' wives in the American dustbowl. She was bony and skinny rather than smooth; the end of her nose was prone to redness and soreness; she was one of those women who can look spectacular, or can look dreadful, if they put on the wrong clothes (and her taste was not infallible, nor did she much care what she wore). But men (some men, enough men for him to fear) liked her. Leggy and gangling, black mascara on gingery lashes, the first signs of ageing (she was forty-five now) naked on her face, she held court: at work, or at home, where there were always visitors, usually male visitors. She said she liked women, but she didn't have many women friends.

He didn't know quite how consciously she held out to her admirers her promise of something they thirsted for, some heady mix of mothering and bossing and sex; standing at the kitchen table with her old faded apron tied round her, serving out like beneficent Ceres to guests and to the children the casserole Graham had cooked and the vegetables he had prepared; sitting up late into the night talking over the problems of some young colleague whose marriage was falling apart until Graham came downstairs in his pyjamas to check on them; dressed in her black suit (which did look good on her) with her battered briefcase stuffed full of disordered papers for a case conference to decide the destiny of one of her forlorn or desperate adolescents. He didn't actually think she liked sex all that much: he believed he had caught fleeting and quickly concealed expressions of disgust on her face at certain crucial moments (which didn't stop him liking sex terribly, needily, with her: in fact her disgust came to be almost, disturbingly, part of what he liked). It was not sex Linda liked but the intoxicating aura of sex, and its power to change things; how could he be sure that it would not come into her head one day to kneel down before one of these admiring men and offer herself, just to see what happened?

He feared, more absurdly but perhaps even more powerfully, that she would go into a convent. She had been brought up by a mother who was superstitiously Catholic (and criminally irresponsible, Graham thought, when he heard tales of Linda and her sisters with one particular lascivious uncle in their teenage years). Although she had gone through the inevitable revolt and now talked the languages of social services and psychotherapy rather than theology, he feared that some deep-laid child-absorbed dream of cold floors and sore knees and wood-faced Madonnas weeping real tears waited concealed, and would break out and recapture her just as Graham thought himself safe from the other men (surely he'd be safe from them when she was fifty? fifty-five?). She had only ever spoken about going into a convent once, when she asked him how it worked: —Can you be chaste again? Can you be married and everything and go through all that and then just be given a clean slate? But ever since then he had been watchful for a certain look, a rapt look of absorbed and even complacent spirituality, like the expression on the face of the Virgin in a Murillo Ascension as she is levitated decorously out of reach of mere mortals. He imagined himself left desperately behind, one of the crowd who gape upwards, grabbing uselessly for a last swirl of drapery.

At the moment, particularly, he feared she might die. She had had two replacement valves in her heart since she was twenty-six (her first husband was the Sikh surgeon who had done the operation), and took Warfarin to keep her blood from coagulating; she had a little machine that looked like a briefcase to do her own blood tests every day, so she could regulate the levels of the drug herself. (Graham nursed a continuous dull ache of accusation against her doctor who trusted her to do this, taken in by her appearance of exceptional and imperturbable competence, blind to the casual extravagance she actually lived by.) Her health in general was not good, she was nervy and prone to infections, although she had surprising reserves of energy. For several weeks now she had been looking ill, her translucent skin was greenish-white and dull, her hair was lank, her eyes could hardly lift themselves to meet his. He had tried to come into the bathroom once and been sure before she slammed the door on him that she was vomiting into the toilet, although she denied it afterwards and shouted at him to stop fussing her. The trouble was that all this was exactly the behaviour he would expect of her if there was something seriously wrong.

But he did try to stop fussing her. His lifework was to keep his fears concealed, and he flattered himself that he did a very good job. She would never know the lengths he went to in order to make her happy: not only the looking after the children so that she could work, and the taking care of the housework because it bored her; but also how he tried to spare her the burden of his absorption in her. He even – hardest of all – worked at his pots sometimes, even pretended to be crusty at being interrupted, even booked extra afternoons for Daniel to go to nursery so he could get on with some commission, even left the door of his studio open in the house so that she could be reassured that he was busy and had forgotten her by the cold mineral smell of the clay that had once been so sweet and stimulating to him. With her complete lack of taste in art, she couldn't see what to him was self-evident: that his familiar, his talent, that slim young gift he had once had to conjure still shapes out of the motion of the air, had left him, slipped out one dark midnight without any fanfare. Or a whole crowd of familiars: ambition, contest, pride in his work, hunger for praise, the aspiration towards the next and finest piece. That

219

whole noisy party had quietly decamped and left nothing but their rubbish round a dead fire. He didn't care: so be it. He only cared that Linda shouldn't know.

He didn't think she knew. Anna, their ten-year-old daughter, knew, or knew something: perhaps not all that grown-up stuff about fame and talent, but knew at least, like him, that if one loved Linda one had better hide it. Anna, who was dark and dainty, used to sew her mother presents and leave her little notes about the house: Linda laughed at them and left them carelessly lying where she found them. It was little stout imperturbable red-haired Katie that Linda took her pleasure in: Anna's lugubriousness (she had called it that to Graham) exasperated her. So Anna stopped following Linda around, into the kitchen, into her bedroom, into the bathroom. ('For goodness sake! Is there something you want?') She took on a transparent, bright, concentrated look that reminded Graham of the little mermaid who walks on knives in the Hans Christian Andersen story: it made him especially careful to be kind to her and treat her with a kind of grave respect, as between equals. She was rewarded for her concentration: now Linda patted her hair and called her 'my *big* girl'. But recently, he and Anna had exchanged involuntary quick glances, when they heard the lock pushed across on the bathroom door, or when Linda left most of her supper pushed to the side of her plate, or when she put Daniel hastily and disgustedly down on the floor for pulling her hair with sticky fingers, which she used to love.

It was May, a windless grey morning with brightness straining to break through the cloud; aeroplanes passed invisibly overhead like smothered thunder. Graham came back from taking Katie to school and Daniel to nursery: Anna was staying at home, she had a cold. He expected to find Linda waiting with her jacket on, drinking black coffee standing up, ready to go as soon as he was through the door. But she was sitting opening letters, smiling, at the table, wrapped in her voluminous ancient maroon dressing-gown that had inkstains on its pockets where biros had leaked and traces of old pale baby-sick still on its shoulders. Anna in her pyjamas was at the table beside her, looking at him with conscious eyes over the tipped-up rim of one of the *café-au-lait* bowls they had brought back from their holiday in Brittany.

—Croissants in the oven, and real coffee, said Linda. —I've decided I'm not going in today. So it's treats. Would you like some?

—I'd love some, he said carefully. —Why? Aren't you feeling well?

—Yes and no, she said. —There's something I should tell you. That's why I wanted to stay here this morning. You two should be the first to know.

—Know what? he said, trying to sound casual. —Did you phone in?

—Yes, she said. —Wait. Wait till the croissants are done. D'you want milky coffee?

She poured him coffee and doled out croissants and put butter and jam on the table: she was drinking peppermint tea, she didn't do any croissants for herself. He was swamped with shame, at the thought that he could not survive his grief, if he lost her. He thought this was just how she would arrange to tell them she was dying.

—I'm having a baby, she said.

—A baby?

—Oh, Mummy! Anna slid from her chair into her mother's arms and dissolved into tears.

—You funny thing! Linda laughed at her. —Isn't it good news?

—You can't be! said Graham.

—That's what I thought. At my age. I couldn't believe it. But I have it on oath from Dr Donald.

—But he won't let you. He'll forbid it. You can't possibly go through that again.

—He says he's got no worries, as long as I take it easy.

—My God! The man's a criminal! What does he think he's playing at?

—Graham . . . Linda slid her hand across his where it was clenched on the table and smiled at him significantly with her head tilted onto one shoulder, as if she was trying to reach a difficult patient. —Don't spoil it. I'm so happy. Don't make it difficult for me. You should be pleased for us. You know I love babies. Eat your croissants.

She did love babies. She adored the whole apparatus of that period of early babyhood, and had never looked quite so completed and triumphant as when she bore home from hospital the latest squalling mite in its white shawls.

Obediently, Graham and Anna began to eat.

—Anna will have to start thinking of names. What shall we have, Annie, a boy or a girl?

—I don't mind, said Anna stoutly, though tears still stood in her eyes. —I love both. I'm so glad it's a baby.

—But it's out of the question, Graham insisted. —Apart from all the medical implications: we don't even have the space.

—Don't be silly. Remember, I grew up with my three sisters in one tiny bedroom.

—Exactly. Exactly my point.

When he thought about what he feared in Linda he often thought about that room. He'd seen it – Linda's mother still lived in the same house – and it was unimaginably too small for the four grown women he knew, all of them near six foot tall, domineering, voluble, two redheads, two brunettes. Fighting when they were teenagers for the space to dress and undress, do their homework, manage their periods, day-dream, they seemed to him to have developed a kind of generous feverheated ruthlessness towards one another with which they proceeded, once they were out of the room, to manage other people in their lives.

—Anyway, said Linda. —I don't know why you're talking as if there's any question. It's not a question. It's a *fait accompli*.

It surprised him afterwards just how long it took for the penny to drop. He must have gone around for several hours that day just worrying about Linda and rehearsing practicalities: he went out to the shops, he remembered, to buy bread and things for supper and cough mixture for Anna, and the sun still hadn't broken through the dirty grey cotton-wool sky. The single thought when it finally arrived – he was bent down unpacking vegetables into the salad compartment in the fridge – dropped like a penny into its slot and on the instant set in motion all its consequences in his mind, coarse and farcical as one of those pier-end automated peep-shows of his childhood.

He and Linda hadn't had sex for weeks.

Weeks and weeks: how many? Certainly not since she had been feeling ill – morning sickness, of course (how could he have missed it?). But before that, for how many weeks? Months, even? He remembered specifics from the last time, little agitating shots and glimpses, he always remembered: but he couldn't place it in relation to anything else that would give him an exact day, or a weekend. Until it came to him that he had opened his drawer to look for clean pyjamas afterwards, and had been pleased at the sight of the Christmas present he'd bought her, a fine grey wool pashmina shawl, still in its plastic carrier, waiting to be wrapped.

—So when's your delivery date? he casually asked her.

—Oh, Dr Donald's not sure, because my periods have been so funny recently. He said to wait for the scan.

Graham wanted to ask, how many periods have you missed, exactly? But he bit his lip.

—So when's the scan?

—God, darling, I don't know. Don't fuss. Two or three weeks or something.

Was he sure, was he absolutely sure that that was the last time, that time before Christmas?

He was almost sure.

The excitement of this almost-certainty, the presence inside him of this might-not-be momentous secret, was bizarre, breathtaking. At moments he almost wanted to catch Linda's eye and giggle with her at this game that they surely could not sustain: as if she had done something naughty which because they were grown-ups she was going to own up to sooner or later. But she didn't give any sign of a desire to own up to anything whatsoever; and meanwhile ordinary life rearranged itself impeccably and convincingly around their new circumstances.

—You should be proud of yourself, she said in the dark one night, snuggled against him, pressing her toes on his.

—Fathering a child in your sixties. Doesn't it make you feel patriarchal? Like Picasso?

He was almost too distracted to answer, he was puzzling so perplexedly over whether she had it in her to say this to him if she knew he hadn't fathered it at all: he thought of how inventively and inveterately those girls in that bedroom must have had to lie in order to protect their secret lives from one another.

He could have asked her, in the dark: —Is it mine?

But the words would not quite form themselves into real sounds in the air between them. And anyway, he never felt sure any longer that anything was his, definitely his.

What happened next depended upon an extraordinary co-incidence. Graham had a problem with the car, the engine was missing and dying at traffic lights. Stan, who had fixed his cars for him for thirty years, had moved premises recently; or rather, he had semi-retired, and now was just doing a few jobs as favours for old customers in the garage at the back of his house. Graham arranged to take the car out there one morning at eleven for Stan to have a look. Stan lived in Stoke Upton, which although it must have been part of the city for a hundred years somehow clung on to a few signs of rusticity: a scrubby patch of grass like a village green in front of a row of failing-looking shops, a field with horses in it beside the Texaco garage, and between the fifties council housing and the Wimpey estates a few little old streets that meandered lazily according to some other logic than town planning. It was a place people came out to walk with their dogs by the river on Sundays: dog shit everywhere.

Graham discussed this very subject with Stan while he was revving the engine and Stan was looking under the bonnet.

—I stand there and watch them, said Stan. —I say to them, this is my front garden, you know. But they've got no shame. I've taken to carrying a plastic bag in my pocket, I offer it to them, to take it home with them, or put it into one of those

225

bins. Some do. But some of them just look right through you, as if they weren't even connected to the bloody dog at the other end of the leash they're holding.

Stan was somewhat diminished, Graham thought, working from home and on his own: he remembered the racier and more anarchic repartee at the place in town. Mrs Stan was just visible, spraying something on her roses, through the trellis that firmly separated the oil-dark garage from the garden.

The problem was spark plugs, Stan decided. He'd have to order some. He'd have them by Tuesday.

As Graham was waiting to turn out of the end of Stan's road, Linda in her red Fiesta passed him without seeing him. There was something almost comical, that first instant, in the sight of the so-familiar face in the unfamiliar place, leaning, frowning intently forward over the steering wheel as usual. He hadn't known that Linda had ever heard of Stoke Upton, let alone knew how to get there: she was notoriously blank about directions and places. He'd told her he was taking the car to Stan's, but there hadn't been any reason to mention it wasn't to the usual premises in town. And hadn't she said she was going to spend all day at the unit? He turned out of Stan's road and followed her. Really, for a moment he was only going to catch up with her, to share the surprise of the coincidence, or in case she was looking for him. Then suddenly instead he was following her, even dropping back so that she wouldn't catch sight of him.

She turned right, then left, without hesitation, as if she knew her way: as if she'd been here before. Now they were on that road which ran past the shops and the green; there was more traffic, he'd had to let a couple of cars turn out in front of him, he was afraid he'd lose her.

She pulled into a space in front of the row of shops. He had no choice but to pass her, then he managed to stop about thirty yards further on, just past a video rentals place that was the last of the little row. Slewing round inside his seat belt with the engine still running, he looked for her through his rear window: he felt so conspicuous, he couldn't believe she hadn't seen him. She was locking her car, she wasn't looking at him. Her hair was pinned up and she had make-up on and dangling earrings: she was wearing her black leggings and some sort of stretchy shiny shirt he hadn't seen before, with her suit jacket. She looked odd, as if she had made an effort to dress up but had chosen wrong things that subtly betrayed her. Perhaps her shape was already beginning to change.

She was parked in front of a hairdressers called *A Cut Above*. He wildly entertained the thought that she was going to cut off her hair. But she crossed the pavement quickly to a pillar-box-red painted door beside the shop that must be the front door to a flat upstairs; she found a key, not on her key-ring but from somewhere inside her bag, opened the door, and disappeared inside. Graham waited for her to reappear. The windows of the flat above the shop were blanked out with bamboo blinds: he stared up at them but they relayed no sign of what might be happening behind them.

It was mid-day.

Graham sat in his car. He felt as if the world quietly came to rest about him. The traffic seemed to ease off, and the desultory shoppers dwindled: was there somewhere left in the world where people still had lunch at twelve o'clock? A couple of blonde child-stylists came twittering out of the hairdressers and returned at the end of ten minutes with sandwiches and bags of cakes, their blonde hair in their eyes and their skirts blowing against their brown bare legs in the wind. One ancient-looking little cavernous sweet-shop and newsagent even shut its door and put up a closed sign. The video shop of course didn't

work to that old rhythm; young well-fed men and women
came and browsed and went away with their next glitter-fix
in its anonymous cover, and Graham repressed a twinge of
rage at the prodigal unimaginable waste of afternoons spent
in front of the television.

He waited. She might have been visiting a client, a difficult
client, who for some reason couldn't come to the door and had
given her a key: perhaps wheelchair bound, or (more Linda's
line) agoraphobic.

After about half an hour he got out of the car. It was quite
a nice day, sunny, although with a cold wind that pasted the
litter up against the tree trunks and the car wheels, and streamed
through the scrappy little trees which had been planted in an
effort to make the place vaguely continental. He walked up
and down past the shops a couple of times, past the red door
which had a bell but no name; he bought some cigarettes in
an eight-til-late store although he didn't really smoke. There
were two empty shops, a butcher and an electrical retailer;
they showed no signs of having been re-let, although their
windows were thickly pasted with posters as though they had
been closed for a long time. The baker's sold sandwiches and
even had a couple of tables squeezed between the counter and
wall at the far end of the shop where presumably you could
order coffee.

He was afraid at first that if he went into any of the shops
he would miss Linda coming out: he didn't know how long
she was going to be. Then he thought that she might take
hours, that she might never come out. Finally he realised that
he knew that she would reappear at about three o'clock: she
had to pick Daniel up from nursery at half past three to take
him to the doctor's for his MMR vaccination, and she would
need to leave half an hour to get from Stoke Upton into town.

Linda had to take Daniel to the doctor's because Graham took Anna to ballet after school on Thursdays; what Linda didn't know was that Chloe's mother had offered to take Anna to ballet, so that he could take Daniel and Katie to the surgery. He had been going to phone Linda on her mobile to tell her she needn't come back early. He supposed her mobile would have rung here, in Stoke Upton, in the flat above the hairdressers, if it hadn't been for the extraordinary coincidence of his sighting of her; and they would have exchanged practicalities without his having any clue that she spoke to him from another side of the world. She would have reached for her phone, he thought, out of a tangle of sheets: for an insane moment he had the sheets vividly in front of his eyes: the bright and flowery type with a little trim of pink and yellow braid (she had had some like this years ago which he had replaced with plain blue ones from Habitat). Then he took firm hold upon himself.

He bought himself milky instant coffee in a polystyrene cup at the baker's and drank it, then went back past the red door to sit in the car. He worried tangentially that someone might become suspicious of his sitting there and call the police, but no one did, although the girl from the video rentals did lean out of the shop door and stare at him a couple of times, as if she was curious about him. Trade didn't really pick up in the afternoon. The sweet-shop didn't re-open. The bamboo blinds at the windows of the flat never stirred.

It was unimaginable that he would fall asleep but he did, perhaps for ten or fifteen minutes. He was woken by the sound of the red door pulled shut; he was sure it was that even before he threw himself around in the car to see, as sure as if it was a sound he recognised because he'd known it all his life. His face felt folded and creased from sleep; his mouth was stale from the cigarette he'd smoked, with repositories of bile secreted along his gums; there was a wet patch on the sleeve of his shirt where he must have dribbled.

It was three o'clock.

Linda was dressed in the same things again (what had he expected?) but she wavered, tottered, in her line across the pavement beneath the agitated trees. Her make-up was smeared, her face was strange, and the red hair was pulled into a perfunctory pony tail. As he watched she paused and fetched out of her jacket pocket not her car keys but her earrings, which she then tried to hook into her ears, missing and persisting, while the wind blew some sheet of junk mail up against her calves. Her face was strange, mobile and raw, because she was crying. Graham glared into the video rentals shop to see if the girl was watching, but she was preoccupied with something behind her counter at the back of the shop. One of the juniors came out from the hairdressers but scarcely looked up from where she was battling to keep her skirt down over her thighs. Linda fixed one earring in and gave up on the other one; she put it back in her pocket and fished in her bag for her keys, her face still distorted with crying. It seemed strange to Graham that she had taken her earrings off in the first place.

—She's not safe to drive, he thought. But then he'd often thought that.

The red Fiesta passed him and she never even glanced in his direction. She looked quite grotesque for that moment as she passed within yards of where he sat staring, quite terrifying really: her face was distorted and working and her mouth was wide open. She must be groaning and moaning: howling, even. He supposed he'd seen her like that, in that extremity, in childbirth; only then she had had right on her side, and all the admiring nurses around her, encouraging her. The Fiesta windows were all wound up and so were his and it was windy, so he couldn't hear anything. Then she was past him. She turned left at the end of the road, on her way back into town to pick up Daniel and Katie.

He got out of the car, walked up to the red door, and rang the bell. After a while he rang again. Someone came down the stairs inside and the door opened. He looked at the man who opened it with astonishment: it was no one he knew, none of the various friends and colleagues of Linda's he'd run in mental review before his fears. This man was in his late forties or early fifties, not tall, with thick neatly combed grey hair and a moustache and a pleasant, wide face, the kind of face you repose your trust in when it belongs to a lawyer or a bank manager, bland and prosperously tanned. Only his nose was rather small: it tipped up at the end and was somehow demeaning, Graham thought, as if it betrayed an effeminacy, or a lack of soul. He was wearing suit trousers and a blue office shirt and a tie, and he was in his socks. There were no marks on him: no traces of turmoil or upheaval to match what Graham had seen a few moments before on Linda.

The man was looking in astonishment at Graham.

—Yes?

Something in his surprise made Graham sure this wasn't his home – it didn't look like a home, anyway, not for a man like him: the stairs behind him were covered in a cheap sagging carpet that smelled, and there were no pictures. He couldn't have expected anyone to have rung the bell for him: he must have thought it was Linda coming back.

—I was looking for Graham, Graham said. —I thought Graham lived here.

He hadn't known he was going to say this: he had had no plan in his mind when he rang the bell.

—No, no one of that name, said the man thoughtfully, warily.

—You don't know where he lives, then? I was sure it was here.

It seemed to Graham that the man began to guess something, then: or at least that a disconcerting but bizarre and unlikely possibility had occurred to him. He must have known what Linda's husband's name was. To his credit he did not begin to shut the door on him; on the contrary, he probably held it open a little longer and more accommodatingly than their conversation superficially warranted.

—I'm sorry. I can't help you.

—Don't worry about it. It doesn't matter, Graham said, and they stood confronted a few moments longer, until it was ridiculous for the man not to begin to close the door.

Graham asked: —And you are . . . ?

The man hesitated. It was absurd to ask, of course.

—I'm Des. Desmond, he said uncomfortably.

—Oh. Thank you.

He never tried that name on Linda. He kept it for himself.

But at the weekend they sat out together in the garden, and he did take the opportunity to mention the spark plugs and the car. They were waiting for Clare, Graham's oldest daughter, who was bringing her children to stay with them for the weekend because her grandfather, her mother's father, had died, and she wanted to help her mother make all the arrangements. Graham had filled the paddling pool and Anna and Katie and Daniel were jumping in and out of it, squealing and shrieking.

—Did I tell you old Stan was retiring?

Linda was sitting on the plaid rug on the grass, rubbing sun cream into her legs and feet.

—Oh dear, she said sympathetically. —Does that mean we'll have to find someone else to do the cars? We'll never find anyone else as nice as Stan. Or as cheap.

—It doesn't exactly. He's going to go on doing a bit of work from home, he's got just about enough room in their place at Stoke Upton. That's where I took the car on Thursday, actually, only I forgot to tell you.

—Do my shoulders? she said, handing him the sun cream, piling her hair up and holding it out of his way, bending her neck. —Stoke Upton? Where's that?

He didn't answer, he concentrated on massaging the cream into her freckled white shoulders and the tops of her arms until it disappeared. He rolled the straps of her T-shirt carefully down off her shoulders so as not to miss any place where she might burn.

—I need a hat, she said. —A sunhat for this summer. One of those wonderful great big cartwheel ones, a sort of Audrey Hepburn hat, you know, joyous and exuberant. Do you know the kind I mean?

—A hat?

—A hat. A really special hat.

—I see.

Clare in dark glasses and laden with bags emerged with her children out from the passage down the side of the house and Graham sat back, screwing the top onto the tube of cream.

—So when did Stan say he was getting the spark plugs in? Linda asked him hastily, as if in a last, binding, exchange of domestic necessity before the frivolities of sociability intervened.

233

—Tuesday, Graham said.

—OK.

—I'll go out there Tuesday morning.

—OK.

—Otherwise he said the engine's fine.

Clare put down her bags on the rug, looking lean, distracted, impatient (she had embarked on an unpromising new relationship with the supervisor for her PhD). Rose was already tearing all her clothes off for the pool, Lily was stamping her foot and starting a sulk because they hadn't brought their bathing costumes. Clare looked at them, frowning, as if she was looking through them.

—Wear your knickers, she said.

Lily winced and delicately coloured. —Mummy! How can you?

—How are you all? Linda commiserated. —How's Marian? Is she coping? Your grandfather was such an extraordinary man, a beautiful spirit. We all should have venerated him. I can find Lily a costume, don't worry about it.

—Mum is so bereft and distraught, Clare said to Graham. —When you think what a burden Grandpa's been. And he could be so horrid to her. But she's in a dreadful state.

—Poor dear old Marian, said Linda. —She's such a saint.

There was a certain way Graham's older daughters had of sometimes staring hard and smilingly at nothing, widening their eyes (he could tell Clare's were widening even behind the dark glasses); he knew very well this was their comment on Linda. Their disapproval was another thing he had imperceptibly to protect her from.

—But you'd be surprised, said Linda. —Some of these very independent-seeming career women, the extent to which they've actually bought in to the whole patriarchal thing.

—I suppose I would, said Clare. —Be surprised, I mean.

Anna and Lily became inseparable for the afternoon. Solemn-faced and with arms draped round one another's shoulders, they maintained a dignified distance from the wild game of plunging and throwing water which the others had begun in the paddling pool.

—Aren't you just dreading when they start mooning around over boys? Linda said to Clare.

She brought out a heap of old clothes from the house for the girls to dress up in, including her wedding dress, the one she'd been married in the first time, to the surgeon-husband: it was long and white and Princess-Diana-inspired, and Anna and Lily dragged round the garden magnificently in it in turns until it was covered in grass stains.

That night Linda woke Graham, urgently, out of deep sleep.

—Gray? Wake up! I'm frightened! I've had a really horrible dream.

It was dark, he couldn't see her face, she was sitting over him pinching his arms painfully in her fingers. She pinched him until he was awake and listening.

—I was in a car, with two men, she said. —One in the passenger seat beside me, one in the back. I was trying to park, I had no reason to think anything was wrong. Suddenly the man in the passenger seat brought out a gun, and shot me. I felt such pain, and I was astonished: what did he want to hurt me for? He shot me more than once, there was blood fountaining everywhere. Then the man in the back seat got out a gun too, and I thought: but why didn't you do this earlier, now it's too late to protect me? Only then he shot me too, maybe because he was so angry with me or something, for being the victim, angry because I was hurt. Through a curtain of blood

I was pushing my face towards the man in the front seat, I was dying, my mouth was open in a terrible sort of groan, trying to find breath, I was reaching out with my mouth for him, I just wanted to touch him and cling to him because he was the last human being I'd ever know . . .

They lay silently.

—The man in the back seat, said Graham, —plays a somewhat inglorious role.

—I need to pee, said Linda, —only I'm too frightened. Will you take me?

He padded downstairs after her and waited while she used the toilet with the door open. Afterwards he got her settled in bed in the position she always liked in pregnancy, on her right side, right leg bent under her, left leg stretched out; then he stroked her back and shoulders until she went to sleep. He put a hand on her abdomen: hardly distended yet, no more than at the time of her normal period. He was interested in this baby. He found himself more interested in this pregnancy than he had been with any of his other children. He wondered whether when it was born he would be able to see himself in its wrinkled face, or whether he would find traces of the soulless Desmond with the upturned nose. It seemed to him that either way – or, more likely, if there was never any certainty, if he could never quite persuade himself conclusively of either case – the baby would need his especial protection. Strangely, he imagined himself dandling it – when it was tiny, with its little bird limbs of that brick-red colour only the new ones had – with a certain special plastic tenderness he had once felt in his fingers towards the clay things he made.

Falling asleep, he found himself imagining Linda at his father-in-law's funeral, his ex-father-in-law's, which must take place sometime in the next few days. (He had never acquired any further father-in-laws, after that first one: his second and third wives had come to him without fathers, one way or another.) In his fantasy Linda was wearing a tight black dress and it was stretched across her stomach, which was unmistakably prominent. Perhaps a wind, too, was blowing the dress clingingly against her, outlining her bump. Yes, there must be a wind because with one hand she held in place a huge cartwheel hat which threatened at every moment to blow away, so that in spite of the solemnity of the occasion she cast a laughing glance at him from across the open grave. He fastened on the glance, its out-of-place mischievousness, its playful promise of adventure; and it sustained him while he allowed himself to fall off the edge of consciousness into the dark.

Bomb Scare

It was Saturday afternoon, October, raining. Clare was upstairs in the city library, where she had come to check a couple of references. While she waited for a book that had to be fetched from the stacks, she browsed randomly across the shelves, took down a volume of Chekhov's letters, and sank into the soothing miscellany of money matters, sickness, arrangements for travel, family vexations, gripes with friends. All musty and done with and long dead.

A librarian was talking to two policemen whose white and fluorescent lime plastic waterproofs dripped onto the carpet; one held a motorbike helmet behind his back and fingered its strap in huge fingers while he elicited information with a practised questioning.

—How old would you say he was?

The librarian, small and excitable, rocked onto his toes and searched the ceiling in an effort to imagine. He brimmed with nervous importance.   —Oh . . . I should say about thirty-ish . . .

—Twenty-five to thirty. And how tall?

—Tall. Not as tall as you. But tall.

—About six foot then.

—His hair was thinning on top. I wouldn't have taken any

notice of him if I hadn't happened to look into the bag: it's quite a standard request, for them to leave their bag of shopping behind our desk while they choose their books. But I did notice his badge.

Clare thought she ought not to be eavesdropping: she might be going to witness some unseemly arrest, someone's humiliation. She dropped her attention back into the receding tide of the life of the book: money matters and travel and sickness and more sickness.

Ten minutes later while she waited at the check-out downstairs with her books there came an announcement over the library intercom.

—Please evacuate the building. Please evacuate the building.

The man at the check-out desk who was stroking the codes on the books with an optical read-out pen stood up, not surprised but relieved, as if he knew something and had been expecting it.

—Leave all your books, he said. —Please leave your books where you are and evacuate the building.

Clare clung onto her books for a reluctant moment; they had gone to all that trouble fetching her that one from the stacks, and anyway she had already begun the process of taking these books in through the skin and making them her own. Her afternoon without them looked bleak. Then as people obediently and without any sign of panic began to file out through the doors and down the stairs she caught sight in the crowd of an intensely familiar little knot of people: her own three children out with Bram and Helly. It was a dizzying sensation, to see the little knot from the outside whose inside feel she knew so vividly. Bram was carrying Rose, and calmly without pushing he was striding ahead making a path for the others to follow; Jacob was hurrying close behind, staring at the back of his father's jacket with pale fixity, bracing himself for the worst. Helly was holding tight onto Lily's hand. Clare knew how Helly felt, gripping tight, steadying herself; you believed that if you could somehow hold them firmly and tightly enough you could stop anything happening to them, physically hold the world still and whole for them against disaster. She put down her books and filed after them, through the glass doors and down the staircase to the foyer. Everyone was subdued and sensible. At most they smiled meekly at one another, because without a real explosion or a fire the drama of emergency was faintly embarrassing.

They looked a handsome family when she saw them full on at the turn of the stairs, Lily's brows and lips delicately marked as a little deer, Rose's cheeks curved like a Victorian doll's, Jacob with the bridge of freckles across his rather flat nose and the serious light in his eyes, the firmly closed pale lips. They all had new haircuts; she had known Helly was going to take them for haircuts, but she had not known how much it would make them look like Helly's children. Bram was wearing a new brown leather jacket, something he could not possibly have afforded and never would have chosen for himself. With his closed dry blond good looks it made him seem a member of some officer class, commanding and self-deprecating and heroic. Out in the street where some of the people evacuated were stopping and waiting to find out what was happening, he signalled to the family that they should walk on, and said something to Helly with a chaffing fond irony that Clare had never seen. Helly's face in return was full of concessions and eagerness to listen.

It looked utterly desirable – and unimaginable – to be part of that family.

It was still raining; rain perfumed with tarmac hissed and drizzled up off the road as the cars passed. Without knowing why she was doing it, Clare trotted after them through the rain, strangely without burdens, without books, without children. Helly put up her big striped umbrella – Clare knew it, the one from the Guggenheim – and tried to hold it up over them all, putting Lily and Jacob between her and Bram. They headed away from the library to join the main pedestrianised thoroughfare into town. Clare was so close behind them that it was almost odd they didn't turn round and see her: Rose might so easily have looked back over Bram's shoulder, but instead she sat straight-backed on his arm and scouted out ahead. Clare willed them not to turn round and see her as if her survival depended on it, and yet she could not tear herself away.

This is the worst thing I'll ever feel, Clare thought; this is the worst moment I'll ever have, about leaving.

She knew, of course, that this picture, this composition of wholeness, was not all it seemed. She knew from the children that it was not all going wonderfully well between them and Helly: she knew that Lily had cried herself to sleep one night she was spending over there, wanting Mummy; and that Rose had played Helly up when Bram had to go out somewhere. She noticed that as they hurried along Jacob never looked Helly in the face even when she spoke to him and put her hand on his shoulder to hold him in under the umbrella. And Helly had taken out her lip ring. Who had told her they didn't like it? Jacob? Bram?

The children were still hers, she hadn't lost them. It really wasn't quite as bad as this seemed.

★   ★   ★

241

They stopped; a few paces behind them Clare stopped abruptly too, and had to apologise to someone who walked into her. Helly must be suggesting they went to shelter from the rain into a cheap place with big plate glass windows that did burgers. It was not the sort of place Bram or Clare would ever have chosen, but it seemed a good idea. As if she could hear them Clare knew the children were asking excitedly if they could have chips. This would make up for the disappointment over the books.

As the others went in Helly paused on the threshold to shake out her umbrella. She saw Clare standing there.

—I was behind you at the library, said Clare.

Helly looked caught out; guilty and apologetic and also even fed up, as if being followed by Clare was the last straw. It must be hard work, spending the afternoon trying to make up to someone else's children.

—Oh, she said. —What was all that about?

She looked different, as if Bram's absorption in her was actually changing her into a creature of his kind of flesh. Her face was pale and scrubbed clean, she didn't have make-up on, she was letting her hair grow out into its natural light brown, her eyes seemed wider apart and paler and startled. Without wanting to, Clare imagined this face with its new fragile tentativeness against the pillows of her old bed. She could even imagine the particular flavour, the excitements – sensitive and nervy and confessional – of their intimacy. These excitements didn't seem to have much to do with the golden Helly of the ice cream advertisements.

—Bomb scare, said Clare. —They found a suspect package. I overheard them talking to the police.

—What a bore. I mean if it's just a hoax. After choosing all the books.

—I followed to make sure the children were alright, said Clare. —Just in case it wasn't a hoax.

—Do you want to join us? We're just going to get them some chips.

—No thanks. I have to meet my father. We're having lunch.

—No news of Linda's baby?

—Not yet. Any day now. Dad's very jittery about it. You'd think he'd be pretty blasé by this time. The Earth Mother pops them out effortlessly enough.

Helly made a quick grimace of sympathetic understanding.

Babies, thought Clare. She's started thinking about babies.

—Don't tell the children you've seen me, she said. —It'll only make things worse.

Now Clare put up her own umbrella. The noise of cars in the rain was constant as a river in her ear, and then there was the thrumming of the rain on the tight nylon of the umbrella, the city smoking upwards with wet and dirt, the frozen bright tableaux of the shop windows. She had to go past the end of the road the library was on, and she saw that the police had moved on to evacuating the frozen food store next door. She wasn't due to meet her father for another half an hour. She wandered into a crowded clothes shop and was immediately deeply absorbed in serious consideration of skirts, tops, trousers.

How could this be? Why wasn't she considering rather the lostness of her children without her?

She carried a mixed armful of things to try into the little changing room, a corner of the shop inadequately screened off by a hessian curtain on big wooden hoops. Behind the curtain there were hooks for the hangers and a hot unflattering spotlight. Sweatily, hastily, she tried one garment after another, peeling things off inside out, not even taking time to put one thing back on its hanger before she was dragging the next one over her head. She swivelled and postured as best she could in the cramped space, simpering and posing, cheeks hectic, wet hair leaving smudges on the fabrics, making that long phony-sultry face at herself in the mirror which Lily and Rose could send up to perfection. She interrogated each outfit feverishly, searching for the absolutely right thing with an abandon as though she expected any moment to be interrupted once and for all. How would she first know if there had been an explosion? Did one feel these things through one's feet, coming up out of the earth like a quake? How much of the city would the bomb take down with it if it went off?

She tried on an electric-blue blouse with frills down the front in what her mother would have called chiffon: she loved it immediately and with passion. It had that derisory edge of ugliness without which nothing ever looked truly good; it managed to be ironic and flattering at once. In it her glance was sharp and dark as a knife; she was veiled, mysterious, she burned with a cold fire. It was the least practical garment she could have found to spend money on, money she didn't even have. It was transparent, too, she would have to buy something to wear underneath it. But it was already indispensable. Without it now she would not be complete; this self that had only arisen for the first time in the changing-room mirror would never get to walk the earth with the gift of her powerful veiled knowingness.

When she came out of the shop with the blouse in a bag it was like emerging blinking back into light and focus from the underground maze of some debauchery. She felt so ashamed she even considered putting the carrier bag down somewhere and leaving it.

She thought Tony would like her in the blouse, though.

Mostly, Tony was a problem. He didn't want to meet her children, and he didn't want her to move in. She was on the edge, the very edge, of being desperate about him, of stepping off from the safe ground of her self-possession. Yet last night, in the chaotic front room of his flat, among the boxes of books he'd never unpacked since his last move, he had put on for her version after version of Miles Davis playing 'So What', and had written something with his finger in wine on her throat (he wouldn't tell her what it was), and had said to her that if once he let himself go he might fall for her so heavily that he would never be able to stand on his two feet again.

She stopped in the rain and looked around for a phone box so that she could call him. She felt the need to reassure somebody that she had survived: even though there hadn't actually been any disaster.